UNFORGETTABLE

Special Edition

Melanie Harlow

USA TODAY BESTSELLING AUTHOR

*For Sammy and AJ,
with love and gratitude*

You have to let go of who you were to become who
you will be.

CANDACE BUSHNELL

CHAPTER 1

Tyler

ONCE UPON A TIME, I might have been the hero of this story.

After all, I had everything a hero needs.

Wicked fastball. Killer instinct. Cocky grin. Full package.

(And believe me, I knew how to score.)

I even had a nickname—they called me "The Rifle" because I pitched with such relentless speed and accuracy. Back then, I could dot a gnat's ass from two hundred feet away. From sixty feet, six inches, I could break the webbing on the catcher's mitt—and I did. Plenty of times.

At my high school, I held the record for strikeouts *and* home runs. They retired my number and hung my jersey in the gym. My coach said I was a once-in-a-generation player. My senior year, I was San Diego's first-round draft pick with a fucking two-million-dollar signing bonus.

Did you catch that?

Two. Million. Dollars.

That night, I signed autographs for kids in Little League uniforms at the ice cream shop on Main Street—then I paid for all their double scoops. Three months later, I was in Arizona for Instructional League. A few months after that, I was in spring training. And before I could even legally buy myself a beer, I made my Major League debut.

I had a locker in the clubhouse. A uniform on the hook. My entire future ahead of me . . . a future I wanted, a future I'd earned, a future—I was convinced—I deserved.

Point is, I was fucking invincible.

Until one day I wasn't.

FORMER LITTLE LEAGUE COACH: Sure, I was watching that game. Who wasn't? It's not every day a hometown kid plays in the World Series. I just wish I knew what happened. One minute, he can throw a baseball; the next, he can't. I mean, what the hell?

HIGH SCHOOL TEAMMATE: It was the curveball. He hung onto it too long. Or maybe he rushed it. But he was done after that. I mean, six wild pitches in one inning? In the World Series? Damn. You gotta feel bad for him. Poor bastard.

CHEMISTRY TEACHER: He lacked discipline. That was his problem.

LOCAL CHURCH LADY: He lacked Jesus.

HIGH SCHOOL RIVAL: His ego brought him down, plain and simple. Tyler Shaw thought his [bleep] didn't stink, but what stinks now is his arm. They shoulda drafted me instead —I coulda thrown better that day. Hell, my dog coulda thrown better that day.

LOCAL BARBER: You'd think with all the millions they paid

him he could just throw straight. I mean, why couldn't he just throw strikes like he used to? I ever see him around these parts again, I'm gonna ask him.

CLIENT CURRENTLY IN BARBER'S CHAIR: I bet his underwear was too tight. That always makes me anxious.

RANDOM GUY AT THE CORNER BAR: I saw him pitch his senior year. He struck out the first nineteen batters in a row. Nineteen! [Bleep] unbelievable. Sad what happened to him, with millions of people watching too. I heard he's some kinda recluse now. Lives alone, won't talk to nobody.

RANDOM GUY AT THE CORNER BAR ONE SEAT DOWN: I dunno, maybe he can make a comeback or something. Do some hypnosis. See a shrink.

RANDOM GUY AT THE CORNER BAR TWO SEATS DOWN: Nah, a shrink can't help him. And no team will touch him. The yips are a death sentence, and everyone knows it. That guy's finished in baseball. He's a cautionary tale.

Of course that fucking documentary was on in the airport bar. No matter where I went, I couldn't escape it.

Changing my mind about a post-flight beer, I pulled my ball cap lower on my forehead and kept my head down as I moved through Cherry Capital Airport. Chances were that nobody was going to recognize me—I hadn't been back to my small northern Michigan hometown in years—but I didn't want to risk it.

There was a time in my life when I'd loved being recognized. I'd lived for it. People would stare, and I didn't mind one bit. They asked for selfies, and I obliged with my signature cocky grin. They asked for autographs, and I happily signed whatever napkin, hat, or ticket stub they handed me. They'd raise a glass to me across a crowded bar.

"Great game against Atlanta!"

"Congrats on Rookie of the Year!"

"You've got an arm like Koufax!"

"Fuck, you can throw the ball."

"Jesus, you've got a gift."

"You're a phenom, Shaw."

"You're a genius."

"You're a god."

I rode that high for a goddamn decade, completely addicted to the rush.

Man, it was some life. I had millions of dollars in the bank. I had women trying to sneak into my hotel room in every city in the country. I drove a car that cost more than the house I grew up in—which I paid off for my dad, who refused to move to something bigger. I put my sister through college.

But three years ago, I blew it. I didn't even have the dignity of a torn rotator cuff or fucked-up elbow to blame—just the faulty wiring in my own head.

The goddamn *yips* got me, and I couldn't throw a strike to save my life. I went down hard and took my entire team with me, during the World Series.

Did you get that? The *World Series*.

After that, the narrative about me changed—I went from hero to head case.

"What the fuck, Shaw?"

"Why can't you just throw the ball?"

"Are you injured?"

"Are you drunk?"

"Is it because of your mother?"

"Is it because of your father?"

"Is your jock strap too tight?"

"No comment," I repeated over and over to the sports reporters greedy for the scoop.

"Get the fuck out of here," I said to the pushy cameramen jostling for the shot.

"Just leave me alone," I said to teammates who offered to play catch where no one would see. "I'll fucking figure it out."

And I'd tried. Every single day, all I'd wanted was to wake up from the nightmare and feel like myself again—I wanted my arm back, not this alien stone limb attached to my body at the shoulder that wouldn't do what I told it to.

But it never came back. My pitching career was over.

Which meant my *life* was over.

Humiliated and pissed off, I quit baseball and spent most of my time hiding out in a cabin I bought in the mountains, brooding about what the fuck I was supposed to do with the rest of my life. I had money, sure, but I also had *time* stretching out like a fucking eternity ahead of me. I wasn't even forty yet.

Then, as if the universe hadn't crushed me hard enough, that damn documentary came out, the one about stellar sports careers that ended because of mental breakdowns, and the spectacular implosion of my career was plastered all over the media *again*. Not a day went by when some jackass didn't see fit to give me his opinion on what I'd done wrong, what I should do to fix it, or just generally tell me I sucked.

People. I wasn't a fan.

"Tyler Shaw?" The guy at the car rental desk looked down at my driver's license and then up at my face.

"Yeah?" From beneath the brim of my cap, I gave him my meanest stare, the one I used to give batters before throwing a fastball right by them.

He turned his attention to his monitor. "And you're renting . . . an Elite Luxury SUV for five days? Returning on Sunday?"

"Yeah." I relaxed a little. This guy didn't recognize me. He was just doing his job.

"Great. Just give me one minute."

"No problem."

His fingers tapped away on his keyboard for about fifteen seconds. And then, "You're not the *pitcher* Tyler Shaw, are you?"

"Yeah," I said through clenched teeth.

"Oh, shit." The guy shook his head. "I saw you play all the time in high school. I was only in Little League back then, but my brother and I used to go to all your games. You were amazing."

Were. "Thanks."

"We just saw that documentary about you. Brutal, man."

"Can we just finish up with the rental please?"

"Oh, sure. Sure." He went back to typing again, but kept talking. "It's just so crazy, you know? One minute you're, like, one of the greatest pitchers in the game, and the next minute, it's all gone."

"Yup."

"I mean, what happened?"

My hands curled into fists. My left eyelid twitched. "Wish I could tell you, buddy."

"Seriously, that had to suck so bad."

Fighting for control of my temper, I took a breath. "Look, do you need me to sign something? I'm in kind of a hurry." Actually, I wasn't—I didn't have to be anywhere until six o'clock and it was barely four, but fuck this guy.

"Yeah, it's printing now." He gave his keyboard a final tap and looked at me again. "Did you ever try meditation? That worked for my mom when she kept forgetting where she put her car keys."

I glowered at him. Steve, his name tag said. "Yes, *Steve*. I tried meditation. And I tried tapping and hypnosis and psychoanalysis and cognitive behavioral therapy and celibacy and Jesus. Nothing worked. I didn't *forget* how to pitch—I just can't do it anymore. Now, I'm happy for your mom, but right now I'd really like you to mind your own fucking business and give *me* a set of car keys so I can get the hell out of here!"

Steve looked offended. "Geez. Maybe you should try anger management."

I backed away from the counter so I wasn't tempted to throw a punch. "I'll be outside."

"Tyler!"

The second I walked into Hop Lot Brewing Co., I heard my name. I took off my sunglasses and saw my little sister Sadie rushing toward me. When she reached me, she threw her arms around my neck and held on tight.

Although we didn't see each other often enough, my sister was the most constant presence in my life, the most supportive, the most loyal. She could read me better than anyone, even over the phone, which was both annoying and reassuring. I'd been fiercely protective of her since the day she was born, and she'd idolized me. We'd lost our mom in a car accident while Sadie was still in diapers, and we'd lost our dad to pancreatic cancer eight years ago, so she was the only family I had left.

I hugged her back, lifting her right off the ground. "Hey, you. Long time no see."

"That's because you never come home anymore." On her feet again, she stepped back from me with tears in her eyes. "God, I missed you, you asshole."

"I missed you too." I hooked an arm around her neck and

ruffled her dark hair the way she'd hated when we were young. "You know, you can always come visit me more often. Planes do fly both ways."

"Stop it!" Laughing, she tried to swat my hand away. "Don't make me sorry I invited you to my shotgun wedding."

"Are you even old enough to get married?"

She rolled her eyes. "Tyler, I'm twenty-eight."

I pretended to think about it. "No way. That would make me thirty-six."

"Exactly. You grumpy old man." She grinned, suddenly looking exactly like the pigtailed, gap-toothed, dirt-under-her-fingernails little girl who used to play in the park on summer afternoons while I was at practice. Before games, she used to give me a shamrock she'd plucked from the ground, telling me it was for good luck. No matter how many times I told her that *four*-leaf clovers were good luck and shamrocks only had three, she'd insist her gift would be my lucky charm that day and made me promise I'd keep it in my pocket. I always did.

When I left home at eighteen, she'd given me a shoebox full of them as a going-away present. I probably hadn't cried since elementary school, but that day, I came damn close.

"Come on," she said, tugging at my hand. "We've got a table already. I can't wait for you to meet Josh."

I let her drag me toward the back of the place, where her boyfriend—now fiancé—sat at a picnic-style table with long benches on either side. He stood up as I approached, looking a little nervous for a guy with so many tattoos. Then again, I could be pretty intimidating. I might not have had my pitching arm anymore, but I was tall, broad-shouldered and muscular, with a menacing glare honed by years of staring down men from sixty feet away. Just to be an asshole, I decided to give Josh here a little taste of it—he was more than likely a perfectly good guy, but he *had* knocked up my kid sister. I wanted him to know he couldn't mess with her —or me.

"Tyler, this is Josh. Josh, this is my brother, Tyler." Sadie looked on anxiously as her fiancé held his hand out and I waited *just* a second longer than necessary to extend mine.

"Nice to meet you," Josh said. His grip was firm, his smile tentative but genuine. He met my eyes squarely. "I've heard a lot about you."

"Oh yeah?" I cocked a brow at my sister, wondering what her stories about me were like.

"All good stuff," she said, gesturing to the bench across from Josh. "Why don't you sit there?"

I did as she suggested, and Sadie sat next to Josh, scooting close enough to loop her hands around his heavily inked bicep. She gazed up at him adoringly, and he planted a kiss on her forehead. I was simultaneously grossed out, baffled, and happy for them. I mean, I sure as hell wouldn't be able to do the whole *'til death do us part* shit, but good for them, I guess.

The server came by, and we ordered drinks—beers for Josh and me, water for Sadie—and while those were being poured, we looked over the menu. Josh recommended the tacos, and Sadie loved the turkey club. I decided on a burger and fries, but mostly I just wanted that beer. When it arrived, I tipped it up and took several long, cold swallows.

"So Ty," my sister said, "there's something I want to ask you." She glanced at Josh. "Something *we* want to ask you."

"What?"

She took a deep breath. "Will you be the baby's godfather?"

I froze with the beer glass halfway between my mouth and the table. Then I lifted it again and took another drink. "Me?"

"Of course, you." Sadie smiled at me and shook her head. "How many big brothers do you think I have?"

"You really think I'm qualified?" I looked from one to the other. "Josh, you don't have a brother?"

He shook his head. "Just a sister. She'll be the godmother."

"I don't even go to church," I told them.

"That's okay." My sister shrugged. "It's not so much a religious thing for us. We just like knowing that if anything happened to us, the baby would be taken care of. We want someone we can trust."

My chest grew tight, and I quickly took another sip of my beer.

Trust. I used to have trust. In my arm. In my mind. In the knowledge that a baseball would fucking land where I threw it.

But I did my best to smile. "Of course I will. I don't know the first fucking thing about babies, so you better stick around, but I'm honored. Thanks."

Sadie beamed, her eyes tearing up. "God, I was so scared you'd say no."

"She wasn't even going to ask," added Josh.

"Well, it's a lot of pressure." My sister wiped her eyes. "Sorry, I'm emotional these days. It's hormones."

"A *lot* of hormones." Josh lifted his beer to his lips.

Sadie elbowed him and went on. "Anyway, it's a big ask, and I didn't want you to feel obligated to say yes. Wait." Her gaze turned suspicious. "Did you say yes because you feel obligated?"

"No," I lied, praying that this *one time* she wouldn't see through it. "I said yes because I wanted to."

My sister sighed with relief. "Oh, good. So tell me what you've been up to."

"'Scuse me." A kid maybe ten years old stood at the end of our table holding a pen and a scrap of paper in his hands. He was looking at me. "Are you Tyler Shaw?"

"Yeah."

"Can I please have your autograph?"

"Sure." I took the kid's pen and paper and scribbled my name on it. "You a ball player?"

The kid nodded. "I'm a pitcher, too. My dad says you were the best there was around here."

"It's true," said Sadie proudly.

"He says you're a bum now," the kid went on, scratching his head, "but he said back in the day, no one could touch you."

Scowling, I handed him the autograph. "Well, here you go."

"Thanks," he said and wandered off.

"What a little shit." Josh stared after the kid.

I grabbed my beer and took another long drink. "I'm used to it."

"Well, we're going to raise our children with better manners," Sadie said defiantly.

"It's fine." I tipped up my amber ale again, nearly finishing it. "Josh, what is it you do? Sadie said something about boats?"

"I'm the head mechanic at Miller Boat Works."

"Must be getting busy this time of year. Summer right around the corner and all."

He nodded. "Yeah, we're swamped."

I looked at Sadie, who taught fifth grade at our old elementary school. "And how about you? School's almost out, right?"

"I've got one month left. I just hope I can keep the belly hidden until then." She glanced down and shook her head. "I'm wearing looser and looser clothing, but I feel like the kids are starting to look at me funny."

"So tell me about the wedding." I finished my beer and looked around for the server so I could order another. "Since you dragged me all the way back here for it, I should probably know when and where to show up."

Sadie sat up tall and pouted. "It's Saturday night at

Cloverleigh Farms, you big jerk, which you should *know*, because I sent every single detail to you already in an email."

"Sorry. I'm avoiding my inbox."

"You also got an invitation in the mail."

"I'm avoiding my mailbox too."

She sighed heavily. "I'll text you."

"Perfect."

Her eyes narrowed. "You brought a suit, right?"

"You mean I can't wear jeans?"

"No. A dark suit." Clearly not in the mood for jokes, she frowned, studying my head. "And could you get a haircut?"

"Is that really necessary?"

"Yes, please. And maybe a little closer on the shave?"

I looked at Josh. "This is why I'm never getting married."

"Who'd marry you anyway, you grumpy old man?" Sadie nudged my foot beneath the table. "Oh, by the way, April Sawyer said to say hello."

My fist tightened around my empty beer glass. My stomach flipped over. "You saw April Sawyer?"

"Yes. She's the event planner at Cloverleigh Farms, so she's doing our wedding."

"I didn't realize she still lived here."

"She was in New York City for a while, but she moved back home a few years ago." She looked at Josh. "If he came home more often, he'd know these things."

I swallowed hard. April Sawyer . . . I hadn't heard that name in years.

"Old friend?" Josh wondered.

"April was the best babysitter ever," Sadie told him. "She and Ty went to high school together." Then she looked at me. "And didn't she help you with math or something?"

"English." Which I never would have passed if she hadn't written half my papers. School had never been my thing, especially writing, but somehow April could ask me a few questions and turn my sparse, fumbling answers into sentences that made sense but still sounded like I'd written them. She always said I was smarter than I thought, and if I put half the effort into my homework that I put into my biceps, I'd be a straight-A student.

I'd dumped an entire bag of microwave popcorn over her head for that one.

And she was so good with my sister. Our dad worked long hours at multiple jobs—roofer, truck driver, handyman—to support us, and I was too busy with baseball to look after Sadie, so April was a godsend. She'd pick Sadie up after school and help her with homework. She'd make dinner on school nights. She'd get Sadie to bed. Then she'd stick around if I needed help with an assignment, or sometimes we'd just hang out and talk. I could make her laugh so hard she'd cry, and she had this way of rolling her eyes at my egotistical crap when any other girl would—and did—fall at my feet.

It was easy with us. No pressure. No bullshit. No games. It wasn't always easy to keep my hands to myself, but I did.

Right up until I didn't.

"So she's a wedding planner now?" I asked.

"Yes, and she's amazing. She's working her ass off for me. She looked at all my dream ideas and came up with ways to make them work on a smaller scale. And she called in favors from a bunch of vendors to get everything done fast, because of course, I'm doing everything last minute." Sadie laughed. "You're not really supposed to plan a wedding in three weeks."

"Do you need money?" I asked, still distracted by the thought of seeing April Sawyer after so many years. What did she look like now? Did she still have that cool red hair?

Sadie shook her head. "We're okay. It's a small wedding, less than a hundred guests, and Josh and I want to pay for it ourselves. But thanks for offering."

"Just let me know," I said, finally flagging down the waitress and ordering another beer.

When it arrived, something about the amber ale's rich auburn color reminded me of April Sawyer's hair. While we waited for our food, I found myself glancing at the door every time it opened, wondering if by chance she'd walk in and what I'd do if she did.

I couldn't get her out of my head.

On the drive back to my hotel, I wondered if she was married. If she had a family. If she was happy.

While I undressed and turned back the covers, I wondered if she ever thought about me.

As I lay on my back in the middle of the king-sized bed, I recalled little things about her I'd liked—the sound of her laugh, the dimples when she smiled, the sprinkle of freckles across the bridge of her nose, the surprisingly loud way she could whistle with her fingers, the smell of this lotion she used to wear that reminded me of birthday cake.

Was it that scent that had finally gotten the better of me that night? Was it the long red hair? The way she'd listened to me ramble on about my major league dreams while we sat in the back of my truck under the stars? Was it the fact that I was leaving the next day, and we had to say goodbye?

Or was I just a typical eighteen-year-old kid, fueled by a couple of beers and a fuck ton of testosterone?

Even now, I wasn't sure.

What I'd told my sister and Josh was true—I didn't know the first fucking thing about babies.

But I knew that eighteen years ago, April Sawyer had given birth to one.

And it had been mine.

CHAPTER 2

April

"I DID IT. I wrote the letter."

Without even a hello, I dropped breathlessly onto the couch in my therapist's office and made the announcement.

Prisha Dar, LMSW, smiled at me and lowered herself into her chair. Crossing her legs, she nodded encouragingly. "Go on."

"I did what you said. I went home and listed all the reasons I want to meet my birth son after eighteen years, and all the reasons I don't."

"And what did your lists tell you?"

"Well, the list of reasons *for* was much longer. It included things like wanting to see what he looks like, wanting to know he's happy, wanting to hear about his college plans." I paused, picturing the lists I'd written out on two separate notebook pages. "It also included things like wanting confirmation once and for all that I made the right decision for him all those years ago . . . and wanting closure on that chapter of my life."

She nodded. "And the list against?"

"It only had one word on it," I admitted. "Fear."

Prisha smiled sympathetically.

"And I'm still afraid. But I'm tired of letting that fear keep me from moving on. I always thought keeping my secret and burying all the painful feelings I associated with it—the guilt and the shame and the grief—was the best way to get over it. But maybe I was wrong."

"We often try to protect ourselves that way," Prisha said. "But it doesn't work, does it? Those feelings become anchors that tether us silently to the very pain we need to work through and let go. And even if you make the decision *not* to meet your birth son, which is perfectly okay, you still need to address those feelings. When you first came in here, I could tell you weren't quite ready." Her lips curved into a gentle smile. "But now I think you are."

I nodded. "I think so too. And last night, I wrote the letter to his parents. I even sealed it and addressed it and stamped it, but . . ." Ashamed, I reached into my shoulder bag and pulled out an envelope. "This morning, I couldn't bring myself to put it in the mailbox."

"Don't be too hard on yourself, April. You've come a long way in just a few months."

My throat caught, and I swallowed hard. "Thank you."

She set her iPad aside and crossed her arms. "Do you remember what you told me the first time you came in? The reason why you were seeking therapy?"

I thought for a moment, looking out the window of her office at a magnolia tree bursting with spring blooms. Back in February, when I'd first sat on this couch, the tree had been stark and barren, its branches lined with snow. "I wanted to be happier. I wanted to feel less alone."

"You wanted to be in a relationship. It's okay to say it out loud—we all want to feel loved and accepted."

I wondered what that would be like—to feel loved and accepted, deep dark secrets and all. I only knew what it looked like from the outside. Over the last year I'd watched all four of my sisters find their soul mates. "Yes. I would like that."

"But we have to start by loving and accepting *ourselves*. When we began, you were frustrated because you'd thought hiring someone at work was going to help. You thought less time on the job and more down time would help. You thought taking a vacation would help."

"Right. And then I did all those things—hired a second event planner, joined a gym, took a beach vacation, and I still felt . . ." I threw up my hands and looked at her again. "*Stuck* in this lonely, unhappy place. Like I'm on an island by myself watching everyone else on the mainland being happy."

Prisha regarded me silently for a moment. "April, it was clear to me very quickly that you weren't going to become happier just by working less. Once we explored your past, I felt certain that the isolation you were experiencing, and that sense of feeling *stuck*, was not because of your job, but because of this secret you've kept for eighteen years—this unfinished chapter in your life. You never wanted to tell anyone about the baby you gave up because you were scared they'd judge you the way you judge yourself, so you never let anyone get close to you. It was a protective measure."

I nodded, the lump forming in my throat again.

"Putting that letter in the mailbox—when you're ready—is a step toward writing the end of that chapter, but talking out loud about what you went through will be just as important. I want to encourage you to open up about this to someone in your life that you trust. You've said only your mother and grandmother knew about the baby, is that correct?"

"And my older sister, Sylvia. But I have three more sisters I never told."

She met my eyes. "Is there one of them you can trust?"

"I trust all of them," I said honestly.

"Good. Your homework is to tell one—or all—of them

about this time in your life. As scared as you are, as uncomfortable as it makes you, I believe it's necessary for you to heal. Once that's done, see how you feel about sending that letter."

I nodded, knowing she was right. If I really wanted to get unstuck, I'd have to be brave.

"There's something else," I blurted.

"Oh?"

I looked down at the letter in my hands. "The baby's father—there's a good chance I might see him for the first time since . . . since then. His sister is getting married a week from tonight, and I'm the wedding planner."

"I see." She reached for her iPad. "How does that make you feel?"

"Nervous, I guess." I played with one corner of the envelope. "I'm afraid I won't know how to act. Once upon a time, we were really close friends. But then afterward . . . we never spoke again."

"You've said you're not angry with him."

"I'm not. He felt just as terrible about what happened as I did. He apologized over and over again."

"Have you forgiven him?"

I looked up at her. "Of course. We were both at fault."

She nodded slowly and asked the question I was dreading. "Have you forgiven yourself?"

Two months ago, I probably would have lied and said yes. I might have even believed the lie. But I was trying harder to find the truth these days.

"I'm working on it," I told her.

"Good." She smiled softly. "And perhaps the timing of this reunion isn't ideal from *one* perspective, but may I suggest another way to look at it?"

"Of course."

"The universe works in mysterious ways, April. Perhaps this timing is meant to nudge you in the right direction. To help you let go of regret and embrace change."

"Like a sign?"

She lifted her shoulders. "Call it anything you like. Just don't be afraid of it. Only *you* have the power to hold yourself back or push yourself forward. Decide for yourself which one it will be."

Later that evening, I pulled a bottle of wine from my fridge.

After leaving the therapist's office, I'd texted my sisters and asked if they could come over to my place around eight. I was afraid if I waited any longer to confide in them, I'd lose my nerve.

I heard the front door of my condo open and shut. "Hello?"

"In the kitchen," I called, uncorking the bottle.

My sister Meg walked in, dressed in a skirt, blouse, and heels, as if she'd just come from the office. "Hey," she said, hanging her purse on the back of a kitchen chair. "How are you?"

"Good," I said, taking four glasses down from a cupboard. There were five Sawyer sisters, and we all loved wine, but our oldest sister Sylvia was pregnant. "How's the new job?"

Meg, the middle sister, had recently moved back from D.C. and taken a position as an attorney at a regional branch of the American Association for People with Disabilities. "I love it," she enthused, rolling up the sleeves of her blouse. "It's long hours, and I wish I saw Noah more, but the job is perfect for me. Want me to pour this?"

"Sure."

Noah was Meg's boyfriend and the reason she'd moved home. He was a K-9 cop with the local sheriff's department, and they'd always been the best of friends, but last fall while she was home for our youngest sister Frannie's wedding, they'd finally admitted to themselves what the rest of us had seen all along—they were perfect for each other.

Chloe, the second youngest, arrived as I was putting a platter of cheese and crackers on the table, and she was bubbling over with excitement because our father was finally going to retire for good this month, which meant she'd really get to take over as CEO of Cloverleigh Farms. My parents started the business as a small sustainable farm but it had grown to encompass an inn, a farm-to-table restaurant, a winery, and a brand new small-batch distillery that Chloe and her fiancé Oliver were opening. It was also one of the top wedding venues in the state.

"Dad actually cleaned out his office," Chloe said, kicking off her heels and dropping into the chair next to Meg. "Maybe he wasn't lying when he said the job was mine."

Meg laughed. "Now you don't have to change the lock."

Sylvia arrived next, looking a little windblown but otherwise—as usual—radiantly beautiful. The oldest among us, Sylvia had returned to our childhood home over the winter in order to make a fresh start with her two children after being abandoned by her asshole ex-husband. Henry DeSantis, the vineyard manager and winemaker at Cloverleigh Farms, had taken one look at her and fallen head over heels. They were newly engaged and expecting a baby this fall.

"Hey, Syl. How are you feeling?" I asked.

Smiling brightly, Sylvia took the seat between Meg and me. "Pretty good, thanks. Growing out of my pants quicker than I'd like, but that's okay."

A moment later, our youngest sister Frannie came bustling in. "Sorry," she said breathlessly. "Mack was late getting home from work, and I don't like leaving the girls alone at night." Frannie was married to Declan MacAllister, the CFO at Cloverleigh Farms, who had three daughters from a previous marriage.

"No worries," I said as she scooted around the table and sat in the chair to my left.

For a few minutes, I was silent, trying to work up my nerve to tell them my secret. Around me, my sisters jabbered a mile a minute about Meg's new job and Chloe's fall wedding and Sylvia's new house and Frannie's pastry shop and our dad's big retirement party at the end of the month, which was also a fortieth anniversary party for Cloverleigh Farms . . . the chatter never seemed to die down.

Eventually, it was Sylvia who noticed I hadn't said anything. "April, are you okay?" she asked, looking at me with concern.

"Yes." I cleared my throat and sat up taller. "Yes, but I have something to tell you guys."

The room grew so silent I could hear the crickets outside the closed kitchen windows.

"What's wrong?" Frannie asked.

"Nothing's wrong, exactly, it's just . . ." I reached for my wine glass and took a sip of riesling.

Next to me, Sylvia put a hand on my leg—somehow she knew. I exchanged a quick glance with her, and she smiled softly at me. *It's okay,* her eyes said.

Nodding slightly, I set my glass down. "This is hard for me," I began, "because I love you and I trust you." Another deep breath. "But I've kept something from you for a lot of years."

"What is it?" Meg leaned forward, her elbows on the table. "You can tell us, April."

I placed my hands over my stomach, which was churning. "The summer after I graduated from high school, I got pregnant."

Jaws dropped around the table. Eyes went wide.

"By who?" Chloe asked the question on everyone's mind.

"I'll tell you guys, but please keep his name within our

Sawyer sister circle of trust. He was supportive of the adoption, but he didn't want his name on the birth certificate."

"It was Tyler Shaw, wasn't it?" Meg asked.

I stared at her across the table. "Yes. How did you know?"

"You guys hung out a lot that year. You were at his house all the time." She shrugged. "And he was fucking *hot*. Half the girls in school were in love with him."

"Well, *I* wasn't in love with him," I said. "I was at his house all the time because I was babysitting his little sister. We were honestly just good friends. I mean, I wasn't blind. I thought he was hot too, but he had girls throwing themselves at him *all* the time—literally throwing themselves. I liked that I wasn't one of them. And I think he liked it too. He respected me."

"So then how did it happen?" Chloe tilted her head. "Was it just a random one-time thing?"

I nodded. "Totally. It was right after we'd graduated, the night before he left. We were at someone's graduation party— I can't even remember whose—and he offered to drive me home. But instead of going straight there, we took a detour."

"Where?" Frannie asked, then bit her lip. "Sorry, is this too personal?"

"No, it's okay." I took a breath, letting the memories from that night roll over me like ocean waves. "He wanted to drive by this old ballfield where he'd played a lot of games as a kid. It was completely deserted and dark, of course, because it was so late at night, and we just sat in the bed of his truck and talked. We'd spent a lot of time together, but that was the first time he ever really opened up to me about his feelings. He talked more about his childhood, his mom's death, how much it meant to him to make his dad proud. And he was just so excited to get out of here and go prove himself. The only thing he was sad about was leaving his sister. He thanked me for helping out with her so much." I took another breath. "Then he thanked me for helping him with homework." A pause. "Then he said how he couldn't have made it through senior year without me, and he reached over and touched my hair."

"You do have *awesome* hair," Meg said.

I laughed a little. "Next thing I knew, we were kissing, and after that, everything happened pretty fast. I mean, *really* fast."

"That's an eighteen-year-old guy for you," Chloe said.

"So no condom?" Frannie guessed.

I shook my head. "Nope. Truth be told, that was my first time. I was mostly just terrified I was doing it wrong."

"Even if that were possible, I doubt he'd have noticed," said Chloe. "Eighteen, remember?"

"So what happened afterward?" Frannie asked.

"Well, immediately afterward, we sort of awkwardly laughed and he took me home. Hugged me goodbye on Mom and Dad's front porch. He was off to Arizona the next day, and I left for college at the end of the summer."

"Did you keep in touch?" asked Meg.

"Not really. Maybe the occasional text, but we were both on to the next chapters of our lives. It wasn't until October that I began to suspect I might be pregnant. I'd missed a couple periods by then, but I'd figured it was stress. And I thought the weight gain was the typical freshman fifteen. But then I took a drugstore test, and it was positive." I shuddered at the memory. "I came home at Thanksgiving and told Mom. She made me an appointment with her doctor. When the results were confirmed, we discussed the options. But she told me the decision was mine and she'd support me no matter what."

"God," Chloe said, shaking her head. "I can't believe you went through all this and never said anything."

"I was embarrassed," I confessed. "I'd been careless and irresponsible. I didn't want you guys to know what I'd done. You were barely out of middle school. Meg was just sixteen.

And Frannie was like *ten* or something. I was supposed to be a good example."

"You were, April." Frannie leaned over and touched my shoulder. "You always put other people first. I learned that from you."

I smiled at her. "Thanks." Then I glanced at Sylvia. "I actually confessed everything to Sylvia that Christmas, because she found me crying in my room on Christmas Eve. But I made her promise not to tell anyone."

"Did Dad know?" Meg asked.

I shrugged. "I asked Mom not to tell him, but I don't know for sure if she did or not. At the time, I thought I wouldn't be able to face him, but he probably would have been just as supportive as Mom. Anyway, I thought about it and decided I wanted to give the baby up for adoption. Mom helped me choose a family through an agency, I deferred my second semester at school, and I moved in with Grandma Russell for my last three months. Had the baby in March."

Chloe gasped. "Grandma Russell knew? Damn, she took that secret to the grave, huh?"

"Well, Mom had to put me somewhere," I explained with a shrug. "And actually, Grandma was surprisingly chill about it. She said it had happened to a friend of hers back in like 1950 or something, and the girl had to go to a convent."

"Wow." Frannie shook her head.

"So what did you have, April?" Meg asked softly. "A girl or a boy?"

"A boy." Closing my eyes, I pictured that tiny, wailing, perfect, beautiful baby they'd placed on my chest. "I had a boy."

No one spoke for a few seconds.

"Did you even get to hold him?" Frannie asked.

"For a few minutes. I remember he was wrapped in a white flannel blanket and wore a blue knit hat, and he had huge, dark, serious eyes. He wasn't even crying, but I was." I smiled ruefully and wiped a tear from my eye. "I promised him that I'd never forget him, that I hoped he'd have the best life ever, and that I was sorry I couldn't keep him. Then I handed him over to his mom and dad—his real mom and dad."

They were all silent for a moment, and Sylvia took my hand. "That had to be so hard for you."

"It was," I said.

"Do you know his name?" Chloe asked gently.

I nodded. "They named him Charles, after his father and grandfather."

They were quiet as it sunk in.

"What did you do after that?" Chloe asked.

"I came home for the summer and never said a word to anyone. That fall I went back to Penn State and tried to move on."

"Wait a minute, back up. What about Tyler?" Meg asked. "You said he knew about the baby?"

I nodded. "Yes. He was home that Thanksgiving too. I went over to his house and told him, and he was devastated. I could just see it on his face—he thought his life was over. He wasn't ready to be a dad. He wasn't even nineteen. He'd barely gotten his ticket out of here, and hadn't even played a major league game yet. He didn't want the responsibility of a wife and kid."

"Did he *offer* to marry you?" Frannie wondered.

"No, he just asked me what I wanted to do. I said right away I wanted to give it up for adoption, and he was totally relieved. He offered to pay for anything I needed, but I told him I didn't need money. The only other thing he asked was that his name be left off the birth certificate, and I agreed that was for the best."

"Were you mad about that?" Meg studied me curiously.

"No. I understood. And it actually made things easier, because I didn't have to chase him down to sign anything." I shook my head. "I know we should have been careful. But I've never blamed Tyler. Mostly I just felt guilty and sad."

"Why would you feel guilty?" Frannie asked. "You did the right thing."

I fought a fresh onslaught of tears. "I know. In my head, I know. But something in me still felt like I was shirking my responsibility to this little human life, like I had failed some kind of test of my worth. I was ashamed."

"I wonder if Tyler ever felt any of that," said Meg. "If he ever had regrets."

I shrugged. "Not that I know of. But to be fair, we never talked about it. I don't know how he ended up feeling."

Sylvia squeezed my hand. "You were so brave, April."

"Do you—do you know what happened to the baby?" Frannie asked.

I shook my head. "No. Robin, his mom, offered to keep in touch by sending me updates every six months, or yearly, or however often I chose, but I declined. I knew I couldn't handle it. She said she understood, but that if I ever changed my mind I could reach out. She left me with her address."

"Did you ever do it?" Meg wondered.

"Not until now." Willing myself to be brave, I stood up, went over to the counter, and dug the letter out of my purse. Then I tossed the envelope on the table and sat down again.

My sisters stared at it.

"Are you going to send it?" Chloe asked.

"Maybe." I stared at it too. "But I'm scared. It will change my life."

"But isn't that why you wrote it?" Sylvia asked. "Because you want to change your life? I don't think you would have brought us all here tonight if you didn't."

I struggled with tears, and they let me work through it for a moment.

"Why *did* you write it, April? I mean, why *now*?" Frannie asked.

I took a calming breath, in through my nose, out through my mouth, like Prisha had taught me. "First, it was you guys. Watching each of you find your perfect someone over the last year has been both wonderful and lonely. I don't want you to feel bad about that," I said quickly, because I could see the anguish taking over their faces. "You deserve to be happy. You worked for it. You put yourselves out there and took risks. I needed to figure out how to do that. I started seeing a therapist, and she's been wonderful at helping me unpack some of the baggage I've kept hidden away. I used to think that what was past was past, but it turns out holding on to a painful secret like that has consequences that stick with you. It makes it impossible to embrace the future."

"Of course it does." Frannie had tears in her eyes. "I feel so terrible that you went through this alone for so long."

"Don't," I said, shaking my head. "It was my choice to keep the secret. And my therapist has shown me how I've used that choice to keep myself at a distance from people, not just from you all, but from potential romantic relationships. So my first step had to be talking about that part of my past out loud with someone I trust . . ." I smiled at them. "So here we are."

Meg smiled across the table, her eyes shining. "I'm so glad you told us."

"Me too." Feeling stronger already, I managed a smile. "I'm so tired of being afraid, you guys. I want to be brave enough to face what's ahead—even seeing Tyler again."

Every single one of my sisters gasped.

"Oh my God, at Sadie's wedding!" Frannie squealed, putting both hands over her cheeks. "I didn't even think about that. He'll be there because he's giving her away!" Frannie and Sadie were the same age and had always been friends. She and Mack would be at the wedding.

"Sadie is getting married?" Chloe asked.

"Yes," I said. "She called me about a month ago. She's

unexpectedly pregnant—kind of a crazy coincidence, I know —but she and her boyfriend want to get married. She said she's always dreamed of a wedding at Cloverleigh Farms, so on the off chance we had anything available in the near future, she reached out. When I told her we'd had a cancellation in May, she booked it. Her wedding is Saturday night."

"Wow," Meg said.

"I didn't mention anything about it to you guys, because I've kind of been processing everything slowly, giving myself a chance to take it all in without freaking out. It would have been *really* easy for me to hand Sadie's wedding off to my assistant and not deal with this head on. But I think seeing Tyler again is something I have to do in order to heal."

"So this will be the first time since . . ." Chloe's voice trailed off.

"Since that Thanksgiving when I told him I was pregnant. We never spoke after that."

"Wow. He didn't even reach out to see if you'd *had* the baby?" Frannie asked. "Or what it was?"

I shook my head. "No, and I was glad about that. I was struggling to handle my feelings, and hearing from him would have made it worse. For a while, I couldn't even watch baseball without choking up." I sat up taller and cleared my throat. "But that was me then. And this is me now."

"I'm so proud of you," Sylvia said, sniffling a little.

"Me too," echoed Meg, then Chloe, then Frannie. Each of them had tears in their eyes.

"Thanks, you guys." Looking around the table at them, my throat grew so tight I could hardly speak. "That means a lot to me. I feel very lucky to have you on my side."

"Always." Sylvia took my hand in hers and squeezed hard. "Now come on. We'll all walk you to the mailbox."

CHAPTER 3

Tyler

I TOSSED and turned all night.

I didn't know if it was the thumping noise coming from the room next to me (seriously, the dude had some stamina), or thinking about April, or the terrifying thought that my sister had asked me to be responsible for her child should anything happen to her, but something was keeping me awake. Maybe it was just being back in this town.

Leaning toward the nightstand, I checked the time on my phone. Not even five a.m.

I flopped onto my back again. For a moment, I thought about jerking off, but before I even got my hand on my dick, April popped into my head, and it bothered me so much that I abandoned the project. It wasn't that the memory of being with her wasn't hot, because it was. And back before we'd had sex, I used to get myself off thinking about her all the time. But after everything that happened, fantasizing about April had just felt wrong. Disrespectful. Like I didn't have the right.

Grabbing the remote from the nightstand, I turned the TV on and hunted for ESPN. Maybe some boring replay of a golf tournament would put me to sleep. Or some talking heads getting worked up about hockey playoffs. As long as it wasn't that damn documentary, I'd watch it.

But of course, that's exactly what was on.

WELL-KNOWN SPORTSCASTER: You know, his dad was a ball player. Put in ten years in the minors but never got called up. I interviewed him once, and he was so proud. And Shaw himself once told me how much it meant to him that his father always had time to play catch or talk baseball with him, even though he was a single dad and had to work two jobs to support the family.

(Cut to photo of fifteen-year-old me with my dad, his arm around my shoulders, a wide grin on his face.)

SPORTSCASTER VOICEOVER: They were close. It had to be hard on Shaw when his father died. I always wondered if that was what caused the problem, even though it happened several years earlier. I don't know, I guess we were all just searching for any reason this guy lost his arm.

FORMER MINOR LEAGUE COACH: I thought maybe he had a blister. I *hoped* he did. A blister would heal. (A heavy sigh. A shake of his head.) But he didn't. Poor bastard.

Angry, I switched the TV off, hurled the remote to the floor, and crossed my arms over my bare chest. If I heard one more person refer to me as *that poor bastard,* I was going to put my fucking fist through the wall.

I sat there scowling in the dark for a while, long enough for the thumping in the next room to start up again, as if to remind me that not only was I a washed-up has-been, I was a washed-up has-been who wasn't having sex. Either way, more sleep was not happening.

Tossing the finger at the couple on the other side of the wall, I got out of bed. After throwing on some sweats, I yanked a ball cap onto my head, grabbed my wallet and keys, and stormed out of the room, letting the door slam shut behind me.

I did seven miles on the high school track. I dropped to the ground for push-ups, crunches, mountain climbers, planks. I ran the bleachers.

When I'd first arrived, it had been dark and cool, but now the sun was rising and the air had lost its chill—I was sweating hard, and it felt good to distract myself with physical exertion, to take out all my pent-up aggression on my muscles. But eventually my stomach started to growl, and I decided to call it quits. Maybe there was a diner open early, and I could sit unnoticed and grab some breakfast before cleaning up and heading out for that haircut my sister wanted me to get. Surely there was a barber somewhere in town who wouldn't recognize me, right? I was jogging down from the stands, thinking maybe I'd have to drive a couple towns over, when I saw that I wasn't alone.

A woman was power walking around the track. She wore black leggings and a white zip-up jacket, sunglasses and a ponytail. Her hair was long and reddish-brown, swinging from side to side as she moved. It reminded me of—

Wait a minute.

I stopped and stared as she looped around the near end of the track and started walking toward me—and that's when I knew.

"April!" I shouted.

She looked up at me and stumbled a second later, going down hard on her hands and knees.

I jumped to the ground and sprinted toward her, reaching her side just as she was getting to her feet again.

"Hey," I said, taking her by the elbow to help her up. "Are you okay?"

"I'm fine. Just embarrassed." She adjusted her sunglasses and looked up at me. "Tyler?"

I nodded, letting go of her arm.

"What are you doing here?"

"I'm in town for Sadie's wedding." My heart was thumping uncomfortably hard in my chest—I'd yelled her name without being prepared to actually come face to face with her.

"Oh. Right." She shook her head. "I knew that."

I couldn't read her expression. Christ, this was awkward.

"Well . . ." April fidgeted for a second or two, then surprised me by laughing. "This really is *not* how I thought this reunion would go."

The sound of her laughter took me back to a different time. I relaxed slightly, widening my stance and folding my arms over my chest. I wished my shirt wasn't so sweaty. "No?"

"No," she said. "I thought it would be at Sadie's wedding. I had planned to wash my hair, put on a dress or at least some real pants, maybe wear lipstick. At the very least, I was going to remain upright."

I grinned. "I'm sorry if I scared you. You're sure you're all right?"

"I'm fine. A little startled was all." Then she opened her arms and gave me a smile, the one with the dimples that rolled time back even further. "So . . . hi."

At first I was too shocked to react, but eventually I recovered my senses enough to put my arms around her. "Hi."

She had to rise up on her toes to embrace me—I was a full foot taller than she was—and I leaned forward at the waist so she wouldn't be pressed against my damp shirt, but damn, it felt good. So good I didn't want to let her go right away. She even smelled nice—not exactly the same as she used to, but it reminded me of something warm and sweet, and it made me even hungrier. I allowed myself to hold her for a moment before stepping back.

"So how are you?" she asked.

I crossed my arms over my chest again. "I'm okay. How about you?"

"Pretty good." As she spoke, she pulled her ponytail out and regathered her hair in her hands. "I'm usually alone here this early in the morning, so you surprised me. How was your workout?"

"I'm dragging a bit," I admitted. "Didn't sleep much last night."

"Why not?"

I shrugged. "Just restless, I guess."

Her face was the same and yet different, more mature—sharper cheekbones, soft grooves on either side of her mouth—and yet still girlish, with its freckles and dimples. The dark lenses of her sunglasses covered her eyes, and for the life of me, I couldn't recall what color they were. Blue? Brown?

As I watched her put her hair up again, a memory popped into my head—the night we'd had sex, I'd reached over and touched it. That was how the whole thing had gotten started, right? I'd put my hand in her hair and pulled her head toward mine. I hadn't planned on making a move—that wasn't the reason I'd taken a detour to the field that night—but in that moment, I'd been unable to hold back. I'd just wanted—needed—to be closer to her.

"Josh seems like a nice guy," she said, breaking a silence that had grown a little awkward while I was staring at her. "Have you met him yet?"

"Yeah. Last night. I had dinner with Sadie and Josh after my flight got in."

"How long are you in town?"

"Too long." I sort of meant it as a joke, but the words came out with more bite than intended.

"Why do you say that?"

I shrugged and looked at my feet. "I just don't like coming back here that much."

She looked genuinely confused. "But this town loves you. People are still talking about you around here."

My jaw clenched as I thought about rental car Steve and the kid at the restaurant last night. "Yeah. And I know what they're saying."

There was an awkward pause while she groped for a polite reply. "So what are you up to these days?" she tried. "I heard you, um, retired from baseball."

"Retired? That's a polite way to put it." My words had a sharp edge to them—again, not exactly what I intended, but I hated that I was now an object of pity and scorn when I'd once been worshipped.

She looked confused. "Is there another way to put it?"

"How about I fell apart on the mound during what was arguably the most critical game of my career? How about I tanked my future in baseball because suddenly I couldn't fucking remember how to throw strikes? How about I failed to prove I was as good as everybody said I was—how about I just fucking *failed*, period?"

"Tyler, come on. You didn't fail. You just—"

"Look, I know what everybody around here thinks of me, okay? You don't have to pretend."

She stuck her hands on her hips and cocked her head. "I'm not pretending anything. And the only thing I'm thinking right now is something I'll say right to your face—you're being a real asshole."

Brushing past my right shoulder, she continued power

walking down the track, her arms pumping angrily. It actually reminded me of the way Sadie didn't let me get away with shit—or maybe it was that Sadie grew up to be like April, the closest thing to a female role model my sister had in the house.

I remained rooted in place for another minute, jaw clenched, mad at myself for being a dick to her. It wasn't her fault I'd turned my baseball career into a dumpster fire and didn't know what I was supposed to do with the rest of my life. And after what she'd gone through, she deserved better from me. Turning on my heel, I ran down the track until I caught up with her.

"Hey," I said, grabbing her by the elbow.

She jerked her arm away from me and picked up her pace. "Leave me alone, Tyler."

"I can't."

"Yes, you can. You've done it for eighteen years, so just keep on keeping on."

"No. Come on. I'm sorry." I darted ahead and jogged backward in front of her. "I'm sorry, okay?"

"Okay." She kept right on walking.

"I'm serious."

"Fine."

"Can we stop moving please?"

"Why?"

"Because I want to talk to you." I halted my steps and reached out, attempting to catch her by the shoulders before she crashed into me, but she barreled into my chest anyway before going down on her butt.

"Oof!"

Immediately I knelt down to help her up. "Sorry. I can't seem to get anything right this morning. Are you okay?"

"I'm fine." She brushed some dust off the seat of her pants. "Not really sure what's wrong with my balance today, but I'm fine."

I took her upper arms and looked her in the eye. "You're totally right—I was being an asshole back there. I do that sometimes."

"Why?"

"I don't know. Because I'm not used to people being nice. Because I don't want sympathy. Because I get really mad at myself and want to make other people mad at me too." I shrugged, dropping my arms. "At least that's what my therapist said. I probably shouldn't have fired him."

"You fired your therapist?"

"It was kind of mutual. I said he wasn't helping. He said I wasn't trying. Which I probably wasn't." I adjusted my cap and tried again to explain myself. "Look, being back in this town is messing with me a little bit. I had a lot of dreams when I left that have died on me—or maybe I killed them, who the hell knows—either way, it's really hard to let them go. But that's not your fault, and I didn't mean to take it out on you."

She studied me silently for a moment. "Okay."

"Does that mean I'm forgiven?"

"I suppose."

I exhaled. "Good."

She opened her mouth like she had more to say, but then closed it again.

"What?"

"I was just going to say that letting go of the past is something I've struggled with too. So I get it."

"Yeah?"

"Yes. And I agree, it's painful. But you have to do it, or you're going to remain stuck in a really unhappy place." Then she sort of smiled. "At least, that's what *my* therapist says. And we're still together."

Voices carried across the field, and we both looked toward the opposite side of the track, where three other runners were stretching out.

"I should let you get back to your workout," I said.

"Okay."

But we both stood there a moment longer, and I realized I didn't want this to be goodbye. "Can I see you again?" I blurted, surprising myself. "Maybe for dinner or a drink or something?"

She hesitated, then shrugged. "Sure."

"Are you busy tonight?" I frowned. "Sorry for the late notice, but I'm leaving Sunday, Sadie has me tied up with wedding stuff Friday and Saturday, so tonight is my only night off."

She thought for a second. "I could do tonight. I have a meeting with an engaged couple at five-thirty. Why don't you come by the bar at the inn? I should be free by about seven."

"I could do that."

"Great, I'll meet you there. You remember where it is?"

I gave her my old grin. "I haven't been gone *that* long."

She laughed. "Okay. Let me give you my number. Just text me when you're on your way."

Pulling my phone from the pocket of my sweats, I listened carefully as she recited her number and added her to my contacts. "Got it. I'll see you tonight."

"Okay." She gave me a little wave and continued down the track.

I watched her for a minute, admiring the swing of her hips and the long ponytail, wondering if she was single. My body reacted at the thought of the curves beneath her clothing, the warm bare skin, that deep red hair hanging down her naked back.

Not that I'd ever seen her naked—I wasn't even sure I'd taken both of her legs out of her jeans in the back of my truck. Too bad I couldn't get a do-over. I'd learned a few things since then.

But as I walked back to my SUV, I scolded myself for even thinking about it.

Hands off, Shaw, I told myself as I unlocked the driver's side door. *You've caused that girl enough grief. Buy her dinner, ask her how she's been, apologize for being a dickhead eighteen-year-old who couldn't keep it in his pants, but do not, under any circumstances, lay one finger on her, even if she is more beautiful now than she was then.*

Yet as soon as I got in the car, I brought up her name and number in my phone just so I could stare at it. Eighteen years had gone by since I'd seen her. That was a long time—half my life. Half her life.

And it hit me.

That baby—had it been a boy or a girl?—was just as old now as we'd been the night it was conceived.

But like I always did when my mind started to venture into dangerous territory, I shut it down.

What was past was past.

CHAPTER 4

April

I FINISHED my walk on rubbery legs.

Thankfully, Tyler was gone by the time I looped around the track again, otherwise he'd have seen me stop, put both hands over my heart and take a few slow, deep breaths.

My God . . . what the hell had just happened?

I'd been thinking of him as I walked, wondering what it would be like when I first saw him again, debating what to wear, fretting about whether I should give him a hug or keep it more formal with a handshake, or maybe even just a smile. What if he was bringing a date to the wedding? Sadie had never said whether he was *single* or not, just that he wasn't married and never had been.

And all of a sudden, I'd heard his voice calling my name. When I looked up, he was *there*. Like a ghost from the past, he was *right there*. I'd been so stunned, I'd tripped over my own feet.

Then we were face to face, he was helping me up, and my heartbeat couldn't seem to find its normal rhythm.

And . . . I'd laughed. Maybe it was nerves, maybe it was panic, but suddenly the situation struck me as funny, and I'd laughed. And he'd grinned. Then it was almost as if no time had passed at all. It had felt natural to hug him. *Good*, in fact. Like finding a missing puzzle piece and snapping it into place.

I circled the track a few more times, going over it again and again. Picturing his face. Recalling the solid feel of his arms around me.

Of course, he was still gorgeous. Maybe he had the tiniest hint of gray in his scruff and a slightly broader torso, but he was just as tall, dark, and handsome as he'd been in high school.

But there was something different in his eyes now—I could see it. Back then, he was all lethal intensity when he was on the mound, and all cocky strut when he was off it. Today I saw something else—vulnerability. It was hidden behind some gruff attitude and dickhead bluster, but I saw it. And I knew a little about what he'd gone through the past few years—everyone did. He wasn't wrong about that.

It got to me . . . I knew what it was like to feel as if you'd been put to the test and failed. I knew what it was like to feel haunted by the past. I knew what it was like to be afraid of people judging you. And I wanted him to know I was still his friend. He hadn't failed *me*.

Also? I was damn proud of myself. I'd handled seeing him again even better than I'd expected, and I was actually looking forward to seeing him tonight. After a few minutes of stretching on the grass, I got in my car and drove home, windows down, radio up, a smile on my face.

I was bursting to tell someone what happened, so as soon as I got to Cloverleigh, I went right to Chloe's new office and knocked on her open door.

She looked up from unpacking a cardboard box on her desk. "Hey," she said. "What's up?"

I shut the door behind me and leaned back against it, breathless. "I saw him."

"Who?" She looked confused.

"Tyler!"

Her jaw dropped. "*What*? Where? When?"

"This morning. Six a.m. The high school track. I was walking. He was running the bleachers." My words tumbled out in a rush.

"And?"

"And he said hello."

"*And?*"

"I said hello back. We hugged. It was awkward for a minute, but then it was just . . ." I paused for some air. "Nice."

Chloe gasped. "Really? It was *nice*?"

"Really. He asked if I wanted to have dinner later, and I said yes."

My sister looked me over with a shrewd eye and nodded. "Well, that explains it."

"Explains what?"

"The Beyoncé hair."

"What Beyoncé hair?" I asked, touching the soft waves cascading over one shoulder. As if I hadn't left my hair down today on purpose instead of pulling it back like I usually did at work. As if I hadn't tried on and discarded ten different outfits before leaving the house. As if I hadn't put a pair of sexy heels in my shoulder bag.

But she couldn't even see them!

She eyeballed me for another moment and then sniffed. "Are you wearing perfume?"

I rolled my eyes. "Stop it. It's not like that."

Laughing, she shook her head. "No way I can stop now. And you're the one who came rushing in here to announce your dinner date."

"It's not a date! And I came rushing in here because I was proud of how well I handled seeing him again, thank you very much. I wanted to share it with you."

"Okay, okay. I'm proud of you too," she said, her tone softer. "I don't mean to tease. Although I *am* a little shocked."

"Same." I shook my head. "I was standing there looking at him, thinking he should feel like a total stranger, but he didn't."

"Well, you went through something pretty major together." Chloe took a framed photo of herself and Oliver as kids from the box and set it on a shelf. "Even though you haven't stayed in close touch, that kind of thing is always going to bind you."

"Maybe."

"So did the whole . . ." Turning toward me, she touched her stomach. "*Baby* thing come up at all?"

"No," I said quickly. "We only chatted for a few minutes."

"About what?"

"Different things. He actually got a little testy when the subject of baseball came up. He's definitely aware that people around here remember the way he was, and he's embarrassed that his career didn't turn out the way he planned."

Chloe winced. "Yeah, that documentary was pretty brutal. I haven't seen the whole thing, but I've heard Noah and Mack discussing it. Mack played with him in high school, I guess."

"That's right, I forgot that. Mack was two years ahead of us, but Tyler was so good he played varsity all four years."

"So he won't even *talk* about baseball now?"

"I don't really know. He just said he knows what people think of him, and it's obvious he doesn't like it."

"Well, who would?"

I bit my lip. "I have this feeling he's kind of . . . lonely."

"Really?" Chloe blinked in surprise. "A guy like that? Former MLB player? Plenty of money? I assume he still has his looks."

"He still has his looks, that's for sure." I recalled the dark eyes and broad shoulders, the chiseled jaw and full lips. "But he's lost some of his old swagger."

Chloe snorted. "From what I remember, he had some to spare."

I laughed. "True. But he's older now, and he's been through a lot. He's lost his dad, his career, saw his childhood dream go up in smoke . . . that had to be painful."

"I love that you're thinking of *his* feelings, when seeing him again had to be so tough for you." Chloe shook her head and smiled.

"I did better than I thought I would," I admitted, proud of myself all over again. "And you know, it really wasn't as hard as I'd expected. Maybe because our history wasn't painful in a romantic way—it's not like he betrayed me or something."

Chloe shrugged. "True."

"And you know, I think seeing him struggling with his own emotional baggage made it easier on me—if he *had* still possessed that cocky-teenager attitude, I might have been put off."

"Makes total sense. So maybe you guys will actually be good for each other." Her eyes took on a mischievous sparkle.

Laughing, I shook my head. "No way. He's only in town until the wedding, and I've been there, done that. I love the idea of reconnecting, maybe getting some closure, but that's all this is. What I'm looking for romantically is something more meaningful."

My sister surprised me by coming around her desk and throwing her arms around me. "You'll find what you're looking for. I know you will."

"Thanks." I hugged her back. "But don't mess up my hair. I'm not going to bang him, but I still want him to think I look good after all these years."

"He will," said Chloe, giggling as she let me go. "I promise you, he will."

CHAPTER 5

Tyler

AFTER LEAVING April on the track, I went back to my hotel room and ordered room service for breakfast. While I was eating, my sister texted all the details about the rehearsal dinner and wedding—exactly what I was to wear, when and where I had to show up, what I would be expected to do. I was fine with everything until I got to **Brother-Sister Dance: You/Me, then Josh/Mary.**

Frowning, I called her.

"Hello?"

"I got your text." I took a bite of toast.

"Oh, good."

"What the hell is this brother-sister dance?" I asked with my mouth full.

"Josh is going to dance with his sister Mary for one song, and then you're going to dance one song with me."

"*Alone?*"

"Yes."

I nearly choked. "For an *entire song*?"

"Yes."

I managed to swallow. "No fucking way, Sadie. I'm not doing it."

"Please, Ty? You can even pick the song. Choose a short one, I don't care, but I've always wanted to dance with you at my wedding. Josh is really close to his sister, and you mean so much to me—even though you're being a big jerk about this—having a special moment where it's all about sibling love is something we really want. Please say you'll do it, for me."

I groaned, knowing I couldn't say no to her.

"It won't be that bad, I promise!"

"There'd better be good whiskey at this wedding."

She giggled. "There will be. Hey, what are you doing today? I took today and tomorrow off, but Josh has to work and I'm trying to move some furniture out of the room that will be the baby's. Can you come over and give me a hand?"

"Yeah." I took one more drink of my coffee and set the cup down. "Text me your address. I'll be there in an hour. Do I need to wear a fucking suit for this?"

She giggled. "No. Jeans are fine. But could you please bring the outfit you're planning to wear Saturday night so I can approve it?"

I pinched the bridge of my nose. "Yes. But you're a pain in the ass, and this wedding is already giving me a headache."

"Hey, I went to a lot of baseball games for you. I think I spent my entire childhood on the bleachers."

"I thought you loved going to games," I said.

"I loved *you*. Baseball was just something you did."

After we hung up, I sat there for a few minutes thinking about what she'd said.

She had it wrong. Baseball wasn't just something I did. Baseball was my life. Baseball was my destiny. I was never more *me* than I was when I was on the field, and I didn't know who I was without it.

I'd spent the last year totally adrift, feeling untethered to anything or anyone. I suppose it didn't help that I'd spent much of that time in self-exile, throwing anything that would fit in my left hand at whatever target I could find, trying to find my motion again.

Occasionally, I'd get close to it, and my body would almost feel like mine again. My head would clear a little. I'd latch onto some hope.

But it would never last.

Rising to my feet, I went over to my bag to pull out clothes for the day—jeans, sweatshirt, T-shirt, underwear, socks. I held the pair of balled-up socks in my hand for a moment, staring at it.

I turned sideways. Gave myself the menacing stare in the full-length mirror. Imagined I got the sign for an inside fastball. In my head, I heard my high school pitching coach talking through the physics of a pitch—the mechanics— which he insisted I had to understand if I wanted to be good.

The windup and stride. Elevation of the lead leg. Center of gravity back. Separation of ball from glove. Lead foot to mound, in line with stance foot and home plate. Pelvic rotation and forward tilt. Upper torso rotation. Late cocking. Horizontal adduction. Maximum torque at the elbow. Acceleration. Transfer of energy to upper extremity for maximum velocity.

Release.

Release.

Release.

I threw the pair of socks toward my reflection again and again and again.

But it never felt right.

I spent the rest of the morning helping Sadie empty out a spare bedroom at the house she shared with Josh. Then she sweet-talked me into ripping out the old carpeting, taping off the molding, and priming the walls.

"If you'll stay and put the first coat of color on, I'll love you forever," she cajoled.

"You'll love me forever anyway." I set the roller back in the tray. "And I thought you wanted me to go get a haircut today."

"You'll have time later. What else are you going to do, mope alone in your hotel room?"

I thought about mentioning my dinner plans, but didn't do it for some reason. "Fine."

She smiled sweetly. "And could you also go to the hardware store and pick up the paint? I'll give you the name of the color."

I rolled my eyes, imagining this is what married life was like, a constant stream of do-this, do-that, get-a-haircut, shave-your-face, not-tonight-honey-I-have-a-headache, you-left-the-seat-up-again. Not for me, thanks. "Yes. Anything else?"

"I mean, if you *really* want to, you could pick up lunch while you're out. I've got a craving for Subway."

I wiped my hands on a wet rag, got her in a headlock and gave her a noogie. "You're a pest. And this is the dance move I'm pulling out on the dance floor at your wedding."

"Tyler Shaw! Don't you dare!" she shrieked, trying unsuccessfully to get away from me. "Let me go, you big jerk!"

I grinned, feeling a little like my old self again.

After I hit the hardware store, I picked up lunch at Subway for Sadie and me. We ate, we painted—well, I painted and she watched—we bickered like siblings, laughed at childhood memories, and reminisced about our dad.

"I miss him so much." Sadie sighed, cradling her belly. "I so wish he was going to be here to meet his grandchild."

I swallowed hard. "Me too."

"How about you move back here so you can see your niece or nephew grow up?"

"How about you lay off the guilt trips?"

She sighed in defeat. "Fine. I'll just show him or her a picture and be like, 'Well, you have an uncle, but he's a hermit. I think he's still alive, but he doesn't leave his hidey hole, so I'm not sure.'"

I gave her the finger over my head, and she laughed.

"Hey, speaking of moving, there's a box in my attic I want to give you. I found it in the house after Dad died."

"What's in it?"

"Just some things he saved over the years. I think he'd want you to have them."

I nodded. It was probably memorabilia from my early baseball career, which I wasn't sure I wanted, but I'd take it with me. Our dad had died in the middle of the season, and I'd barely had two days off to attend his funeral. Sadie had been saddled with all the details—arranging the service, settling his affairs, selling the house, emptying it out. I'd paid for everything, but I hadn't been there to help her, which was another reason I wanted to do anything I could for her now.

She rose to her feet and put a hand on my shoulder. "Come on. Let's go sit on the front steps and have a snack while this coat dries. The paint smell is getting to me."

We went outside and sat on the front stoop, where we ate potato chips and watched two little girls across the street set up a lemonade stand.

Sadie waved to them. "Hi, girls!"

"Hi, Ms. Shaw!" they chorused.

"How was school today?"

"Good!"

"Students of yours?" I asked.

She shook her head. "Not currently. I had their older brother last year. The girls are in second grade—they're twins—but it's a small school. Everyone knows everyone."

"Sounds about right."

"Twins." Sadie shook her head. "I cannot imagine that. Two at once."

"I can't even imagine *one* at once," I said.

"Oh, come on." She nudged me with her leg and patted her belly. "Junior here is going to need a cousin someday. Can't you find a nice hermit girl to settle down with?"

"Don't hold your breath."

Another sigh. "Have you even been on a date lately?"

I pretended to think. "When you say *date*, do you mean—"

"I mean you ask a girl to have dinner with you, you pick her up and make polite conversation, you respectfully kiss her goodnight—*if* she says it's okay."

"That sounds boring as fuck."

Sadie elbowed me. "Oh, come on, it does not. Are you really going to be alone forever?"

"Why not? It sounds peaceful to me."

"It's not peaceful, it's *weird*. And it's not healthy. You're going to end up being that old guy in the neighborhood no one likes who's always yelling at the kids to get off his lawn."

"Because it's *my* lawn."

She sighed. "You're hopeless. I give up."

We watched the kids across the street go in and out of the house a few times, returning to their stand with various items—plastic cups, two pitchers of lemonade, a small box I guessed would be their bank, a big sign that said LEMONADE FOR CHAIRITY 50 SENTS.

"Oh, dear. Should we tell them?" Sadie wondered.

"No. Don't be such a teacher," I scoffed. "This isn't school."

The two girls took turns holding the sign, and waving frantically at the occasional passing car, but there wasn't much traffic on the street. Ten minutes went by, and nobody had stopped. Eventually, they sat on the grass, looking a little dejected.

"Oh, look how sad they are. Go buy some, Tyler." She elbowed me.

"I don't even like lemonade," I complained, but I was already getting to my feet. On my way across the street, I took my wallet from my pocket. The twins jumped up excitedly as I approached, huge grins on their faces.

"Would you like some lemonade?" one of them asked with a heavy lisp. And it was no wonder—she was missing both front teeth. Close up, I realized they weren't perfectly identical, but they both had big brown eyes, blond hair, and pigtails. They reminded me of Sadie at that age.

"Yes, I would," I said, taking some bills from my wallet. "How much for two cups?"

"It's fifty cents each, so two would be one dollar," answered the other one. Her T-shirt said Girl Power, and the *i* in Girl was a lightning bolt. "And we're giving all the money to charity."

"What charity?"

"St. Jude Children's Research Hospital," they recited at the exact same time.

"Hmm. That's a good cause. Can you break a hundred?" I teased, holding out a crisp new Benjamin.

The twins exchanged a worried look. "We only have quarters in here," fretted the one with the lisp. *Quarterth.*

I smiled. "That's okay. Tell you what. You give me two nice big cups of lemonade and I'll donate all one hundred dollars. How does that sound?"

This time, the look the two girls exchanged was pure, open-mouthed excitement. "Wow!" said Girl Power. "Thanks, mister!"

I handed over the hundred and watched as they carefully tucked it into their cash box then poured lemonade, one holding the cup steady, the other concentrating hard, the pitcher in both hands. Looking relieved when both cups were full, they each handed me one.

"Thanks, girls. Good luck."

"Thank you! Bye!"

I could still hear them squealing while I crossed the street.

Sadie was leaning back on her hands, a suspicious smile on her face. "How much did you give them? They can't stop looking in their box."

I handed her a cup of lemonade. "A hundred bucks."

"A hundred bucks!" She laughed. "Are you crazy?"

I lowered myself onto the cement. "They're giving the money to St. Jude Children's Hospital. It's a good cause."

She pointed her nose at me. "Softie."

The girls were still laughing and marveling over their good fortune, peeking into the cash box as if to make sure the hundred hadn't escaped. When they saw me looking at them, they waved excitedly.

"I think you have some new fans," remarked Sadie.

I laughed, taking a sip of the lemonade in case the girls were still watching, then setting it aside. "They're a little young for me."

We sat in silence for a moment. I readjusted my cap. "I ran into April Sawyer this morning."

Sadie looked over at me. "Did you? Where?"

"At the track over at the high school. I went for a run this morning, and she was there walking."

She nodded. "Did you say hello?"

"Yeah. We chatted for a bit." I hesitated. "She looks good."

My sister nodded.

"She still has that red hair," I went on.

Sadie gave me the side-eye but didn't say anything.

I waited for what I hoped was an appropriate amount of time. "So is she married?"

"Nope." Again, she stuck her elbow in my ribs. "Why do you ask?"

I moved away from her. "Will you quit elbowing me? I was just curious."

She sighed dramatically. "Too bad. I always wanted you guys to be a thing."

"You did?"

"Sure. At one point, I had this whole fantasy where you two got married and lived next door to me." She giggled. "How come you never dated her?"

I shrugged. "I never wanted a girlfriend—I didn't have time. Plus, I'm not sure she'd have dated me anyway—she was too busy making jokes about my big ego."

"You guys never even . . . you know, hooked up?"

I thought about lying, but then thought, *fuck it*. I trusted Sadie. "Actually, we did. Once."

She bolted upright. "You did?"

I nodded. "The night before I left for Arizona."

"Wow." She leaned back on her hands again. "Wow. I didn't see that coming. Nothing ever came of it?"

Taking a deep breath, I admitted the truth. "Something did come of it. She got pregnant."

Silence.

I looked over at my sister, who was staring at me, her chin practically in her lap. "What did you say?"

"April got pregnant that night."

"Oh. My. God." Sadie sat up tall and put a hand over her heart. "I'm in shock."

"We were too. Believe me."

"So what happened?"

"She gave it up for adoption. We agreed I wouldn't be named as the father to make everything easier."

Her eyes closed and she exhaled, her shoulders slouching. "What did she have?"

"I don't know."

Her eyelids flew open. Her stare was sharp. "You don't *know*? Please tell me you're lying."

I shook my head. "No. We . . . never really talked after that."

"What do you mean, you never really talked after that?" Sadie's voice was getting louder.

I glanced at the kids across the street. "I mean, she went back to school and I went back to Arizona, and that was that. We never talked again."

"You never even called her to make sure she was okay?" Sadie asked, incredulous. "Or in all the years since?"

Again, I shrugged. "No."

My sister jumped to her feet. "Tyler Michael Shaw, what is *wrong* with you?"

"Nothing." I was surprised at her angry reaction. "That's how April wanted it."

"She said that? She specifically told you not to contact her ever again even though she carried your baby for nine months and then had to give it up?"

"Well . . . yeah." Hadn't she? I rubbed the back of my neck. The details were fuzzy in my head. All I could recall was the sheer terror of hearing her say she was pregnant and the utter relief at being absolved of any responsibility.

Sadie crossed her arms over her chest. "For some reason, I have a hard time believing that. How could you completely abandon her that way?"

I frowned. "I didn't abandon her."

She touched her chest. "*I* got pregnant unexpectedly. What if Josh had done that to me?"

"Sadie, you're being ridiculous. I saw April this morning, and *she* isn't mad at me. So why are you?"

"I don't know! I just am!"

"Look, I don't know what you want me to say."

She stared me down. "I want you to say you're the guy I think you are. That's what I want."

I clenched my teeth and said nothing—of course I wasn't the guy she thought I was. Turns out I wasn't even the guy *I'd* thought I was—and she stormed into the house.

For a few minutes, I sat there on the stoop, wishing I hadn't said anything at all. What the hell was wrong with me, digging up this secret baby bombshell and lobbing it at my pregnant sister? Why hadn't I just left it buried in the past where it belonged?

Across the street, the two girls were silently staring at me. Had they heard the argument? Grimacing, I stood up and went into the house to find my sister and apologize—for what, I had no idea. But it felt like that was supposed to be my next move.

Sadie was unloading the dishwasher, angrily tossing silverware into a drawer. I leaned back against the counter. "I'm sorry if I upset you."

"It's not me you should be apologizing to."

I thought about that for a moment. "Look, maybe I should have reached out to April at some point. But at eighteen, I was entirely self-centered and laser-focused on my career. I was an expert at shutting out anything that wasn't going to get me where I needed to go, and I had to be cutthroat. My worth depended on it."

She looked over her shoulder at me. "Your worth as a pitcher maybe. But not your worth as a human being."

"In my mind, there was no difference, Sadie. You have to understand that."

She stopped moving and stared into the drawer, saying nothing. "There's more to life than being good at baseball, you know."

"Maybe for you, there is. Look, cut me a little slack here, okay? I didn't reject her. I offered to pay for everything. I asked her what *she* wanted to do. Adoption was her choice, and it was the right thing. Then we just . . . moved on. It wasn't that I didn't care about her."

She turned to face me. "Then why not call her? Even afterward?"

"I don't know, Sadie. I put it out of my head. And the more time that went by, the more awkward it would have been. I didn't want to go back there. And for all I know, she didn't either. She had my number," I pointed out. "She never used it."

"You never once wondered about the baby?"

"I never let myself. There was no point."

She leaned back against the counter. "I just can't believe I didn't know. Every time I talked to her . . . I feel weird about it now."

"Well, don't. Just forget I said anything, okay? Let's drop it."

She studied me for a long moment. "I don't think I ever realized how repressed you are. It's not good for you."

I scowled. "What the fuck are you talking about? I'm not repressed."

"Yes, you are. You just told me what an expert you are at shutting things out. You can't keep doing that. You need to make your peace with this."

"I have."

She rolled her eyes. "Right."

I folded my arms over my chest. "What makes you think I haven't?"

"Oh, I don't know, maybe the fact that you've kept this buried for, what, twenty years?"

"Eighteen."

"Whatever. There's a reason you're talking about it all of a sudden. It bothers you."

"No, it doesn't." But I was growing agitated. "I'm talking

about it because I wanted to share it with you, although I'm beginning to regret my decision."

She shook her head. "It's more than that."

"I told you, I saw April this morning."

"It's more than that too."

"I'm seeing her again tonight."

Her eyes took on a knowing look, and she nodded. "Aha. The plot thickens."

"Look, it's not a big deal. We're meeting for a drink."

"Just a drink?"

"Okay, dinner and a drink," I admitted.

"Are you going to talk about what happened?"

"No, Sadie. It's dinner. Not a therapy session. I don't want to talk about it."

"Well, be nice to her. Apologize for being selfish." She shook a finger at me. "And if *she* wants to talk, you *listen*."

"I will." I rolled my eyes. "Can we drop this now?"

"Yes. Thanks for telling me." Then the little shit walked across the kitchen and patted my stubbly cheek. "I knew you were in there somewhere. Now go get that haircut. And don't forget to shave."

CHAPTER 6

April

MY MEETING with the engaged couple finished by six-thirty, and I slipped into my office to freshen up.

Nothing drastic, of course. This wasn't a date. But I traded my utilitarian flats for the sexy heels, made sure my black skater skirt wasn't too wrinkled, checked the mirror on the back of my office door to be certain my emerald green blouse was tucked in properly, and gave my hair a little boost with some dry shampoo.

Okay, *maybe* I swapped my regular nude lipstick for something a little deeper and more sultry. *Perhaps* I spritzed myself with a little more perfume. And *possibly* I undid one more button on my blouse, but only so my four-leaf clover pendant showed. I didn't wear a lot of jewelry, but I loved that necklace—it had been a gift from my parents when I first moved away from home.

There was nothing wrong with any of that, was there? I mean, how often did I have dinner with a hot guy? (Borderline never.) When was the last time I'd worn perfume? (Couldn't recall. Bottle was dusty.) What was the harm in a little flirtation with an old friend? (None that I could think of.)

But admittedly, I didn't think too hard. I just wanted to

feel beautiful and have a good time, and if it happened to coincide with being the sole object of Tyler Shaw's attention tonight, so be it.

At a couple minutes before seven, I got a text from an unknown number. **I'm here at the bar. Take your time.**

I added him to my contacts and replied, **See you in a few.**

When I was ready, I grabbed my bag, switched off the lights in my office, and headed for the door. Walking at a leisurely pace, I followed the paved walkway from the wedding barn, where my office was located, over to the inn. It was a mild evening, and I took deep, calming breaths of fresh spring air. But the closer I got to the inn, the more nervous I felt.

What would it be like to be alone with him after all these years? Would the subject of *that night* come up? The pregnancy? The adoption? How would we handle it? Was there enough distance between then and now for us to be able to talk about it without weirdness?

There was also a distinct possibility he could turn out to be a big fat jerk. Maybe that vulnerability I thought I'd glimpsed this morning was all in my head. Maybe he'd snap at me again—I wouldn't be so quick to forgive this time. Maybe I'd need an excuse to duck out early.

Oh for goodness sake, April, I told myself as I pulled open the glass door to the inn's lobby. *Relax.* But just in case, right before I went into the bar, I pulled out my phone and texted Chloe. **Hey, can you check in with me in about an hour or so?**

Chloe: Of course. You okay?

Me: Yes. Just walking into the bar.

Chloe: Completely understand. You got this.

One of many awesome things about my sisters—they understood things like this. I felt much better as I entered the bar.

It was crowded for a Thursday evening, but nothing

compared to the way it would be in a few weeks when all the "summer people," who'd been away through the cold months, started returning to their second homes and cottages on the water. I enjoyed the cozy, quiet atmosphere of Cloverleigh Farms during the winter, when it was all covered with snow and a fire always roared in the inn's fireplace. But I loved seeing it come alive when the snow melted and wedding season picked up again, when the winery tasting room was always full, and the inn was booked up solid. I was always happier when I was busy.

Was that because I was lonely?

I shoved the thought aside.

Right away I picked out Tyler sitting at the end of the bar. Even from behind in the dim light, I knew his wide shoulders, his tall frame, his thick dark hair. Smiling and calling hello to a couple regulars I recognized, I made my way toward him, ignoring the way my pulse accelerated with every step.

When I reached his side, I touched his shoulder. "Hi."

Immediately he stood, offering me his seat.

"You don't have to get up," I protested.

He held up one hand. "Please. I know my manners were AWOL this morning, but I swear I have them. And my dad taught me that a man never sits while a woman stands." He gestured toward the vacant stool.

"Thank you." More at ease—he was still a nice guy—I slid onto it. "I was sorry to hear about your dad. He was such a good guy."

Tyler nodded. "Thanks. He was."

"You must miss him a lot."

"Yeah. It happened so fast. I guess I should be glad he wasn't in pain long, but I wish I'd had more time with him." He rubbed the back of his neck. "Although part of me is glad he went before he had to witness my career ending the way it did."

"Hey." I put my hand on his arm. "He still would have

been proud of you. That's what family does—they love us and they're proud of who we *are*, not just what we do."

"Yeah." He tipped back the rest of his drink and set the empty glass on the bar in front of me. "Anyway, thanks for meeting me tonight."

"Of course." I smiled, taking in his clean white button-down with the sleeves cuffed up, his dark jeans, and brown lace-up boots. His dark hair, which I could see now that he wasn't wearing a cap, was still thick and wavy. Girls had always loved his hair. "You clean up nice."

"Thanks. You look nice too." He leaned a little closer to me, his eyes focused on mine. "Hazel?"

"What?"

"Oh, sorry." He straightened up, looking a little sheepish. "Earlier, I was trying to remember what color your eyes were, because you were wearing sunglasses and I couldn't see them. But it's kind of dark in here, so I'm guessing—are they hazel?"

I laughed. "Yes. They are."

"And you still have your red hair." He tugged a strand near my ear. "That's how I recognized you on the track."

"I do still have red hair, because as any redhead will tell you, it's nearly impossible to color. You have to bleach it, which I tried once with disastrous results." I cringed at the memory. "It was *not* a good look for me."

Tyler seemed surprised. "Why would you want to change it? I fucking love the color of your hair. I always have."

Flattered, I felt the rush of warmth to my face and knew my cheeks had roses in them, as my mother would say. "I don't know. It was in college. I think it was at a time in my life I was trying to change a lot of things about myself—I guess I wanted to feel like somebody else, and the hair color seemed like a good place to start."

"Well, I'm glad it didn't work. What would you like to drink?"

"What are you drinking?"

"Brown Eyed Girl bourbon," he said, moving a little closer to me as he tried to catch the bartender's eye. He smelled good—woodsy and clean—like a combination of autumn and spring. "I'd never had it before, but the bartender recommended it. It's made in Michigan, I guess."

I nodded. "Yes, it's made in Detroit. My sister Chloe is engaged to the guy who started that distillery—his name is Oliver. They're opening one up here at Cloverleigh too."

"Oh yeah? That's cool. I like it a lot. In fact, I'll have another. Want one?"

"Sure." I crossed my legs, clasping my hands around my bare knee. "So what did you do today?"

"Slave labor for my sister," he answered, stealing a glimpse at my hemline.

I smiled. "At her house?"

"Yeah. Josh had to work today, so she asked me to come over and move some furniture, which turned into ripping up carpet, running errands, and painting a bedroom."

"Wow. That's a lot of labor. You get a union break?"

"One." A smile crept onto his full lips. "During which I spent a hundred dollars on lemonade."

"What?"

"These two little girls across the street were having a lemonade stand for charity, and they didn't have any customers. So I gave them a hundred bucks."

I burst out laughing. "They must have been totally shocked. You'll probably see them out there again tomorrow, hoping you come back."

He chuckled. "Probably. They reminded me of Sadie when she was little."

I shook my head. "Hard to believe she's getting married in two days, isn't it?"

"Yes. I still can't wrap my head around it. *Married*." He looked like he'd just sucked a really sour lemon.

"Is it just Sadie and Josh's wedding you're having a hard time with?" I asked, amused. "Or is it marriage in general you dislike?"

"Marriage in general. But hey, if Josh wants to put up with Sadie bossing him around the rest of his life, he can go right ahead."

I laughed and gave him a gentle nudge in the stomach, which was *rock hard*. "Oh, come on. They're in love. Don't you have any sense of romance?"

"I have a sense of *reality*. There is no way I could live with another person day and night forever. She would drive me insane, and I would return the favor."

I was about to argue in favor of true love when we were interrupted by the bartender, an old-timer named Toby.

"Hey, April. What can I get for you guys?" He leaned on the bar in front of us with both hands and smiled.

"Hi, Toby. I'd like you to meet my old friend Tyler Shaw."

Toby's grin widened as he shook Tyler's hand. "I wondered if that was you. 'The Rifle,' right? Damn, you could throw a fastball." He whistled through his teeth. "Had to be, what, like ninety-seven miles per hour?"

"Something like that," Tyler said. "Nice to meet you."

"And that curveball. What a weapon that was. Nobody knew what to do with it." Toby shook his head. "Shame what happened to your arm. You ever figure out what it was?"

Tyler stiffened. "Uh, no."

"I was watching that World Series game. It was the damndest thing. I kept thinking to myself, 'I know how good he is. Why can't he just relax and throw the ball?'"

Next to me, so close I could sense it, tension continued to fill Tyler's long, muscular frame. His jaw was clenched tight.

"Hey, Toby, can we get a couple glasses of Brown Eyed Girl bourbon on the rocks?" I asked, instinctively placing a hand on Tyler's lower back.

"Sure thing, April." He smiled at Tyler. "Nice meeting

you, man. Hey, keep throwing. Maybe it'll come back someday."

Tyler swallowed and nodded curtly.

Once Toby's back was turned, I looked up at Tyler. Rubbed his back a little. "Sorry about that."

"Not your fault."

"But I could tell it made you uncomfortable. I shouldn't have introduced you."

He shrugged. "Doesn't matter. I'm used to it."

Taking my hand off him, I decided to change the subject. "So you're still living in San Diego, huh? You like it out there?"

"Yeah."

"Do you live on the beach?"

"Not far. I also have a cabin in the San Bernardino Mountains on Lake Arrowhead. I spend a lot of time there."

"I bet it's beautiful. Do you . . . do you live alone?"

He nodded. "I like living alone. It suits me."

"Why?"

"My sister says it's because I'm a grumpy old man." A hint of a crooked grin appeared. "I say I just like solitude."

"What do you like about it?"

"Everything. I like silence in the morning and the couch to myself at night. I don't like sharing covers or the Netflix remote. I also drink from the carton and leave the cap off the toothpaste."

I wrinkled my nose. "That last one's a deal breaker. We can definitely never be roommates."

He laughed. "What about you? Do you live nearby?"

"Not too far. I have a condo in Traverse City. And I live alone too, although I'm *not* sure it suits me."

"What makes you—"

But before he could finish the question, Toby showed up with our drinks and assured us they were on him. "I was thinking. Acupuncture." He pointed a thick finger at Tyler.

"That's what you should try. Acupuncture. My sister's anxiety was so bad, she couldn't even leave the house. Tried acupuncture—worked like a charm."

"I'll keep that in mind," said Tyler, taking a quick sip of his bourbon.

"Thanks for the drinks, Toby," I said, picking up my glass and rising to my feet. Then I put a hand on Tyler's chest—also rock hard—and said, "Hey, let's move into the dining room. I bet it's less crowded in there."

Tyler tossed some cash on the bar as a tip. "Good idea."

We walked over to the hostess stand with our drinks. "Hey, Makenna." I smiled at the college student who'd recently been hired on for the busy season. "Any chance we could snag that corner booth in the back?"

"Sure thing, April."

"Great," I said, relieved we'd be able to talk with a little more privacy. The dining room at the inn, with its low ceilings, dark wood paneling, and plush booths, was cozy and intimate. And best of all, there would be no prying bartender trying to serve cocktails with a side of advice.

"Follow me." Giving us a smile, she turned and led us to the back of the candlelit room, where my favorite booth was already set for two. "Here you are. Jacie will be your server, and she'll be right with you."

"Thanks, Makenna." I slid onto the curved leather banquette and smiled at Tyler. "This is much better, isn't it?"

"Definitely." He eased in from the other side, meeting me in the middle. "Can't say I'm much for crowds these days."

"I don't blame you. Do strangers often try to give you advice like that?"

"*All* the damn time. Everybody thinks they've got it all figured out. Believe me, if there was a cure, I'd have discovered it by now."

"Do you still practice throwing?"

"Not on a ballfield. And never in front of anyone."

Sensing it wasn't something he wanted to discuss, I opened the menu and scanned both sides. "What are you going to eat? Everything is excellent, and I'm totally not biased."

That got him to smile again. "Of course not."

Jacie came over a minute later, greeted me warmly, and told us about the night's specials. As far as I knew, she hadn't grown up around here and she was too young to have known about Tyler's storied high school baseball career anyway, but on the off chance she'd heard his name before, I didn't introduce him. We decided on a few small plates to share—burrata with fig and balsamic, charcuterie and olives, a smoked whitefish Caesar salad—and placed our order.

Alone again, we sipped our bourbon and continued catching up, although I did most of the talking. Tyler asked about my parents and sisters, some friends from high school, my job, the changes at Cloverleigh Farms, and whether I liked working with my family.

"Honestly, I do," I told him. "It can be a lot of togetherness, and we're up in each other's business all the time, but I've always been close to my family. I really missed them when I lived in New York, and I was glad when my parents broached the subject of moving back and building up Cloverleigh Farms as a wedding venue."

"I've heard you're awesome at what you do."

I smiled into my glass before taking the last sip. "Thanks. Sadie is such a doll."

"She really appreciates you working so hard and so fast for her."

"It's my pleasure," I said, setting my empty glass down. Tyler's had been empty for a few minutes already. "It's going to be a beautiful wedding. She's an easy bride to work with, and it makes me happy to see her so excited. Seems like yesterday she was a little kid in pigtails needing a Band-Aid for a scraped knee, or help with her spelling words, or a quarter for the gumball machine."

"You were so good to her."

"Well, it was my job."

"You never treated her like she was a job."

My cheeks warmed, and I shrugged. "Being a big sister came easy to me. Plus, I loved hanging out with her. And with you too, of course." It came out a little flirtier than I'd meant it to. Was it the bourbon? Was it how good he smelled? Or was it how close he was sitting, the way he was looking at me like I was the only person in the room, possibly the world?

Something was definitely making me a little lightheaded.

Tyler gave me his old grin. "We had some good times, didn't we? That is, when you weren't giving me shit about my massive ego."

"The only thing bigger than your biceps," I quipped, poking his upper arm.

"Now you know *that's* not true."

Our eyes met, and my heart hiccupped. I crossed my legs —tight.

"Sorry," he said. "I couldn't resist." But that cocky smile stayed put on his lips, telling me he wasn't really sorry.

All at once, I remembered how easily I'd fallen into his arms eighteen years ago—and I knew instinctively how easily it could happen again if I wasn't careful.

Tyler Shaw just *did* something to me.

CHAPTER 7

OKAY, maybe I shouldn't have said it, but I wasn't sorry.

I'd always loved teasing April. And something about being around her had me feeling like my old self again.

Her expressions were the same, her voice was the same, and those dimples just made me happy to look at them. I could still make her laugh, and when she made her usual crack about my biceps, it was like no time had gone by at all, like everything was right in the world. It was giving me an even better buzz than the bourbon.

The food arrived, and Jacie asked us if we'd like another round.

"I'll do one more," I said.

April hesitated, then laughed. "I would, but I'm not sure I should. I'm already a little tipsy."

"Oh, come on," I prodded. "I can drive you home."

She leveled her gaze at me. "I've heard *that* one before."

Happy that she'd been the one to make a joke about it this time, I held up my hands. "No detours, I promise."

She sighed and shrugged. "Okay. Why not? Another Brown Eyed Girl bourbon on the rocks. *Lots* of rocks."

Jacie smiled. "You got it. Be right back."

"Here, try some of this. It's really good." April leaned toward me and put some salad on my plate.

That was when I accidentally looked down her blouse—okay, it wasn't *exactly* an accident—and the glimpse of her black lace bra made the crotch of my pants get a little tight. But then I noticed the pendant she wore around her neck—a small gold four-leaf clover.

"Hey, I like your necklace," I said, reaching for it without even thinking. My fingers brushed her collarbone. "It reminds me of when Sadie used to give me a shamrock for luck before a game."

Her dimples appeared, and she stayed still while I examined the little gold charm. "Oh, I remember that," she said. "So sweet."

I let it go and leaned back. "She used to get so mad when I'd tell her they weren't four-leaf clovers, so they weren't lucky."

"But they made you feel good, didn't they?"

I nodded. "Every time."

"That's what mattered to her. She worshipped you."

"Who didn't?"

That earned me a dirty look and poke on the shoulder, just like we were seventeen again and back at my dad's old kitchen table. I never wanted this feeling to end.

While we ate, I asked her about her time in New York and whether she ever missed living in a big city.

"You know, it was fun, but I *don't* really miss living in a big city," she said, spreading some burrata on a small piece of bread. "I liked it when I was there—the chaos, the energy—but that was my twenties. I don't have that in me anymore—the late nights and early mornings would kill me. And I didn't love the corporate culture. I much prefer where I am now."

"So you'll stay in this area, you think?"

She sighed. "I suppose that depends on what the future

holds. I do like it here. It's home to me. What about you? Ever think about moving back?"

Our drinks arrived, and I took a hefty swallow before answering. "Nah. This isn't home anymore."

"You think of California as home now?"

I shrugged. "I'm not sure *any* place feels like home to me."

"Why not?"

That was a hard question to answer, so I turned it back on her. "What makes this place feel like home to you?"

She took a bite of her bread and thought for a second. "I guess it's the sense that, somehow, I know I belong here. I have history here. I miss it when I'm gone, and I'm always happy to come back. I just . . . feel most like *myself* here."

"I used to feel that way on the field." After another sip, I set the glass down. "But I don't feel that anywhere anymore. Not since I quit playing. And I miss it," I confessed, which surprised me, because it wasn't something I ever said out loud. "I really fucking miss it."

"I'm sorry." She was silent for a moment. "Do you want to talk about it? Baseball, I mean? Or what happened?"

"No. It's fine. I mean, obviously, it's not fine, but if talking about it helped, I'd be on the mound in St. Louis right now."

"Well," she said, offering me a tiny smile, "I might be the only one, but I'm glad you're here with me tonight. It's really good to see you."

I smiled back. "It's good to see you too."

"And it's nice to get out," she went on. "Most nights I'm either working late at events or just grabbing something quick and eating dinner at home by myself."

Looking at her and having spent the last couple hours enjoying her company, it was hard to believe she was single if she didn't want to be. Not only was she beautiful, but she was sweet and funny and smart—so what was the story? What was wrong with the jackasses around here that they weren't lining up to be with her?

"Earlier, you said something about living alone," I ventured. "That it doesn't suit you. What made you say that?"

She sighed and popped an olive in her mouth. "I'd like to meet someone. Get married, have a family."

I nodded slowly. "You'd be good at that. Taking care of a family."

"But you wouldn't?"

"Nah."

"How do you know?"

I shrugged. "I just know. I mean, I was supposed to be good at baseball—the best, in fact—and look what happened there. Turns out, I wasn't shit."

"Tyler, that's not true."

"Sure, it is," I said, frustrated that she couldn't see it. "Maybe once upon a time, I was good, maybe I was even close to the best, but it didn't fucking last. Because nothing lasts. And anyone who says otherwise is a liar." I picked up my drink and tossed back the last few sips.

April pushed some food around on her plate.

One minute ticked by. Then another.

"Say something," I demanded, since I'd already been a jerk.

"Like what?"

"I don't know. What are you thinking?"

"I'm thinking that I don't know whether I want to give you a hug or give you the finger."

That actually made me laugh. "I vote for the finger."

She flipped me off and picked up her bourbon. "You know, I thought Sadie might have been exaggerating about you being a grumpy old man. But I'm beginning to believe her."

Exhaling, I rubbed my face with both hands. "Sorry for the rant. Sometimes I can't stop myself. And I spend so much time alone, I'm not used to having it affect someone else."

She leaned closer to me and whispered, "Maybe you wouldn't be alone so much if you quit all the ranting."

"I don't mind being alone," I said. "In fact, I prefer it."

She sat up straight again and stuck another olive in her mouth. "You should get a kitten."

"Hell, no."

"A puppy?"

"Too hard to train."

"How about a friend?"

I cocked my head. "I thought *you* were my friend."

"I was," she said, widening her eyes in mock seriousness. "But the job is turning out to be tougher than I thought."

Laughing, I draped one arm along the top of the booth and looked at her. Was it terrible that I sort of wished she'd suggested a blowjob instead of a kitten? She was so fucking cute. "Giving up on me already, huh?"

"I didn't say that." She took another sip of bourbon. "But I do think you need to deal more effectively with your emotions. And I'm just drunk enough to try to help you."

I groaned. "I think I need another drink."

Jacie came to the table and I ordered a beer, but April said that since she wanted to leave here on her feet, not her hands and knees, she was definitely good with the half-glass of bourbon she had left. She did, however, put in an order for cherry ice cream with amaretto sauce, which she said was her favorite dessert on the menu. "I'll share it with you," she promised, briefly putting her hand on my thigh.

My cock jumped, and I moved a little farther away from her. The *last* thing I needed was an erection right now. I was determined to be a gentleman tonight.

But she wasn't making it easy.

While she was waiting for her dessert to arrive, she touched my leg at least three more times, leaned close enough for me to accidentally look down her blouse again, and gave me several enticing whiffs of her perfume. And she must have kicked off her shoes, because she'd tucked her legs beneath her and was sitting on her bare heels—exactly the way she used to sit on the chairs at our kitchen table when we'd do homework. Then later I'd jerk off thinking about her getting up from her chair and straddling my lap.

Which was not a helpful thought at the moment.

At one point, she checked her phone and started laughing as she typed something.

"What's funny?" I asked.

"I forgot that I asked Chloe to check in on me earlier, in case I needed an escape hatch. I just looked at my phone and she's texted and called like five times to make sure I'm okay. I'm letting her know I'm fine."

"An escape hatch?"

"Yeah, you know . . ." She tossed her phone back into her bag. "In case you turned out to be a jerk or a pervert, I would have an excuse to leave."

"Ah."

"But since you're not a jerk, I didn't need to escape."

I cocked a brow at her. "The jury is still out on *pervert*?"

She lifted her shoulders and grinned mischievously. "The night is young."

I gulped my ice water.

When my beer and her dessert arrived, April clapped her hands like an excited kid, grabbed a spoon, and dug into the mound of pinkish ice cream with caramel-colored sauce dripping down the sides. She moaned at the first taste, her eyes closing. "Oh God, this is so good." Then she moaned again, even louder this time.

Jesus, that sound. It was sexy as fuck.

She stuck her spoon into the ice cream again, but this time lifted it to *my* mouth. "You have to try this. And don't say no."

I set my glass down and let her feed me a bite. She was

right—it was delicious. *And it would be even more delicious if I could lick it off her naked body.*

"Good, right?" she asked happily. She took another bite for herself, moaned again, then licked both sides of the spoon, while I suffered in agony watching her.

Christ.

Was she doing this on purpose?

I shifted on the booth seat, trying not to think about my tongue on her skin while surreptitiously adjusting the giant bulge in my pants. Thankfully, she was either too buzzed or too obsessed with her ice cream to notice.

"The cherries in this are from our farm," she announced.

"Yeah?"

"Yeah. Want another bite?" Then she started to laugh. "I know how much you like local cherries."

Tipping back my beer, I narrowed my eyes at her, then set the bottle down with a thunk. "What is that supposed to mean?"

She shrugged. "You liked mine, didn't you?"

"*What?*"

April laughed even harder and sucked on the spoon.

"Wait a minute. Wait a minute." I sat up straight and blinked at her. "Are you serious? You were a *virgin* that night?"

"Hush," she said, looking around, although we were practically the only people left in the dining room. "Yes. I was pure as the driven snow before you got me in the back of your truck."

I groaned, squeezing my eyes shut. "Why didn't you say something?"

"Because I didn't want you to know, obviously."

"God, now I feel like an even bigger prick."

"Tyler, I can't be the only rookie you initiated."

"You were different."

That made her smile. "Are you saying you wouldn't have done it?"

I thought for a second. "Nah, I probably still would have done it. But I might have tried to make it last a little longer."

She dug into the ice cream again. "It *was* pretty quick."

I groaned again.

"But you were a gentleman, as far as I was concerned. And it's not like I knew any better back then." She started laughing. "I mean, after all, your nickname *was* 'The Rifle.'"

"Because I *pitched* fast, dammit!"

"Oh, come on, that's funny. Admit it." She leaned over and nudged me with her shoulder. "And I was glad you were my first, despite everything."

I ran a hand through my hair, sat up a little taller. "Good. But I just want it on the record"—I held out one hand—"I *have* learned some self-control in the ensuing years. And some skills. Some very valuable skills."

"Duly noted," April said with a nod. "Now let's talk about your feelings."

I frowned and picked up my beer. "Do we have to?"

"Yes. You're very angry."

"Don't I have a right to be? You saw it tonight. I feel like I can't turn a corner without someone telling me how great I *was*, what a *shame* it is that my career ended the way it did, or wondering why, for the *love of God*, I just couldn't relax and throw the ball."

"So tell them to fuck off."

"I do. All the time."

"But then you have to actually *let it go*."

I exhaled. "That's a lot harder. Because deep down, I'm asking myself the same damn thing."

"Okay, so what's next? Look ahead. If you can't play ball anymore, what are you going to do to show everyone that you're still a badass?"

Um, put my tongue between your legs? But I didn't say that. What I said was, "I've got no idea."

"Hmm. You need some clarity."

What I needed was her naked body against mine. That moan in my ear. "You think?"

"Yes. And some inner peace. Deep down you're craving it."

Deep down I was craving a taste of her pussy, but I didn't think I should mention it. "Okay."

"Maybe you should try yoga," she suggested. "Learn to find your center."

The only center I wanted to find was hers. "*Yoga?* No way."

"Well, we have to think of something to decrease your stress level. What about sex?"

I froze. "What about it?"

"Does it relax you?"

"You know, you don't have to try to fix me. I'm fine." *And you definitely shouldn't talk about sex—I'm hanging on to gentleman by a very thin thread here.*

She sighed dramatically and held up her hands in surrender. "Okay, okay. I'll stop bothering you."

"Thank you. You know, when you're not trying to poke at my feelings, hanging out with you tonight is the most fun I've had in a long time."

Her face lit up. "Really?"

"Really."

Her cheeks turned pink and her dimples appeared, making me even warmer beneath my clothes. "That makes me feel good."

"Here you go." Jacie appeared and dropped off the check, which I grabbed before April could get her hands on it, although she tried, getting up on her knees and practically crawling onto my lap.

"Will you stop?" I held it way out of her reach with my right hand. "This is on me."

"No! You don't have to buy my dinner."

"I know I don't."

"This is my family's restaurant!"

"Don't care."

"Can we at least split it?"

"Fuck off. See? I said it."

"I didn't mean say it to me!" She laughed and made one final lunge for the small leather folder that sent her sprawling across my thighs.

Snaring her waist with my left arm, I set her upright again, tucked firmly against my side. "Hey. Enough. You're gonna knock those candles off the table and set us on fire."

She stopped struggling, but I didn't let her go.

Our eyes locked. We were practically nose to nose. I could see the quick rise and fall of her chest. One easy slant of my head, and I'd know the taste of bourbon and cherries on her lips. If it were any other night, any other circumstance, any other girl, I'd have kissed her.

But it was April, and I couldn't.

Tonight was my opportunity to do the right thing, be a better man—the kind of man my sister thought I was. Maybe I had been a selfish asshole back then, but I didn't have to *keep* fucking up this friendship. April mattered to me, and I needed to act like it this time.

I released her from my grip and took my wallet from my back pocket. "Let me get this paid. They're probably ready to get rid of us by now."

"Okay." She put a little distance between us and felt around beneath the table for her shoes. "Thanks for dinner."

"You're welcome."

The vibe between us shifted toward politeness, and I was both relieved and disappointed.

When the bill was settled, we walked into the inn's lobby,

where April called goodnight to the woman at the front desk. I held the huge glass door open for her, and once outside, she tipped her head back and took a few deep breaths of cool night air. "Whoa, I'm dizzy. I'm definitely not used to bourbon."

"It's potent stuff."

"I think I'm going to sleep at my parents' house tonight. I definitely can't drive."

"Let me take you home. I don't mind driving you—and no detours. I promise."

She smiled at me. "I trust you. But I'd have to figure out how I'm going to get back here in the morning. I have to work."

"I'll come pick you up and bring you here. Whatever time you want," I said, thinking she should not trust me at *all*.

"Stop it. You're busy tomorrow."

"I'm not too busy to help you."

She sighed. "I *would* like to sleep in my own bed. Are you sure you don't mind?"

"I'm positive." I took her arm and started leading her toward my rental. "And driving you around doesn't begin to make up for all the nice things you've done for me."

When I said it, I'd been thinking of all the homework help, but as soon as the words were out of my mouth, it occurred to me how small that stuff was compared to her willingness to handle the adoption on her own and leave me out of it. Without a doubt, that had to be the single kindest thing *anyone* had *ever* done for me my entire life. It had allowed me to chase my dreams without guilt, without responsibility, without the inconvenience or distraction of a media shit-storm. I'd never even had to tell my father. I'd gotten off completely scot-free. And April . . . she'd weathered that massive storm on her own. For *me*.

Jesus, how had it taken me eighteen years to think of it

that way? And how could I show her how much I appreciated it?

You can start by keeping your hands, your mouth, and your dick to yourself.

Immediately, I let go of her arm. "I'm over there. The black SUV."

As I drove down the long, winding driveway leading from Cloverleigh Farms back onto the main road, April gave me directions to her condo. When I turned into the lot of her complex, she pointed to a row of townhouses over to the left. "I'm over there. The one on the far end. You can use the spot right in front—that's mine."

I pulled up in front of her place, where she slept alone but didn't want to, and wished more than anything I could go in with her. Treat her right this time. Show her I wasn't selfish. I'd undress her all the way this time, slowly. I'd use my tongue and my hands. I'd tell her how beautiful she was. I'd spend all night long making her come.

Oh, and I'd fucking wear a condom. Maybe two.

Don't you dare, asshole. You stay on your side of this vehicle and you let her get out of the car. You're not even allowed to walk her to the door, got it? You will remain in your seat with your seatbelt fastened.

"Thanks for the ride," April said as I put the SUV in park. "And for the food and drinks. This was really fun."

"It was." *Get inside, April. Now.*

"And it's so good to see you."

"You too." *But you need to get out of my sight this minute.*

"We should have done this sooner. It wasn't nearly as scary as I thought it was going to be."

I laughed nervously, gripping the steering wheel tightly with both hands. "Yeah."

"Well, I guess I'll see you tomorrow." She opened the door, and I put a hand on her leg.

"April, wait."

CHAPTER 8

April

I HESITATED, staring at his hand on my thigh.

"Shut the door," he said.

Confused, I pulled the door shut. "What is it?"

"I don't know." He looked at his hand on my leg too. "I just know that I don't want you to go."

My heart began to beat faster. "Tyler."

He took his hand away. "I'm sorry. I know I have no right to touch you."

"It's not that."

"For the last hour, I've been telling myself to be a gentleman. That this is an opportunity to do right by you. A chance to be a good guy."

"You *are* a good guy."

His eyes seared mine in the dark. "You wouldn't say that if you knew what I was thinking right now."

My stomach whooshed. "Why don't you tell me and let me decide for myself?"

"Christ, April," he said through clenched teeth. "Don't say those things to me."

"Why not?"

"Because I promised you there would be no detours.

Because you've been drinking. Because I told my sister I'd be nice tonight."

I laughed. "You *have* been nice."

"Yeah, well, it hasn't been easy."

It struck me what he'd said a moment ago. "You told Sadie you were seeing me tonight?"

"Actually . . ." He paused. "I told her everything."

"What do you mean, *everything*?"

"I told her. What happened with us. I'm sorry if I betrayed your confidence."

"It's okay. I trust Sadie." But I couldn't believe it—he'd told her about the baby? "What did she say?"

"She was pretty shocked. And she was mad at me."

"Why?"

He didn't answer right away. Then he said, "April, I need to ask you a question."

"Okay."

He looked over at me. "Did I abandon you?"

"Of course not."

"Because if I did, I'm sorry."

"Tyler. Listen to me." I leaned toward him and spoke quietly, putting my hand on his arm. "What happened was a careless mistake, and God knows I've struggled with the fallout, but that's on me—not you, okay? I think we handled it the best way we could."

He ran a hand over his jaw. "I thought so too, at the time. But now . . ." His hand fell into his lap. "My sister made me wonder if I'd been totally selfish. When she first said it, I shot the idea down, but it's been in the back of my head all day."

Sighing, I took my hand off him and stared straight ahead. "I don't know, Tyler. I think everyone is selfish at eighteen."

"*You* weren't."

I almost laughed. "Do you know how often I've questioned that? How many nights I lay awake wondering if *giving away* that baby was the ultimate selfish decision?"

"April, it wasn't." His voice was firm. "You did the most selfless thing I can think of, and you did it alone."

"I wasn't alone."

"But I wasn't there for you like I could have been. Like I should have been. All I cared about was baseball. And I can see how, in my sister's eyes, it doesn't seem fair that I walked away so easily. Especially since she's pregnant now."

"That's a really different situation—Sadie and Josh are grown adults who belong together. They have a home together. They're in love. You and I were two hormonal kids who got carried away in the back of your truck."

"Yeah."

"Hey. Look at me."

He angled his head in my direction.

"I was *not* a victim, Tyler. I could have said no to sex in the first place. I could have asked you to put on a condom. It was fast, yes, but it wasn't so fast that I couldn't have stopped it. You would have stopped if I'd asked, right?"

"Yes. I would have."

"And I knew it. The truth is, I didn't want you to stop." I wasn't sure whether it was the bourbon or the dark interior of the car or the years of keeping that night a secret that was loosening my tongue, but it was a relief to say the words out loud. "It felt so good to be wanted that way—by *you*. You'd never looked at me like that before. Deep down, I had always wanted you to, but I was too scared to admit it. And you were leaving the next day, so it felt like my last chance . . . I *wanted* that chance, so I took it."

"That's how I felt too. I'd wanted you for a long time, but I'd told myself again and again to keep my hands off you. Then that night, I just lost my grip on control. And I'm not sorry it happened—I'm only sorry about the consequences. But if I could go back, I'd have called and made sure you were okay." He reached over and took my hand. "I'm sorry I didn't."

We were quiet for a moment, studying our fingers laced together.

"Think of it this way," I said quietly. "We made another family really, really happy."

He nodded slowly. "Can I ask you something?"

"Of course."

"Was it a boy or a girl?"

I swallowed, fighting the little lump that had jumped into my throat. "It was a boy. They named him Charles, after his father and grandfather."

He exhaled. "I wasn't sure I ever wanted to know."

"Are you glad now that you do?"

"I'm not sure."

I laughed gently. "I know all about mixed feelings on this topic, I promise."

"Was it hard? To give him up?"

"The hardest thing I've ever done. But the parents who adopted him were wonderful, and they wanted him so badly. I knew right from the start they were *his* parents. That helped."

"Good."

For a moment, I considered telling him that I'd reached out to Charles's parents about meeting him, but decided against it. It seemed like too much for one night. I felt like we'd crossed a hugely important bridge—individually and together—and I didn't want anything to set us back. Besides, he was leaving in three days. It wouldn't affect him at all, and I could always tell him in the future. Hopefully, we'd stay in touch when he left.

"You know what?" he said.

"What?"

"I decided. I'm glad I know. And I'm glad to hear that he was adopted by wonderful parents who really wanted him. That makes me feel good."

"Me too."

We sat in silence for another minute, but it wasn't awkward. It was . . . nice. Familiar. Comfortable.

Tempting.

"Well, I should go in," I said, reluctantly taking my hand from his. I loved that he'd reached for it. How long had it been since anyone had taken my hand? Kissed me in the dark? Held me close and whispered all the things he wanted to do to me? And why was I wishing Tyler would do all of those things? Was I that lonely? Or just *insane*?

"Can I still pick you up tomorrow and drive you to work?" he asked.

"You don't have to. I could ask Chloe to get me on her way in."

"I want to. I'll pick you up about eight, if that works? That way I can still get an early run in."

"That works. Thanks." I put my hand on the door handle but didn't pull it. "And thanks for talking about this with me. I know it's not easy, but in all honesty, I needed this."

"You're welcome." His eyes held mine. "Now get the fuck inside, April, before I forget I'm the good guy tonight."

Smiling, I hopped out of the car and slammed the door behind me.

That smile lingered on my lips as I let myself into my condo. As I watched him drive away through my living room window. As I floated upstairs to my bedroom. As I undressed myself, got ready for bed, and slid between the sheets. As I recalled the moment at the restaurant when he'd held me close. As I remembered the way he'd taken my hand in the car. As I heard in my mind his deep, hushed voice asking whether I'd had a boy or a girl.

I was so glad he'd asked. I would have been fine if he hadn't, but it had been such a relief to acknowledge out loud the piece of my past I constantly carried around with me but could never discuss. It felt like a huge weight had been lifted from my shoulders.

And speaking of shoulders . . . I closed my eyes and pictured Tyler's body, imagining what it might look like naked. The broad chest. The sculpted arms. The solid abs. The night we'd been together, everything had been so fast and furtive and threaded with fear—Would we get caught? Would I bleed? Would he guess that I'd never done it before? Would he stop? Was this going to hurt? Was I supposed to make noise or be quiet?—that my memories had taken on a blurry, unreal quality. More like a movie than a life experience.

I only recalled two things with any clarity—the moment he reached over and touched my hair, and the way he said, "Come here." A second later, his lips were on mine and I was in heaven.

God, I wished he'd kissed me goodnight.

Was I losing my mind?

I mean, what would be the point of messing around with him? Nothing could come of it. He was only in town for the wedding. He lived all the way across the country. He wasn't interested in a relationship. And our history was *all* kinds of complicated.

But . . . it hadn't felt complicated tonight.

Being with him had actually felt easy, just the way it used to. Easier than it had ever felt with any other guy, because I didn't have to hide anything. And I was *proud* of us. We'd managed to tread softly through a landmine of emotional baggage and come out the other side hand in hand.

He still made me laugh. He still had that cocky grin that made me want to take him down a notch. He still had the biceps, but now he had maturity too, the kind that comes with age and life experience and finally learning that life doesn't always go the way you planned.

Sighing, I hugged my pillow.

Good thing he was a gentleman.

The next morning, I woke up at six-thirty and got in the shower, humming a tune and wondering if Tyler would have time for breakfast before running me up to Cloverleigh. I decided to text him and ask.

Me: Hey. How was your run? Do you have time for breakfast?

Tyler: You caught me. I skipped the early run and slept in. Totally down for breakfast.

Me: I know a great spot. See you at eight.

Since I wouldn't have time to come home before Sadie's rehearsal, I dressed a little more formally than usual, in a black and white gingham pencil skirt, black blouse, and heels. My hair still held some of its Beyoncé waves, but I knew it would be a busy day, so I tied it back in a ponytail, leaving just a few pieces loose around my face.

A few minutes before eight, I heard his knock. I raced down the steps to answer it, but when I hit the landing I made myself slow down, take a breath, chill. When my heart stopped pounding so fast, I opened the door.

Seeing Tyler on my doorstep made my pulse spike right back up again. He was dressed casually—jeans, sneakers, and a navy zip-up sweatshirt—and he hadn't shaved. But the smile was what got to me.

"Morning," he said, his eyes traveling over my outfit. "Damn. You look awesome. I'm a little underdressed."

I laughed. "You're fine. Thanks for coming to get me."

"No problem. You ready?" He glanced over his shoulder. "I think it might rain soon, so if we don't want to get soaked, we should move."

I nodded. "Let me just grab my purse. Want to come in for a sec?"

"Sure." He shut the door behind himself and looked around. "I like your place."

"Thanks." I moved toward my kitchen and dining area, which was open to the living room. From the counter I grabbed my keys and phone, tucking them into my purse.

He wandered toward the fireplace and studied the framed photographs on the mantel. "Whose wedding is this?"

"My youngest sister, Frannie's."

"She was a friend of Sadie's, right?"

"Yes. She still is."

"I feel like I recognize the groom too."

"You probably do—he was two years ahead of us in school, and he played baseball. Declan MacAllister. Goes by Mack."

"Oh, right." He took the frame off the shelf and looked more closely. "Outfielder. Good arm."

I walked over and stood beside him. "They got married last fall. He's actually the CFO at Cloverleigh Farms. He had three daughters from a previous marriage—that's who those young girls are."

"Wow. Three girls." He set the photo back on the mantel.

I laughed. "She's trying to convince him to have more."

"He's probably a great dad."

"He is." I threw my bag over my shoulder. "Okay, ready to go."

Outside, the sky was completely overcast and the air was slightly humid. Off to the west, I could see dark gray clouds moving toward us and knew Tyler was right about the rain coming. He unlocked the passenger door and opened it for me.

"Thanks," I said as I climbed in. "The place I want to take you for breakfast is Frannie's pastry shop. But they have eggs and sandwiches and all kinds of things. Plus, the coffee is amazing."

"Sounds good. Just tell me how to get there."

Once he was behind the wheel, I gave him directions and he nodded, but I could tell he was distracted by something. He leaned toward the driver's side door, elbow on the window, hand rubbing his jaw.

"Everything okay?" I asked.

"Yeah. Fine."

But he went silent again for the rest of the ride downtown—so silent that I knew intuitively something was wrong. We parked along Main Street and hurried down the block, thunder rumbling softly over our heads. Tyler opened the pastry shop door for me just as the first fat, heavy raindrops were starting to splat on the sidewalk.

Coffee Darling was always busy in the morning, but we snagged a table for two toward the back. The server came over right away and asked us what we'd like to drink. Caitlan, her name tag read.

"Coffee please," I said. "With cream."

"Sure thing. And for you?" she asked Tyler.

"Coffee. Black."

"You got it."

"Hey, is Frannie here this morning?" I asked her.

Caitlan nodded. "She's in the back."

"Can you tell her that her sister April is here, and to come say hello if she gets a moment?"

"Of course. Be right back with your coffee. The menu is on the chalkboard behind the counter."

"Thanks."

As soon as we were alone, I sat back and looked at Tyler. "So what's on your mind?" I asked. "And don't say nothing or I'm going to personally go out and buy you a kitten."

He gave me a barely-there smile. "Sorry. That picture of Mack and his kids reminded me of something."

"What?"

"Sadie and Josh asked me to be their baby's godfather the other night."

"Really?" I sat up taller. "That's so exciting, Tyler!"

"I said yes, but I didn't want to."

"Why not? I think you'll be an awesome godfather! You'll love being an uncle, I promise. Being an aunt is so much fun. And I'm actually my niece Whitney's godmother. It's a really cool relationship."

"But it's a lot of responsibility too. If something were to happen to Sadie and Josh—"

"Don't even think about it like that," I said quickly. "No point in stressing out about things you can't control. Focus on the good part. Your sister trusts you with the most precious thing in her world—the life of her child. That's an incredible honor."

"But what if I'm not qualified? What if I, like, drop it? Or leave it somewhere? Or screw it up somehow?"

"Screw it up how?"

"I don't know—that's the point. But if I can screw up baseball, I can screw up a kid."

I laughed. "You'll be fine. I have faith in you."

Caitlan appeared, setting down two cups of coffee and a tiny pitcher of cream. "Now what can I bring you to eat? Frannie is just putting something in the oven and then she'll be right out."

"Great," I said. "I haven't even looked at the menu, but I'll just have a cinnamon roll. They're my favorite."

"Mine too." Caitlan looked at Tyler. "And for you?"

He was squinting at the chalkboard menu. "I'll try the farmer's omelette."

"Greens or potatoes?"

"Potatoes, please. And a side of bacon. Oh, and some toast."

"White or wheat?"

"Wheat."

"Coming right up."

When she was gone, I laughed as I poured cream into my

coffee. "I forgot about your appetite. My God, you used to eat so much when you'd come home after a game. Like an entire pot of spaghetti."

"That was your fault. You made good spaghetti sauce."

"In those days, I could make two things reliably— spaghetti and chicken parmesan casserole."

"Oh yeah, I remember that." Tyler picked up his coffee. "I used to eat it for breakfast the next day."

"What? Ew!"

He shrugged. "I liked it."

I sipped my coffee. "Do you cook?"

"The only thing I can make reliably in the kitchen is a mess. Yet another reason why my sister should think twice about putting me in charge of her kid. The poor thing would probably starve."

"Hey, you guys!" Frannie called, making her way toward our table.

"Hey, Frannie." Setting my cup down, I stood up and gave her a hug before gesturing across the table. "Do you remember Sadie's brother, Tyler Shaw? Tyler, this is my youngest sister, Frannie."

Tyler rose to his feet and extended his hand. "Nice to see you again."

"Nice to see you too." Frannie beamed at him. "My husband Mack played baseball with you in high school, and he's always talking about how good that team was."

"We were pretty damn good," Tyler said with a shrug.

"You should come by while you're in town if you can. But don't be surprised if he drags you outside to play catch or something." Frannie rolled her eyes. "None of his girls are too into sports and he's always begging for someone to go with him to games or toss a ball around in the yard or even just watch the playoffs on TV." She giggled. "One time, before we were married, they said they would watch with him as long as he'd let them paint his nails."

I laughed. "And did he?"

"Totally," she said gleefully. "Then they pretended they didn't have any remover, and he had to go to the store to buy some with hot pink fingernails."

Tyler looked at me but gestured at Frannie. "Did you hear that? This is why I don't want kids."

Frannie grinned. "They're really not that bad. I should get back to work. You guys enjoy breakfast. Nice seeing you, Tyler."

"You too," he said, taking his seat.

"Call me later, April."

I said I would and sat down, but we'd barely started to eat when my phone started blowing up with texts. I glanced at the screen to make sure there wasn't some kind of emergency at work and saw they were all from Frannie.

OMG!!!!

He's SO HOT.

Is this a date?

I'm dying.

Call me ASAP!!!!

Shaking my head, I dropped my phone back into my bag.

"What's up?" he asked.

"Nothing. My sister is ridiculous."

"So is mine. Did I tell you that in addition to believing I am a responsible adult, she's insisting I *dance* with her at this wedding?"

I smiled and licked some icing from my finger. "You don't like dancing?"

He gave me his grumpy old man face. "No."

"Well, the father-daughter dance is a tradition," I said gently. "You're playing that role for her. And it's two minutes—three at the most. You can get through one song for her, right?"

He stabbed a potato with his fork and stuck it in his mouth.

"*Right?*" I repeated forcefully.

"She wants me to pick the song," he complained. "I don't know any songs that would be right for that."

"I'll help you."

"Everyone will be watching me."

"Everyone watched you for years on the field and it never bothered you. In fact, I am pretty sure you enjoyed it."

"That's different." He picked up his coffee and took a drink. "I was *good* at baseball. I have never been good at dancing."

I tore off a doughy piece of cinnamon roll and popped it into my mouth. "Will it make you feel better if I show you a few simple moves to show her off so no one focuses on you?"

"What do you mean?"

"I mean, I can teach you a few easy, partnered dance steps so you feel like you know what you're doing. I've done it for brides and grooms before."

He looked confused. "Like, twirls and shit?"

Laughing, I took another bite. "Something like that."

"Excuse me," said a scratchy voice to my right.

I looked up to see an elderly man standing to the side of our table. He looked like he might be in his eighties or close to it—his posture was stooped, his belly was round, he needed suspenders to hold up his pants, and he wore thick glasses. His ears looked too big for his head, on which he wore a bright red ball cap. Tufts of white hair stuck out beneath it.

"Coach?" Tyler blinked at the old timer.

"Is that you, Shaw?"

"It's me."

"I thought so. But my wife says I can't see shit, so I wasn't sure. Came to take a closer look."

Tyler laughed as he rose to his feet and held out his hand. "Good to see you, Coach."

The old guy shook it but pulled him in for a hug too.

Whacked his back a few times. "Good to see you too, son. You playing any ball?"

"Nah, I'm retired."

"Where you hanging your hat these days?"

"I'm still in San Diego," answered Tyler. "Just in town for my sister's wedding." He nodded at me. "This is April Sawyer. April, this is Virgil Dean, one of my old coaches."

"His favorite one," added Virgil.

Smiling, I stood and offered my hand. "Nice to meet you, Mr. Dean."

He took my hand, and I noticed how his trembled. "Nice to meet you too," he said. Then he looked at Tyler. "This your wife?"

Tyler shook his head, and we exchanged an amused glance. "No, just a friend."

"I was gonna ask how you got someone like her. She's too good-looking for you." Virgil winked at me.

"She is," Tyler agreed, folding his arms over his chest. "So how've you been?"

"Oh, you know. Got some back pain. Some blood pressure trouble. Had one knee and both hips replaced. Can't see shit —my wife is right—but I don't hear too well either, so mostly I can ignore her carping at me." He shrugged. "I'm still walking around, so I guess that's good."

"Are you still coaching?"

"Not too much. I get out there every now and again and help my son David over at the high school—he's the head coach at Central now—but mostly, I try to stay out of the way. He doesn't like his old man to interfere too much."

"He'd be lucky to have you interfere." Tyler nodded toward his old coach and spoke to me. "You're looking at the man responsible for my fastball. Taught me everything I know."

"Really?" I raised my eyebrows. "I'm impressed. People are still talking about that fastball around here."

"Hell of a pitch." Virgil nodded proudly, then looked at Tyler. "Hell of an athlete. Say, you're not sticking around here for any length of time, are you? They think *I'm* an old fart over at the school, but they could use a good pitching coach. The last one didn't know his ass from his elbow."

Tyler shook his head. "Nah, I'm leaving Sunday."

"Why so soon?"

He shrugged. "I gotta get back."

"Thought you said you retired."

"I did, but—"

"So stay a while. What else you got going?"

Tyler paused. "Maybe you haven't heard, but baseball just isn't my thing anymore, Coach. I lost my arm."

"Bullshit. Baseball isn't here, son"—Virgil tapped Tyler's shoulder—"it's here." He thumped a gnarled fingertip on Tyler's chest. "And here." He tapped his head.

Tyler pressed his lips together. "I'll think about it."

His former coach lifted off his red cap, scratched the back of his head, studied Tyler with a shrewd eye, and looked at me as he replaced it. "See if you can get this guy to stay a while, get over to the high school. The kids could use his knowledge."

I smiled. "I'll try."

"All right, I guess I'll go back and tell my wife she was wrong. I love doing that. Good seeing you, son. Don't disappear so long." Virgil patted Tyler's shoulder and shuffled back to his table.

When we were seated again, Tyler dug into his breakfast.

"He seems like quite a character," I said.

"He is."

"Think you'll go over to the high school like he asked?"

"Nah. They don't want me over there."

"I thought you missed baseball."

"I do." He picked up a slice of bacon and tore a piece off with his teeth.

"And you aren't sure what the next move should be."

He gave me his best menacing glare as he chewed.

"You don't think you have something valuable to offer the next generation of players?"

"I know I do." He quirked a brow at me. "I never said I wouldn't be *good* at it."

"So what are you afraid of?" I pressed.

"I'm not afraid of anything."

I said nothing, just picked up my coffee cup and took a sip.

He rolled his eyes. "I've decided. You are officially worse than my sister."

"At what?"

"Pushing my buttons."

"Does that mean you'll stop by the school before you leave?"

"If I do, will you stop trying to boss me around?"

I grinned and picked up my cinnamon roll. "I'll consider it."

CHAPTER 9

Tyler

AFTER BREAKFAST, I dropped April off at Cloverleigh Farms and headed back to my hotel to get in a workout at the gym. It was still raining, and I wondered if Sadie was going to panic about that. April had been fretting on the ride back, checking the radar app on her phone with her bottom lip caught between her teeth.

I wanted to bite that lip too.

I hadn't thought anything could be more difficult than keeping my hands off April in the car last night, but watching her lick icing off her fingers this morning made me want to flip the table between us, throw her legs over my shoulders, and bury my face between her thighs.

Probably not the kind of behavior the crowd at Coffee Darling was used to, but hey, it would have been fun.

I was hoping a good hard weight session and some serious inclines on the treadmill would help me work off some of the sexual tension, but they didn't. I kept thinking about her while I worked out, imagining how she'd taste. Sweet, no doubt—like that cherry ice cream last night. But she'd be warm, not cool.

I'd go slow at first—I bet she liked it like that—so slow I'd drive her crazy. She'd moan and she'd sigh and she'd plead —*Tyler. Just like that. Don't stop.* And she'd put her hands in my hair and dig her heels into my back, and I wouldn't stop until I made her come.

Then—I had all the details worked out because I'd spent a fair amount of time last night jerking off to them—then, I'd move up her body and slide my cock into her while she was still wet and hot and murmuring softly. *Yes,* she'd say. *Fuck me, Tyler. You're so big. You're so good. You're the best I've ever had.*

Suddenly I heard myself groan out loud, and I quickly turned it into a cough so the other two people in the gym wouldn't think I was a fucking weirdo.

But Jesus. I couldn't remember the last time I'd been unable to get a woman out of my head. Was it because she was so completely off limits? Did I just want what I couldn't have? Was it because she reminded me of the me I used to be, and actually gave me back some of that feeling? Or was she just gorgeous and sexy and totally my type? I was a man, not a machine—a man in the middle of a tragic dry spell. Why wouldn't I find her tempting?

After I showered and dressed, I texted Sadie and asked her if she wanted to have lunch with me. I needed a distraction. She replied that she had to run a few errands downtown, but she'd meet me afterward, and gave me the name of a diner on Main Street.

I was sitting at the table waiting for her when I heard a voice.

"Excuse me. Tyler Shaw?"

I looked up and saw a young woman standing beside my table with a notepad and pen in her hand—a reporter. I'd learned to recognize them. "No," I told her.

She laughed like I'd said something really clever and tossed her Barbie hair. "My name is Bethany Bloomstar, I'm a local reporter for—"

"I'm not interested." I gave her the menacing glare.

"I was hoping to ask you a few questions."

"I know what you were hoping." I'd dealt with these people day in and day out in San Diego. "And I have nothing to say to you."

"Well, we're doing a story on you, and we'd like to give you an opportunity to comment. Any idea what caused your mental breakdown?"

"Look, I'm asking you politely."

"Asking me what?" Her eyebrows rose suggestively.

I frowned, feeling my grip on politeness about to go the way of the pterodactyl, and spoke through gritted teeth. "Fine. I'm *telling* you politely. I have nothing to say."

"Are you aware that some people are referring to the yips as Tyler Shaw Syndrome?"

"Please go away."

"Look, we're *doing* the story. Don't you want your voice on the record?"

"Here's something for your record—fuck off." Okay, maybe I shouldn't have said it, she was only trying to do her job, I get it . . . but she was like the eleventy-billionth reporter trying to get in my head, and it wasn't a space I shared with strangers.

"That's your comment?" she asked.

"That's my comment."

She sighed. "Okay, if that's the way you want it."

"That's the way I want it."

After she left, I pulled out my phone, thinking of texting Sadie that I'd changed my mind about lunch in a public place. Hadn't I learned my lesson by now?

"Tyler?"

I looked up from my phone, ready for another fight, but it wasn't another reporter. It was Virgil's son David, the coach at the high school. He'd been an assistant back when I was playing, and he'd also taught social studies, if I remembered correctly.

"David. Hey." Setting my phone on the table, I stood up and shook his hand.

"Good to see you, Tyler. I heard you were in town."

"News travels fast. I just saw your dad this morning."

David chuckled. "He was so glad to see you. Called me right away."

"So you're still at the high school?"

He nodded. "Dad said he tried to convince you to stop by."

"He did, but—"

"You should. The kids would love it. You're a legend at Central. And it would mean a lot to my dad."

For some reason, I found myself considering it. "My schedule's pretty tight. I'm only here until Sunday."

"We've got practice tomorrow morning," he said hopefully.

"Do you?" I rubbed a finger beneath my lower lip.

"Yes. Just think about it. I got this new kid, a senior, just moved here beginning of this year. He's a lefty. Fantastic arm, lots of speed, great power. But—"

"No command?"

He shook his head. "Very little."

"Sounds familiar."

David laughed. "You had more than he does."

"Well, I had to learn it. Your dad taught me that. Made me slow down and rededicate myself to the mechanics." I was sort of warming to the idea of passing on the knowledge. "I might be able to come by."

"That would be awesome. I'm not even gonna say anything to the guys, because they'll fucking lose it, and we've got a game tonight."

"Oh yeah? Where?"

"At home. You should come check it out. Chip, the lefty, is pitching."

For a second, I thought about it. Maybe April would come with me. "Oh wait—I can't. I've got my sister's rehearsal dinner tonight. She's getting married tomorrow. That's why I'm in town."

"Oh. Well . . ." He shrugged. "We'd love to see you at practice tomorrow if you can fit it in. Ten a.m."

"Sounds good. But David." I squared my shoulders and spoke firmly. "I don't throw in public. Not even for practice."

"That's okay. You don't have to throw. You could just talk to them. Help Chip with his motion."

Just then, my sister appeared at the table, her hair damp from the rain. "Hey."

"Hey, Sadie. You remember David Dean, my old coach?"

She smiled at him. "I do, but he was Mr. Dean, geography teacher, to me. Nice to see you."

"You too, Sadie," he said. "Congratulations on your wedding."

"Thanks." She closed her eyes and sighed. "I'm not going to stress about the rain. I'm not going to stress about the rain. I'm not going to stress about the rain."

David grinned. "Nope, not at all. Well, I'll let you two have lunch. Good seeing you both. Tyler, hope you can make it tomorrow."

I nodded and sat down, and Sadie dropped into the chair across from me. "What's he talking about?" she asked.

"Baseball practice. He and his dad—I ran into Coach Dean this morning at breakfast—are on me to stop by the team practice tomorrow morning."

"What time?"

"Ten."

She nodded. "That works. You should do it."

"I'm thinking about it."

She shrugged out of a light jacket. "God, this weather better break."

"April thinks it will."

Sadie looked up at me and tucked her wet hair behind her ears. "How did it go with her last night?"

"Good."

"Good?"

"Yeah. It was fun."

She stared at me. "No. Do not give me the man version of events—I want the details."

I rolled my eyes, prepared to give her only a slightly longer man version, but I was saved by the server who came to take our order. Once we were alone again, though, Sadie persisted.

"Well?" she prompted, giving me a gentle kick in the shin for good measure.

"I met her at Cloverleigh's bar. We had some food and drinks. We talked about old times. It was nice."

She digested that. "Did you apologize?"

"Actually, I did. But you were wrong."

"About what?"

"I didn't abandon her. I specifically asked her if I had."

Her eyes widened. "What made you do that?"

"I don't know. I guess you got me thinking about it." I leaned on the table with both elbows. "I started doubting my recollection of the events and realized maybe it wasn't the only version of the story."

"Wow." She blinked. "I'm impressed. I didn't really think you'd do it."

"I wasn't going to. But . . . I don't know." I sat back and shrugged. "At the end of the night, the question just sort of slipped out, and we wound up having a conversation about it."

Her brows shot up. "Interesting."

The server returned with our drinks, and Sadie took a sip

of her herbal tea. I probably should have let the subject drop right there, but for some reason, I didn't.

"It was a boy," I said.

Sadie looked up at me in surprise, nearly choking on her tea. "You asked that too?"

"Yes."

"Wow. *Wow.*" She sat back and studied me. "And how do you feel about that?"

"Fine." I shrugged. "It doesn't really affect me, you know?"

"It doesn't?"

"No. She told me he was adopted by two amazing people who really wanted a baby, and she knew right away they were the mom and dad. I told her I was glad to hear it."

My sister nodded slowly. "Well, I'm glad to hear that too."

"Good. So now we never have to discuss it again."

"Okay, but one more thing."

"What?"

"Did she tell you his name?"

"Charles."

"Charles," she repeated softly. "What's his middle name?"

I shrugged. "I didn't ask."

"Why not?"

"I don't know." I frowned, scratching my head. "Look, I didn't ask about him for *him*, I asked about him for April. I wanted to hear that *she* was okay."

"And is she?"

"Yes."

"Okay. Good." Sadie took another sip of tea. "She's such a good person. I want her to be happy."

"Me too." I took a drink of my iced tea. "Any idea why she never got married?"

"No. It's really surprising to me, actually, because I know she always wanted children. She used to talk about it when she'd babysit me."

"Huh."

Sadie shrugged. "Maybe she just hasn't met the right person."

"Maybe."

"Maybe it's you." One of Sadie's eyebrows peaked.

I rolled my eyes. "It's not me."

"How do you know?"

"Because I *know*," I told her, picking up my iced tea again. "Believe me. We talked about this last night too—she and I are very different, and we are not looking for the same things."

"What's she looking for?"

"A husband, two-point-five kids, maybe a cat."

"And you?"

"A club sandwich. And look at that, dreams do come true." I leaned back as the server set a plate in front of me.

My sister sighed dramatically. "I don't even know why I bother."

I picked up a French fry and stuck it in my mouth. "Me neither."

After lunch, I drove by my old barber shop, but at the last minute I kept on driving, deciding instead to try a salon up the street that said "Walk-Ins Welcome." I figured I had less of a chance of being recognized there, and the encounter with that reporter was fresh on my mind.

Thankfully, I was right. The salon was full of women who either didn't recognize me or didn't give a shit, and I got a pretty nice haircut too. Not only that, but it came with a shampoo and a scalp massage that—not gonna lie—made me miss a woman's hands in my hair. I closed my eyes and imagined the hands were April's.

At five o'clock that night, I reported for duty at Cloverleigh Farms. Sadie had told me I didn't have to wear a suit but to please look nice, so I'd added a blue sports jacket and tie to my dark jeans and a white button-down.

April was standing in the entrance hall of a building Sadie had called "the wedding barn," which was the designated meeting spot for the rehearsal. The way she looked me over—kind of the way she'd gazed at her dessert last night before devouring it—put a little swagger back in my game.

"Hi," she said, her eyes traveling over me. "You look great."

"Thanks." I gave her a kiss on the cheek without thinking if that was okay or not. She looked great too. It was amazing how she could make such a long skirt—it came down to at least her knees—look sexy. Maybe it's because it hugged her butt so tight. And the blouse she wore didn't show any cleavage—it tied around her neck, in fact—but somehow, the whole effect of the outfit was making me sweat.

Was it the heels? They were the same ones she'd been wearing last night—black and high and shiny, with a little hole at the top where the barest suggestion of red polish on her toes peeked out.

I loosened my tie.

The rehearsal was pretty straightforward, although we had to run through it indoors instead of out because of the rain. I stood where they said to stand, moved where they told me to move, and stayed out of the way as much as I could. Mostly I watched April, impressed by the way she handled everything and everyone so smoothly. My sister's constant questions and requests would have driven me fucking bananas, but April's patience seemed endless.

By six o'clock, it was over. Sadie seemed happy with

everything but the weather, which wasn't even that awful now that the storms had quieted to a drizzle.

"My weather app says no more rain tonight," assured April. "And everything should be nice and dry by tomorrow."

Sadie still looked nervous. "I hope so."

The dinner was being hosted by Josh's parents at a restaurant downtown, and on our way out, Sadie invited April to join us.

"Thanks, but I can't," she said. "I've got a lot of things to get done here."

"Can't you get away for a little bit? You still need to eat," I told her, disappointed she wasn't coming along.

She shook her head, smiling wistfully. "I wish I could. I'll grab something to eat later. Go have fun."

"Okay." I glanced out the glass door and watched Josh and Sadie walking arm in arm next to his parents. "Hey, what about the dance stuff? My sister was bugging me about it at lunch today, and I told her you were going to help me."

"Oh, right." Her forehead wrinkled for a moment.

"Can I come back here later? How long will you be here?"

"A few hours, for sure. That could work." She looked up at me. "You don't want to go out with the wedding party?"

I gave her a look. "Are you serious? They're like twelve. They'll probably want to go drive go-karts or play paintball or something."

April laughed. "Okay. Meet me back here after dinner. In the meantime, I'll think of a song."

"Something short, please. And not too fast. But not too slow either."

She pushed me toward the exit. "Trust me. Sheesh."

"I do trust you." I stopped in front of the door and looked at her. "Thank you for this."

"For what?"

"For everything you're doing for my sister. And for me."

She shrugged. "It's my job. And you guys are like family to me."

I couldn't resist pressing my lips to her soft pink cheek once more. Her skin was warm, and I left my mouth there for a little longer this time. When I picked up my head, I saw that her face had gone full-on flushed. "I'll see you soon," I said, pushing open the door.

She raised one hand, looking a little dazed. "Okay. Bye."

The cool air felt good on my skin as I walked toward my car. That girl made me hot all over, and I was growing concerned about my ability to stay in control when we were alone later tonight, especially if I had to put my arms around her.

But I couldn't fucking wait.

CHAPTER 10

April

I WATCHED Tyler walk across the parking lot with his long, easy strides until I couldn't see him anymore. Then I bolted for my office, snatched my phone off my desk, and called Chloe.

"Hello?"

"Are you still at work?"

"Yeah, but I'm about to leave."

"Can you come over to the wedding barn first?"

"Why?"

"Because I'm afraid I'm going to make a really big mistake and I need you to talk me out of it—or into it. I can't decide."

"Okay, okay. Give me ten minutes."

While I waited for her, I paced back and forth in front of my desk, even though there were a million things I should have been doing. But I couldn't concentrate—all I could think of was that Tyler had kissed my cheek *twice*! And he was so handsome! And it had been so sweet watching him walk his sister down the aisle! And he was coming back later tonight and we were going to be alone and I'd promised to show him how to dance, which meant he'd have to touch me, and I wasn't sure I could take it.

Which reminded me—I'd better start looking at songs. I had a few ideas, but I wanted to listen to them.

I had just perched on the edge of my desk, phone in hand, when Chloe knocked on my open office door. "Hey."

"Oh, thank God." I set my phone aside. "I need a voice of reason."

"So you called *me*?" She cocked her head. "I feel like another sister might have been a better choice."

"Well, they're not here, so you'll have to do. Come sit."

She sat in one of the chairs in front of my desk while I resumed pacing. "So what's up?" she asked. "Is it Tyler?"

"Yes."

"How did it go last night?"

"Great."

"Did he want to bang you after all?"

"Yes. But we didn't."

She made a face. "Why not?"

"Because he said he wanted to be a gentleman this time."

"Like he was trying to make up for last time?"

"Exactly. He said he saw it as an opportunity to do the right thing, like a good guy would. He drove me home because I drank a little too much, and he said he'd promised me no detours this time, and he was determined to keep his word."

Chloe sighed. "Can't fault him for that, I suppose."

I turned and faced her. "It's not that I fault him, Chloe, it's that I *want* him. I think I want him even more *because* he was such a nice guy last night. If he'd tried to put his hand up my skirt or something, I probably would have been mad. Tonight could be a different story though."

"You're seeing him again tonight?"

I nodded. "After the rehearsal dinner he's coming back here. For a dance lesson."

"A dance lesson?"

"He's nervous about dancing with Sadie tomorrow. I

promised to show him a couple easy moves. It's not *that* I'm worried about—it's what could happen afterward."

"What's the problem? If he wants you, and you want him..."

"But *why* do I want him, Chloe? It doesn't make any sense." I tapped my head.

"Uh, yes it does. He's ridiculously hot. And you guys have history."

"But it's stupid—he's only in town for two more days."

She cocked her head. "How long do you think sex takes?"

I stopped moving and looked at her. "You know what I mean. I'm not interested in a weekend sex fling. At least, I shouldn't be."

"Why not?"

"Because I'm supposed to be trying to find *the one*." I threw my arms in the air. "I want the damn *one*! But if he could just hurry up, that would be great, because I haven't had sex in a really, really long time, and I'm getting a little desperate!"

Chloe laughed. "That's exactly why this attraction to Tyler makes sense. Even though your mind knows he's not the one, your orgasm is like, 'Hey, remember me?'"

"What's an orgasm?" I asked irritably. "I vaguely recall one from 2015, but it might have been self-inflicted."

"Exactly."

I crossed one arm over my stomach and chewed the thumb of the opposite hand. "You don't think it's a terrible idea?"

"It's a terrible idea if you're looking for something deep and meaningful out of it. But if all you're looking for is a good time, and it won't mess with your head, maybe it's part of the closure you're looking for. Like maybe you need to get him out of your system once and for all. On *your* terms."

I perched on the edge of my desk again. "Maybe."

"But for the love of God, use protection if you do."

I laughed. "I'm pretty sure Tyler would be all over that. The man does *not* want children."

"No?"

I shook my head. "We talked about it last night."

"Really." Chloe crossed her legs. "*That's* interesting. Did you guys discuss the adoption thing at all?"

"We did, actually. Not until the end of the night when he took me home, but then he came right out and asked me about it. He wanted to know whether the baby I had was a boy or a girl."

"Wow. How did he take the news?"

I shrugged. "He was quiet at first, but when I told him about the couple who adopted him, he said he was glad he'd asked. It's so weird, Chloe. I really think he was able to move on from it just like that"—I snapped my fingers—"and never feel anything about it again."

"Yeah, well, in general, guys are better at that than women. They can file their emotions away in a box and not allow them to seep into other parts of their lives. Especially a guy like Tyler, who had a fuck ton of pressure to deal with."

"Yeah."

"But that doesn't mean they're not still there," she said, surprising me. "It just means he doesn't like opening that box. Most men don't."

"What about Oliver?"

She rolled her eyes. "Oliver was excellent at keeping the box locked up. But he is learning that opening it up is not going to kill him, and in fact, science has shown it leads to increased blowjobs and occasional butt stuff."

I burst out laughing. "Okay. Good to know—sort of."

Chloe smiled and stood up. "I better get home. We have dinner plans with Mack and Frannie tonight. Did this help at all?"

"I think so," I hedged. "I guess I have to just learn to feel the things I feel without judging myself, no matter what they are."

"I agree one thousand percent," she said, coming forward to give me a hug. "And you're going to be okay no matter what."

After my chat with Chloe, I stayed busy checking tasks off my list, including setup for Sadie's wedding and thinking about potential songs for Tyler and Sadie's dance. I stayed away from anything slow, sappy and overdone, and gravitated toward songs that reminded me of their sibling relationship—playful, loving, timeless. In the end I had a short list of suggestions that included tunes by Frank Sinatra, Stevie Wonder, Amy Winehouse, and John Legend.

I was sitting at my desk when a text from Tyler came in around quarter to eight. **I'm bored.**

Smiling, I messaged him back. **Why?**

Tyler: I'm done eating. Now I'm just listening to people I don't know make speeches and eyeballing the door.

Me: I'd be bored too.

Tyler: I'd rather be with you.

I was still thinking about how to respond when another text from him came in.

Tyler: Can I still come by?

Me: Sure. I have some song suggestions for you.

Tyler: Okay. I'm either going to make a run for it when no one is looking or fake appendicitis here in a minute.

Me: Haha. Good luck. The outside door of the wedding barn is locked, so text me when you get here, okay?

Tyler: Okay. See you soon.

I set my phone aside and put both hands over my fluttering stomach.

About twenty minutes later, he messaged me that he was outside, and I went to open the door. My heart raced at the sight of him.

"Hey," I said, catching the scent of his cologne as he came in. "You escaped."

"I escaped."

I locked the door behind him. "So which was it? Did you ghost or fake an illness?"

"I ghosted. But I texted Sadie what I was doing so she wouldn't get mad."

"Ah. Smart."

"What have you been up to?"

"Working. Come with me. I have some songs to play for you, then once you choose we can work on some steps." I led him into the dimly lit reception room, where I'd cued up the sound system. Plugging my phone into it, I invited him to sit with me on the band platform and listen to a little of each song. He ended up choosing "Isn't She Lovely?" by Stevie Wonder, because he said their dad had been a fan.

"She'll love that," I said, happy with his selection. "And it's a nice mid-tempo song that will make everyone smile, not cry."

"They might cry when they see my moves," he said.

I laughed and slapped his shoulder. "Will you please trust me? This is not going to be difficult. I'm going to edit this to be a short version, two minutes max. And I'll make sure it's the version the deejay has."

"Good."

I put the song on repeat and stood up, offering my hands. "Okay, now come here."

He rose to his feet and took my hands, letting me pull him forward onto the empty dance floor. Just one overhead chandelier was lit, and I'd turned it down low. "Dark in here," he said.

"I thought it might make you less self-conscious."

He glanced around. "Are you sure we're alone? I don't want anyone to see this."

"Yes. Okay now, you put your right hand on my back, and keep your left in mine." I placed my left hand on his shoulder, leaving plenty of space between us.

"Got it."

"Now just step to the rhythm of the song."

He swayed me side to side, pretty stiffly, but on the beat, at least.

"Good."

"We have now reached the top of my skill level."

I laughed. "Now you're going to turn me. Raise your left hand, and gently push me under the arch with your right. Keep my hand in yours."

"That sounds complicated."

"It's not. And it will be nice and smooth because you're so tall. I'll be able to get under the arch without even ducking, and so will Sadie."

He did as I asked. "Now what? You're way out there."

"Now bring me back."

"How?"

"Raise the arch again, and turn your wrist a little." I showed him what I meant. "That tells me where you want me to go." A couple seconds later, I was back in his arms. "Perfect. See? It's easy."

"I don't think I did that," he said skeptically. "I think that was all you."

"So *you* do it this time. Three motions—lift the arch, push me through, bring me back."

He did it a few more times, each time a little more smoothly. "Hey, I think I've got it."

"Congratulations. Now one more step."

He groaned. "Don't push it, Sawyer. One step might be all I can handle."

"Listen, if you can strike out nineteen batters in a row, you can learn two dance steps."

He stopped moving. "You remember that day?"

"Of course I remember that day. I'm pretty sure I cried when they gave you the standing ovation."

"Did you really?" His arms slid further around my back, pulling me closer to him.

"Yes." I swallowed hard. We were now hip to hip. "And later that night, we went to a party, and you kissed Jenna Holmes."

"I did?"

I nodded, my palm moving from the shoulder of his jacket up the back of his neck. "I was so jealous."

"You never showed it."

"I couldn't. I didn't want to be just another girl to you."

"You were never just another girl to me, April."

"Because I never let on that I wanted you to kiss me."

His head dipped lower, until his lips were just inches from mine. "I don't even remember Jenna Jones."

I smiled. "Jenna *Holmes*."

"See? But I remember you always smelled like birthday cake. I remember the way you'd play with your hair while you did math problems. And I remember this one little skirt you had, the way it would ride up your thighs when you sat on your knees at the kitchen table."

Forget about dancing. I couldn't even feel my feet on the ground anymore. "Tyler?"

"Yeah."

I slid my hand into his thick dark hair. "I want you to kiss me."

"It's about fucking time." That cocky grin flashed for a fraction of a second, and then—finally—his lips were on mine.

The music continued to play, but I barely heard anything above the pounding of my heart. Tyler's right arm tightened around my back, and his left hand moved to the back of my head. He opened his mouth wider and stroked between my lips with his tongue, sending a tingle straight between my legs. His hand gripped my ponytail and pulled my head back as his mouth traveled down my throat. "Your hair drives me crazy," he growled.

"Pull the elastic out," I urged. "Take it down."

A few seconds later, my hair tumbled down around my shoulders, and he threaded his fingers through it, cradling my head in his hands as his mouth collided with mine once more. I looped my arms around his waist and pulled his torso against mine, feeling the bulge in his pants thick and hard against my abdomen.

Suddenly he broke off the kiss and rested his forehead on mine. His breathing was ragged. "Fuck, April. This is where I'm supposed to leave—alone. This is where I remind myself that I'm the good guy. This is where I should remember to do the right thing. However, this is also where I'm the bad guy who wants to rip your clothes off and make you come a thousand different ways."

A breathless laugh escaped me. "A thousand? Really?"

"Really."

Excitement and desire ricocheted through my body. "Tell me more about this bad guy."

"He's good with his hands."

"Does he say dirty things?"

"*Filthy* things."

"Does he take his time?"

He paused. "He will really try."

I laughed. "Come on, bad guy. Let's go."

I got the sound system shut down, the lights off, and the building locked up in record time. Within five minutes, Tyler and I were racing hand in hand across the parking lot as quickly as my heels would allow.

"Your place or mine?" I asked.

"Mine," he answered. "There's a guy in the room next door to me who needs to be taken down a notch."

"What?" I shrieked as he opened the door to his SUV for me. "We're not inviting the neighbors, are we?"

"No." He shut me in and ran around to get in on the other side. "It's just you and me. But if he happens to hear us, I will not be upset."

Tyler sped the whole way back to his hotel—I cannot believe he didn't get pulled over. I had to cover my eyes because I was positive he was going to run a red light. When we reached the resort where he was staying, he left the car at valet—with the keys in the ignition—even though we didn't even see anyone there. Then he grabbed my hand and pulled me through the lobby toward the elevators.

The doors opened right away, and he yanked me inside, punching the Close Doors button furiously. When they came together, leaving us alone, he spun around and crushed his lips to mine.

The kiss knocked me breathless. His arms came around me—tight. His body forced me back into the corner while his mouth ravaged mine without mercy. When the elevator pinged and the doors opened, he reached for my hand again and raced down the hallway on his mile-long legs toward his room. I stumbled after him on much shorter legs, panting and laughing and out of my mind with desire.

I was so far off the ledge, I couldn't even see it anymore.

Tyler struggled with the key card, but finally the green light flashed, and he threw open the door, pushing me inside the room. By the time I heard it slam shut, he'd swept me off my feet and was carrying me over to the bed.

The drapes were shut but one bedside lamp was on, illuminating his dark, hungry eyes as he tossed me onto the spread and removed his jacket.

I propped myself up on my elbows and watched him yank off his tie, pull his shirt from his jeans and unbutton it, ditch his shoes and socks and belt . . . all in the space of about ten seconds. Finally, he peeled off the button-down and whipped his T-shirt over his head. For the first time, I got a look at his bare chest.

Let me just say, it was worth the wait.

But I barely had time to admire it before he launched himself onto the bed. I squealed as his body sprawled over mine.

"Maniac," I teased, putting my hands on that chest. It was hot and hard and made my body shiver with anticipation. "You're going to crush me. And I've never seen anyone get undressed so fast. Are you *sure* you know how to take your time?"

"Listen," he said, sliding down my body and getting onto his knees. "The only thing I'm doing quickly tonight is undressing you." He pulled off one of my heels, then the other.

"Yeah?"

"Yeah." He flipped me onto my stomach, unzipped my skirt, and tugged it off, leaving my black panties in place. They weren't my sexiest underwear, but they weren't Netflix and nachos either, and they still made his jaw drop when he flipped me onto my back again. He ran a fingertip along the lace at the top, making my belly quiver.

Next, he untied my blouse at the neck, then worked his way down the row of buttons. It took him a little while because the buttons were tiny and his hands were so big.

"Want help?" I offered.

"Nope."

When he finally reached the last button, he opened the blouse and looked down at my chest. I was wearing a black bra, nothing special, but the way his eyes traveled over my skin made me feel infinitely beautiful. He grabbed my wrists and pinned them to the mattress over my head, stretching out above me.

"No fair, I can't use my hands," I told him, wrapping my legs around his hips.

"You put your hands on me, this could be over before it begins, babe. You gotta at least give a guy a chance." He kissed me in that slow, deep way that awakened every nerve ending in my body and made my back arch beneath him. Through his jeans I could feel the hard length of him rubbing against me, and I was anxious for more. But he took his time, moving his mouth down my neck, my chest, my stomach, running his tongue along the lace edge of my panties where he'd brushed his fingertip before.

"Tyler," I said impatiently. "Take your pants off."

"Not yet, my pet." He moved all the way down so his head was between my legs. "While I appreciate your eagerness to get where we're going, I'm going to enjoy the ride a bit."

"The ride?"

"Yes." He kissed his way up one inner thigh. "See, some guys might be all about the shortcut . . ." He kissed his way down the other. " . . . but I myself like a detour."

I half-laughed, half-panted as he centered his mouth

between my legs, using his tongue on my clit through the thin, soft satin. "I know this about you."

"Oh," he said confidently. "But you don't."

He was right.

I'd had no idea what it was like to be so thoroughly ravished by him—or by anyone else, for that matter. No one had ever made me feel so good. He used his mouth in ways that had me clawing the sheets and pounding the mattress and begging him not to stop. He tugged my panties off with his teeth. He licked his way all the way back up my thighs. He stroked me with his tongue again and again and again— soft and slow, hard and fast, gentle one minute and greedy the next. He told me my pussy was the sweetest thing he'd ever tasted, that he couldn't get enough, that he might come just from fucking me with his tongue. He used his fingers, sliding them inside me while he sucked my clit, flicking it with the tip of his tongue while I writhed and rocked beneath him. And when the orgasm tore through my body in glorious, rippling contractions, he moaned just as loudly as I did, as if he could feel it just as deep.

I had barely caught my breath when he moved up my body, wiping his mouth with the back of his wrist. If it were anyone else, I might have been self-conscious—but I wasn't. For once, it hadn't even occurred to me to worry that I didn't taste right or wasn't wearing the perfect underwear or moved too much or not enough. I never once contemplated faking an orgasm just so I could stop being so anxious and try to enjoy myself more. With Tyler, I felt at ease with my body and everything he was doing to it.

And *good lord*, he was hot. I didn't know where to look, between the hair and the eyes and the jaw and the shoulders and the chest and the abs. He braced himself on his hands above my shoulders, and I ran my palms down his arms and up his chest. "I *love* your body. I never saw it that night."

He kissed my cheek, my shoulder, my collarbone. "That's because I didn't even bother to take my clothes off."

"Nope, it was minimum nakedness, that's for sure."

"Sit up."

I did as he asked, and he removed my blouse, unhooked my bra with an easy flick of his fingers, and tossed both aside. Then he gently pushed me back again and looked down at me. "Good thing I didn't get you naked that night. I could come just looking at you."

My core muscles tightened. "Tyler. Take off those fucking pants."

His hands were on the zipper before I even finished the sentence.

CHAPTER 11

Tyler

I'D BEEN WRONG—SHE didn't taste like cherry ice cream with amaretto sauce. She tasted better.

And the flavor of her was still on my tongue as I put my mouth all over her body. I loved the sounds she made, the way she moved, the feel of her skin against mine.

I went slow, just like I'd planned, but I knew it was only a matter of time until I lost control. Something about her just made me want to get inside her—I didn't know whether it was her scent or her taste, her hot little moans or her deep-throated cries, the gorgeous red hair spilling over the pillow or the alabaster skin flushed pink with heat.

Christ, she was beautiful.

And the way she touched me, a little shyly, like she'd always wanted to but never dared—her hands running over my chest and back, my stomach and arms, and finally wrapping around my cock—with that bottom lip caught between her teeth and her eyes open wide. Like she couldn't believe this was real.

We tipped to our sides, and I groaned against her lips as she stroked me, soft and playful at first, her fingertips brushing over my crown, then harder and faster, her fist tight around my shaft. I ran my hand along the curve of her hip, up between her thighs, slipped my fingers inside her again. God, I wanted to be there. I needed it, and I couldn't wait a second longer.

"Wait," I told her. I rolled away from her and hurried into the bathroom, where I'd seen at least two condoms in my travel kit earlier. They'd been in there a while, mocking me, but now I thanked Jesus I hadn't taken them out.

And if Jesus didn't approve of what I was doing, he could look the other way.

I took both condoms back to the bed, tossed one on the nightstand, tore open the packet of the second, and rolled it on. My heart was thundering in my chest.

April was on her side, chin resting on her fist, watching me. "Are you going to wear both?" she asked.

"I wasn't planning on it. I only have the two, and I figured we'd save one for later."

She arched a brow. "Pretty optimistic of you."

I jumped back into bed, and she squealed as I flipped her onto her back, circled her wrists with my fingers, and held them tight to the mattress. "You trying to turn me back into a grumpy old man?"

"No!" She shook her head violently. "Please let me keep this Tyler. He's hot. And sexy." She lowered her voice to a whisper. "And he has a really big dick that's going to do deliciously naughty things to me."

"You got that right." I eased inside her and began to move, fighting for control. If I wasn't careful, I'd explode like a teenager in under a minute.

Her eyes fluttered shut and she turned her face to the side as I plunged in deeper, her mouth dropping open.

"Are you okay?" I asked.

She nodded. "Yes," she whispered. "Just keep going slow for a minute, okay?"

"Okay." I did as she asked, watching her discomfort

subside and her desire take over. Her back began to arch. Her gasps turned to sighs. Her hands traveled down my back and over my ass, pulling me in deeper. When her hips began to rock beneath mine, I knew she was getting close.

"Tell me how you want me to fuck you." I spoke low in her ear, my voice ragged with the fight for control. "Do you like it deep? Hard?"

"Yes," she said, holding out the *s* in a long hiss. "Yes, I like it deep and hard. Just like that," she rasped as I started to move with more muscle, more aggression. She cried out with every savage thrust, and I couldn't get enough—of her tight, wet pussy, of the smell of sex, of the sound of the headboard banging against the wall.

Take that, asshole! I have stamina too!

God, it felt so fucking good to command my body and have it obey. To experience that surge of power and pleasure that came from peak physical performance. To work up this agonizing tension and know the release was *right fucking there*, and it was going to deliver the way it was supposed to —for both of us. I hadn't been in this place for so long, *so long*.

But I had to take her with me. "Come for me," I growled, or maybe begged, as I dangled from the edge, losing my grip. "Come for me. Now, now, now—"

"Yes!" she cried out, her body contracting around my cock as it throbbed inside her.

I kept moving until I couldn't anymore, until my muscles gave out, until I collapsed on top of her in complete and utter bliss. Her hands came up to my head and threaded into my hair, and we stayed just like that for a moment, our skin slick with sweat, our breath coming hard and fast, our bodies still connected.

But after a minute, I realized I must be crushing her, and I lifted my chest from her upper body. "Sorry. You okay?"

"Um, I just had two orgasms in like twenty minutes. I'm amazing. Well, *you're* amazing."

I grinned down at her. "Thanks. Want a third? Because I think I could do it."

She laughed and swatted at my chest. "Whoa there, cowboy. This pony needs a little rest. I think you might have bruised my spleen or something."

"Sorry."

Her eyes narrowed. "Liar."

"You're right." Rolling off her, I carefully extracted myself, kissed her shoulder, and stood up. "Be right back."

When I returned from the bathroom a few minutes later, she was lying exactly where I left her, on her back on top of the covers, one arm across her stomach, the other above her head. Her forehead was wrinkled, like she was fretting about something. I got back on the bed and lay on my side, my head propped in my hand.

"Hey." I tugged a strand of her hair.

"Hey."

"That's a serious face you're wearing for someone who just had two orgasms in twenty minutes."

She smiled sheepishly. "Sorry. I was just thinking."

"For fuck's sake, don't do that."

She rolled to her side and faced me. "Do you think this is crazy?"

"No."

"Not even *kind* of crazy? I mean, given our history?"

"I mean, maybe a little. But I don't think it's *bad*—unless one of us has strange expectations about what it is. Wait—we don't, do we?" Suddenly I was nervous that we hadn't laid out the parameters before we jumped into bed.

She laughed. "You should see how scared your face is. Don't worry, no strange expectations here. I know *what* this is, and it's okay. We're still friends."

"Okay." I paused. "So what don't you know?"

"I guess I was just lying here wondering why this feels so good with you."

"It's supposed to feel good."

"I know. But for me, it hasn't always. And I've been working through some stuff for the last few months—well, really, if I'm honest, it's been a lot longer than that—so I'm trying to sort of fit us into that bigger picture."

"What do you mean?"

She reached out and brushed her fingertip over a small scar on my chest. "My therapist believes I've kept people, especially men, at a distance, because I don't want to reveal my past. I'm scared of being judged for my decisions."

"All of your decisions? Or one in particular?"

"One in particular." She kept her eyes on my chest.

"Meaning . . . the baby?"

"Yes. Because I felt a lot of guilt about giving it up, I never let anyone get close enough to tell them about it. I purposely put up a wall—this thing that prevents me from really letting someone in. But with you, it isn't there."

I brushed a piece of hair off her face. "No. It isn't."

"I guess—I guess it's a relief to feel like I have nothing to hide. No reason to put up the wall. You already know the deepest, darkest piece of me, the part I've kept concealed from everyone else, so I have nothing to feel anxious about. It freed me up to just feel . . . *good*."

"So what you're saying is, my dick isn't just big, it's therapeutic."

Laughing, she gave my chest a push. "God, your ego really never quits."

"I can't help it. I'm around you, and I'm eighteen again."

"But smarter. And safer."

"Don't forget slower and more skilled."

She giggled. "Definitely slower and more skilled. No more rifle."

I took her hand, and automatically, our fingers interlocked. "So I decided to go over to baseball practice tomorrow morning."

Her eyes widened. "Really? What made you decide that?"

"I ran into Coach Dean's son David this afternoon. Virgil had already told him I was around for the weekend, so he was making the hard sell too. He told me about this kid, a new kid—a lefty pitcher like me—who's got a great arm but struggles with control. I thought I might go over and watch him throw a little bit. See if I can help him out."

"I think that's awesome. Those kids are going to love having you there."

"Maybe. But it's not really the kids I'm concerned about. It's the asshole parents, the ones who'll ask why a fuckup like me is coaching their kids." I shrugged. "Guess you were right about me being afraid of something."

"You can ignore them."

I grimaced. "I can try."

She sat up and got feisty with me. "Listen, you are not a fuckup, and you don't have anything to be ashamed or afraid of. You *made it*. You left here and did exactly what you said you were going to do—pitch in the major league. How many people can say that? You were a superstar for, what, like ten years? That's a long time. And you probably made a bazillion dollars doing it, so you have plenty of money and can do anything you want with your second act. You just have to decide what it's going to be."

"It won't be anything as great as the first, that's for sure."

She poked my shoulder. "You don't know that. It could be even better. Ten years ago, I was living in Manhattan planning super ritzy parties for ridiculously wealthy clients, and I thought it was the epitome of success in my career. But you know what? I got bored. It was the same kind of people, and they weren't always good people, and I started to feel like my life didn't have the kind of purpose I wanted. When my parents offered the job here, I said no way at first. I'd worked really hard to make it in the big city—why would I come back to this little town? For a pay cut, no less. And dealing with *brides* all the time? No, thanks."

"Why did you?" I wondered.

"Because I had the opportunity to build something of my own here. To grow it and watch it take off. I also realized how much I missed my family—and even this little town, where everyone wants to know your business and no one is shy about poking into it. Because they can also be really generous and loyal. I like that so many people around me know my name, know my family, care enough to ask about my dad's health or compliment my mom's hospitality or tell me how beautiful they heard so-and-so's wedding was at the farm."

I shook my head. "You're a much better person than I am."

She laughed and tried to push me again, but this time I flipped her onto her back. "You are. Just admit it."

"I'm only trying to show you that your second act might not look like you thought it would, but it can still make you happy. I mean, you weren't going to play forever, were you? What was the plan?"

"I didn't have one," I told her, settling my hips over hers. "I was going to die on the field."

"Of what?" She wrapped her arms and legs around me.

"Heart attack? Lightning strike?" I planted kisses on her shoulder, her collarbone, her breast. "I don't really know. Never gave that part much thought."

"Well, I'm glad you had to retire before that happened. I would've been very sad at your funeral."

I picked up my head and grinned at her. "You'd miss my big therapeutic dick?"

"I wouldn't even know about that. If your pitching career hadn't ended, I bet you wouldn't even be here. You'd be on the field in some random city tonight, you'd fly here tomorrow to see Sadie get married, and fly right back out again."

"St. Louis," I told her, lowering my lips to her other breast. "I'd be in St. Louis right now."

And it shocked me to realize that I was actually glad I wasn't.

We made good use of the remaining condom, then fell asleep almost immediately. That was another surprise—normally I didn't like sharing a bed. I preferred sleeping toward the center of the mattress, I tended to hog the blankets, and I really didn't like to be touched while I was sleeping. And since I was a light sleeper, other people always seemed noisy to me during the night. Back when I'd had a sex life, I'd had a strict no-sleepover rule.

But I didn't mind having April next to me at all. For one, she stuck to one side of the bed. Two, the only sound I heard was her breathing, and I liked it. Three, she smelled so good, it was like aromatherapy or some shit. I found myself snuggling up behind her just to get more of the scent. And I slept hard, even better than I had the night before.

When I woke up, I was alone in the bed. The room was still dark, but I could see a slash of light coming from under the bathroom door. I checked my phone and discovered it was just after seven. Then I lay back, hands behind my head.

The toilet flushed, the sink ran, and a moment later, she came out of the bathroom, leaving the light on. She stood at the foot of the bed, looking mussed and adorable and a little apprehensive.

"Hi," she said.

"Hi."

"You shared the covers."

"I did."

"Was it terrible?"

I shook my head. "Just the opposite, actually. So why don't you come back to bed and I'll work on sharing some more."

She laughed. "I wish I could, but I should probably get home. I have a big day ahead."

"Me too. And I promise I'll take you home in a minute. But first, come here." I reached for her with one hand.

Smiling, she took my hand and let me tug her back into bed. Pulling up the covers, I wrapped my arms around her and tucked her head beneath my chin.

She rested her cheek on my chest and tossed an arm and a leg across me. "That's what you said to me that night, you know."

"What night?"

"In your truck. On the detour. You said 'come here' right before you kissed me."

I laughed. "Did I? That was my big line?"

"Mmhm. And it worked."

"I thought it was something with your hair."

"Well, it was that too. You put your hand in my hair and then you said it."

"That was all it took, huh?"

"That was it."

I kissed the top of her head. "I have better game now."

"You know what? I liked it. It didn't feel like game. It felt real."

"It was." I held her a little tighter. "It was real."

After a quick room service breakfast—fruit and coffee for April; eggs, bacon, fruit, waffles, and coffee for me—I dropped her off at Cloverleigh Farms to get her car and told her I'd see her tonight. The weather was beautiful already—sunny, mild, cloudless—and the temperature was supposed to reach the low seventies by later afternoon. She was thrilled because Sadie was going to be happy.

Afterward, I went back to the hotel, worked out at the gym, grabbed a shower, and headed over to the high school field.

A thousand memories flooded my brain as soon as I got out of the car and looked up at the lights, the stands, the dugouts, the mound. It was just after ten, and the team was warming up by running sprints.

David saw me approaching and lifted a hand. I waved back and walked over to where he stood along the fence. "Morning," I said.

"Morning." He shook my hand and smiled. "Glad you could make it."

"Thanks for inviting me." I stuck my hands in my pockets, watching as the team finished up the sprints and another coach yelled instructions at them. They scattered, grabbing their gloves and spreading out on the field.

"The kid I wanted you to see is the last one down on the right," he said. "Come on, let's mosey in that direction so you can take a look."

"Sure." We ambled slowly along the fence, and a nice, familiar feeling settled over me as I watched the team playing catch in the morning sun. I'd missed being around baseball.

As we walked, David pointed out different players, told me about the team's record, what the remainder of the season looked like, which guys might have a shot at college ball. "No one is like you, of course—never has been and never will be another Tyler Shaw—but we've got some talent. Chip there, the lefty, has been talking to a few schools."

I watched the kid throw—he *did* have a good arm. "Oh yeah? Which ones?"

"Clemson, LSU, Florida State."

"Nice."

"Yeah, he's got talent." David squinted at the field. "Got kind of a tough family situation though. I think it's messing with his mental game."

Nobody knew better than I did how critical the mental game was. "How so?"

"Well, his dad died suddenly a year or so ago. Mom moved them up here to be closer to her family. But I think he worries about leaving her alone. There's a little sister too."

Immediately, I felt sympathy for the kid. "That's hard."

"Yeah. He's talking about sticking around here, but his mom really wants him to go away to college. She's trying to talk him into it."

"An education is a good thing," I said. "Since all this happened with my arm, I've wondered a few times if I should have gone that route."

David nodded, and I braced myself for the usual barrage of hindsight advice. But it didn't come. "Nah, I think you did the right thing for you. But I agree with his mom, and I hope he gets a good enough offer from one of those schools. I think he will, if he can gain a little more control before the season finishes up." He looked at me. "Want to watch him pitch?"

"Sure."

"Hey, Chip!" he hollered.

The kid turned around. "Yeah, Coach?"

David waved him over. "Come here. I want to introduce you to someone."

The kid, tall and trim with long limbs, came jogging over. He wore a cap over his shaggy brown hair, but tipped up the bill a little to meet my eyes.

"Chip, the man standing before you is none other than—"

"Tyler Shaw." The kid grinned. "I recognize you."

I wasn't sure if that was good or bad. "Nice to meet you," I said, holding out my hand.

He shook it, looking a little awestruck. "You too."

"This is your lucky day, Chip. Tyler is only in town for today, but he says he's got a little time to watch your motion and give you some feedback."

The kid's eyes widened. "Seriously?"

I shrugged. "Sure."

"Oh, man." He adjusted his cap, his expression anxious.

David clapped him on the back. "Don't be nervous, son. Just listen and try to do what he says."

"Okay." Chip's voice cracked.

"I hear you've got great power and speed," I told him. "But you're struggling a little with command?"

"Yeah."

"I had the same issue, and my coach was able to help me by breaking down the mechanics and making sure I understood every step. You have to focus on the process, not the result. Because if you can't control your body, you can't control the ball, right?"

He considered that. "Right."

I nodded, getting kind of excited to watch this kid pitch and help him out. Maybe I couldn't fix myself, but I knew this game—especially from the pitcher's mound. "Let's do it."

CHAPTER 12

April

AFTER TYLER DROPPED me off at Cloverleigh, I drove home to shower and change for work. The previous night replayed in my head like a dream, and I must have stood in the shower for an extra fifteen minutes just recalling the way he'd used his mouth on me. And his big, strong hands. And his massive, therapeutic erection.

Giggling, I rinsed my conditioner out and realized how much we'd laughed all night long. I'd never had a sexual experience that was both really intense and really fun at the same time. Was it because we knew each other so well? And how was that even possible? We hadn't seen each other for *years* and had only reunited three days ago. It was incredible how you just felt a connection to some people—and it never went away, no matter how much time or distance came between you.

I dressed in jeans, a comfortable top, and sneakers, but I packed a garment bag with a little black dress and heels for Sadie's wedding later on so I wouldn't have to come home.

I did my hair and makeup, tossed my cosmetics case in my shoulder bag, and headed back to Cloverleigh. It was an absolutely gorgeous day, and the sunshine made my smile even bigger.

Once I was in my office, I checked in with Sadie, who was already at the salon, and confirmed delivery times with the florist and the bakery. Then I texted Frannie to ask what time she wanted to bring over the favors—Sadie had flipped for the tiny boxes of pastel macarons we'd shown her as an option, and Frannie had offered them as a wedding gift. She texted back that they were all ready to go, and said she'd bring them over after the morning rush at the shop was over, in about an hour.

When she arrived, I was setting up a guest book on the table in the entry hall. I saw her approaching the glass door and opened it for her, since she was pulling a wagon carrying two crates full of little white boxes.

"Morning," I said.

"You never called me back yesterday!" Frannie admonished, dragging the wagon inside.

"Sorry." I laughed and gestured into the reception room. "I had the rehearsal and things got busy. Let's set those up and I'll tell you all the things."

"You better. Chloe says you saw him again last night."

"When did you talk to Chloe?"

"We had dinner with them."

"Oh, right. She mentioned that." Together we started stacking the favor boxes into a pyramid on the table. "Yes, I saw him."

"And?"

"And I saw him *naked*."

"Oh my God!" she squealed. "So how was it?"

"Amazing."

"Better than the time in the truck?"

I added another box to the table. "Um, yeah. Less frantic and clumsy. Plus, we took our pants all the way off."

She laughed. "He probably has a really good body."

"He does. But he's also really patient and funny and generous."

"Were you at your place?"

I shook my head. "His hotel room."

"So what now?" she asked, turning around to perch on the edge of the table. "He has to go back to California, right? Will you see him again?"

"We haven't really talked about it." I looked in the wagon, where there were at least fifty boxes left. "Don't stop working. We have to get this done."

"Sorry." She reached into the crate for another box. "I'm just flustered. And happy for you. But also worried that he's going to leave and take your glow with him."

I laughed. "My *glow*?"

"Yes! You're positively radiant right now!"

"It *was* a fun night. And I think it was good for both of us. In more ways than the obvious."

"What do you mean?"

I placed another box on top of the pyramid. "Just that I think we've both been struggling with something. He needed to feel like his old self again. And I needed closure on a chapter of my life. I feel like we both got something we needed, not just something we wanted."

Frannie was silent as we finished arranging the favors. When the crates were empty, she turned to me. "Are you seeing him naked again tonight?"

"Probably."

"Okay, don't be mad at me for asking this, but are you *sure* sleeping with Tyler is going to give you closure?"

I sighed. "I'm not sure of anything, Frannie. I just know that it feels really good to be with him. I'm trying not to read into it too hard."

"Okay, okay." She held up both hands. "I don't want to

rain on your parade, I just want you to move forward, not backward. Fun and games is one thing, but feelings are another."

"I know. But this honestly doesn't feel like a backward move." I stuck my hands on my hips, shaking my head. "I can't explain it, but it really does feel like I'm getting myself unstuck."

She smiled. "I'm happy for you. I'll see you tonight."

Frannie's question lingered in my head the rest of the day. My answer had been the truth—I wasn't at all sure that sleeping with Tyler was going to give me closure, since my issues really weren't with *him*, they were with my feelings surrounding the adoption. In order to really have closure, I needed an answer to my letter.

But I had no control over that, and the reality of it was, I never would. If the family chose to ignore my letter, I'd have to move on without ever knowing the boy I'd given birth to and be okay with it.

In the meantime, I didn't see the harm in flexing my sexual muscles a little bit with a guy who made me feel like a million bucks, whether he was a piece of my past or not. It wasn't like we were hurting anyone.

I was in my office changing into my dress when Tyler called me.

"Hello?"

"Hey, you. Whatcha up to?"

"I'm taking my clothes off. Wish you were here."

He groaned. "Will you take them off again for me later?"

I laughed. "Not unless you buy more condoms."

"Already done. I went to the drugstore and got an entire box. We can have very, very safe sex many, many times."

"Then I'll think about it. How's your day?"

"Good. I worked out, then went over to the high school and watched practice."

"Oh yeah? How was it?"

"It was better than I thought. The kids were really cool, and there were no asshole parents around."

"Glad to hear it. Did you watch the one lefty kid pitch?"

"I did, and he's good. He needs work on his motion, but he's got a lot of potential."

I sighed. "I haven't been to a high school game in years."

"Well, what's the point if *I'm* not playing?"

"Oh, Jesus. Can you see my eyes rolling back in my head from where you are?"

He laughed, and the sound made my heart quicken. "Just about. Anyway, I just wanted to say hi. I'm back at the hotel getting ready now. I have to go over to Sadie's and take pictures soon."

"And you have to be there precisely at three o'clock, so you better get going. I'll see you here after that."

"Okay."

But neither one of us hung up.

"April?" His voice was quiet.

"Yeah?"

"I had a really good time last night."

I smiled as a tingle swept up my spine. "Me too."

I went a little weak in the knees when I saw him walk in. He looked great in a baseball uniform, hot as hell in nothing at all, and downright delectable in a suit and tie. Watching him come through the door and walk toward me, my jaw dropped open and I may have drooled.

But that was nothing compared to watching him lead his sister down the aisle.

From my position over to the side, I motioned for the string quartet to start the song Sadie had chosen for her processional. His gorgeous face had been stoic as he'd walked arm in arm with Sadie from the building over toward the orchard. But they'd exchanged the most adorable affectionate look at the foot of the aisle as everyone stood, and my heart melted. I knew they were both thinking of their father, maybe even their mom too, and my throat grew tight.

When they reached the end, he kissed her cheek before shaking Josh's hand, and she smiled at him one last time before he took his seat in the front row.

Wishing I could go sit at his side, I observed the ceremony from the back, then coordinated the recessional and directed the wedding party one way and the guests another. Tyler looked at me as he walked by, and I put my hand over my heart.

Mack and Frannie came over to say hello, and as she hugged me, she whispered, "Holy shit, he looks good in that suit."

I laughed. "I know."

"Mack's dying to talk old times with him. I saw we're seated at the same table."

"You are. Sadie asked me to put him with you guys, since Tyler wouldn't really know a lot of people here." I turned to Mack. "He'll love talking about old times. Just do me a favor —don't mention the documentary, don't give him any pitching advice, and don't ask why he can't just relax and throw the fucking ball."

Mack looked angry. "What the hell? People do that?"

"All the time. Everywhere he goes."

"Jesus. People are such assholes."

I laughed and patted Mack's lapel. "You sound just like him."

Inside, I oversaw more wedding photos, checked in with the kitchen and head server, went over the night's schedule with the deejay, who was serving as emcee, and then sought out Tyler. I found him standing out on the patio by himself, sipping a glass of whiskey and looking out over the farm.

"Hey," I said, coming to stand next to him. "Hiding out?"

He smiled. "Just enjoying the view."

"Well, don't go too far. Dinner will be served soon. And then it's dancing time."

He took a big swallow of his drink. "Do I have to? We never finished the lesson. I only have one move."

"Which you mastered. You're going to be great, and Sadie will love every moment. And don't worry, I cut the music so it's under two minutes long."

He grumbled something into his whiskey and took another sip.

I patted his shoulder. "Come on inside. You're sitting with Mack and Frannie. You guys can discuss your glory days from high school."

He followed me to his table, shook hands with Mack and Frannie, and sat down with them. Several times during dinner, I looked over and saw them chatting animatedly, and one time I heard Tyler burst out laughing. For a moment, I thought of how nice it would be to hang out, the four of us. Or have dinner with Meg and Noah. Grab drinks with Chloe and Oliver. Or hang out with all of them over at Henry and Sylvia's new house while everyone's kids played in the yard. I felt a little sad that it would never happen.

Right before the bride and groom's first dance, Frannie found me over by the deejay's table. "Hey," she said. "How's everything going?"

"Good. Just waiting for Sadie to get back from the bathroom so the dancing can start."

"Oh yeah, the dancing. Tyler's pretty nervous about that." Frannie glanced back toward her table, where Tyler was sitting with Mack and a few other guests. "He keeps threatening to make a run for it." Then she laughed. "And he offered Mack a thousand bucks to take his place."

I shook my fist. "I'll kill him."

"He's also mentioned *you* about, ohhh, 5,862 times. That is, when he's not speechless, staring at you across the room."

"What?" My face got a little hot.

"You heard me. You guys have serious chemistry. It really stinks he has to leave tomorrow."

"Yeah." I didn't want to think about it, so I was glad when I noticed Sadie entering the ballroom. "Do me a favor. Can you go tell Tyler to come over here? And don't let him drag his feet. Tell him I said right now."

"Well, you might not want to boss him around like that if you're hoping he'll ever come back."

"He needs it." I gave her a gentle shove. "Go, please. I have to get these dances going before the guests get restless."

A minute later, Tyler appeared at my side, and together we watched Josh and Sadie take the floor as husband and wife. "Am I next?" he asked, fussing with his tie.

"Yes."

As their song wrapped up, Tyler glanced at the door.

I grabbed his arm. "Don't even think about it."

"How do you know what I'm thinking?"

"I saw you looking at the exit!"

"Oh." His expression turned anxious again.

"Listen, you're going to be great, and then afterward, I'll give you a prize."

His brow cocked. "Oh yeah? What kind of prize?"

"I'll think of something good."

The song finished to thunderous applause, and Josh brought Sadie over to Tyler.

She took Tyler's hand. "Ready?"

He glanced at me. "I hope so."

I gave him a reassuring smile. "You're ready."

The deejay announced them, and Tyler led his sister out onto the floor as their song began. I held my breath as he took her in his arms just like we'd practiced and began swaying her side to side. I exhaled when I saw that not only was he moving right on the beat, but he and Sadie were both laughing and enjoying themselves. I almost cried when he spun her out exactly the way I'd shown him, and spun her back just as effortlessly. The crowd cheered and snapped photos with their phones. At the end of the song, Sadie threw her arms around her brother's neck, and he lifted her right off the ground in a huge bear hug and held her there several seconds. I wasn't the only one who had to wipe my eyes.

Afterward, he waited with his sister while Josh danced with his sister Mary. Then he delivered Sadie to Josh's dad, who brought her out to the dance floor for one final number, while Josh danced with his mom. Then he made his way over to me, his smile one of total relief.

"You did it," I said, unable to resist giving him a hug.

He held me close. "Thanks for the help. It actually wasn't as bad as I thought."

"See?" I didn't want to let him go, but I stepped back so no one would speculate about my koala grip on the bride's big brother.

"So? Do I get to claim my prize?" His dark eyes glittered.

"Oh, that. Hmm." I checked the time. "Yes, but you have to give me a few minutes. Just until the dancing gets going and the cake is served."

He frowned. "Can't people serve their own cake?"

I laughed. "Ten minutes. I'll meet you in my office."

"Does the door lock?"

My stomach jumped. "Yes."

"Is it soundproof?"

"No." Then I rose up on tiptoe to whisper in his ear. "But

you won't have to worry about me making a lot of noise, because I'll have something in my mouth."

He gripped my elbow—hard. "*Five* minutes. Go."

It ended up taking me more like fifteen minutes, because I had to locate a missing cake knife, return a diamond earring found on the dance floor to its owner, find the head server and let her know I was taking a short break (I lied and said I had to run over to the inn for a few minutes), and duck into the bathroom to wipe off my lipstick. By the time I snuck down the hallway to my office, I was practically running.

I pushed open the door and walked in, expecting to see him in there, but my office was dark—which was weird, because I was certain I'd left the lights on.

That's when the door slammed shut behind me and I heard the lock bolt click.

I whirled around. I couldn't see a thing. "Tyler?"

"Expecting someone else?"

"No." I laughed. "I just can't see anything. How do I know it's really you?"

"Come here. I'll prove it to you."

My pulse kicked up as I moved toward his voice, and then I felt two strong hands reach out and grab me. He pulled me against his chest. Then his lips were on mine, and I knew it was him for sure—*I knew* that mouth, that tongue, that kiss. I reached down and stroked him through his pants, feeling him grow thicker and harder, his erection bulging against my palm.

"I only have a few minutes," I whispered, unbuckling his belt.

"So let's make good use of them." He started pulling up the bottom of my dress.

"No!" I put my hands on his chest and pushed back. "It's my prize to give. I told you what it is." Then dropped to my knees in front of him, continued undoing his pants. "Do you want it?"

"Your mouth on my cock? Hell yes, I want it. But I want to *see* it." He flipped a light switch next to the door, which turned on an overhead light.

I looked up at him. "Better?"

"Much." He took my face in his hands. "You're so fucking beautiful."

I smiled and freed his hard length from his pants, taking it in both hands, licking it from bottom to top. "Can you do me a favor?" I asked in my best sex kitten voice before swirling my tongue around the crown.

"Does it involve dancing? Fuck it, the answer is yes, I don't care what it is."

I laughed throatily. "It does not involve dancing. Would you mind holding my hair back?"

He put his hands farther into my hair and lifted it away from my face. "Like that?"

"Perfect." I lowered my mouth down his shaft, and he sucked in his breath. I kept going, taking him deeper, sucking him harder.

"Good thing the music is loud," he said, his voice thick with desire. "Because I'm not sure I can be quiet. Jesus *Christ*."

"You don't have to be quiet," I told him, pausing for a breath. "But you do have to be fast."

That wasn't really a problem either.

I don't even think a full sixty seconds went by before his fists were tight in my hair and he was rocking into me with quick, short thrusts that hit the back of my throat and threatened to choke me. I willed myself to keep going because I could feel and taste and hear him getting close, and finally he gave me the warning.

"Fuck, April. I'm gonna come, so if—"

But I wanted it just like that, so I gripped him hard by the hips and stayed right where I was. Five seconds later, I heard his deep, guttural moan, felt the pulsing between my lips, the hot surge in my mouth. He stopped moving, and eventually his fingers loosened in my hair.

I let him go and swallowed, sitting back on my heels to finally catch my breath.

His head banged back against the door. "Shit. Are you okay? Did I cut off your air supply?"

I shook my head and laughed, still a little breathless. "I'm fine. Maybe a little oxygen-deprived, but fine."

"I'm going to pay you back later." He offered his hand and helped me up.

"Thanks, but this isn't about trading favors. I wanted to do that."

"Okay, maybe *pay you back* isn't the right way to put it. I'm going to fuck you with my tongue later because I want to, and you wouldn't let me do it here. How's that sound?" He started doing up his pants.

My insides tightened. "Good. But I'll be here late."

"I'll wait for you."

"I'm always the last one out on a night like this. It could be a long wait."

He finished buckling his belt and put his arms around me. "You are worth a long wait, and don't fucking forget it. And besides, I've got less than twenty-four hours before I have to get on a plane, and I want to spend as many of them as possible making sure you don't forget me."

I smiled, even though the thought of him leaving made me sad. "No argument here."

It was after one a.m. by the time we walked out to the parking lot hand in hand.

"Want to come over?" I asked him.

"Of course I do. I've got promises to keep—some of them you don't even know about."

I laughed as my stomach swooshed. "Follow me to my place."

With Tyler's SUV in my rearview mirror, I drove to my house as quickly as I dared, and we parked next to each other in front of my building.

On my front porch, his mouth was on my neck, his hands already pulling up my dress as I tried and failed like five times to get the key in the lock. Finally, I managed to get the damn door open, and we stumbled into the front hallway, slamming it shut behind us.

I dropped everything I was holding and heard my keys hit the tile floor. Tyler spun me by the shoulder and backed me into the wall, caging me in with his arms and devouring my mouth with a searing-hot kiss that set fire to every nerve ending in my body. I reached down between us and slid my hand over his bulging cock, desperate to feel him inside me again. "God, I want you," I whispered. "I've never wanted anyone so badly."

When he stepped back to wrestle off his suit coat, I dashed for the stairs, ditching one shoe and then the other so I could move faster. But he caught me around the waist when I was halfway up, taking me down to my hands and knees. From there he hiked up my dress and yanked off my panties. "I can't wait. I need you now. Right here." Bracing himself with one arm on a step above my head, he reached around and slipped his hand between my legs, groaning when he felt how wet I was already.

Trapped by his size and strength, I panted beneath him, torn between wanting to get him out of that suit and feel his naked skin against mine and wanting to let him have his way with me on the stairs. God, he was *so good* with his hands. His fingers had me on the verge of an orgasm in no time at all.

Then he snared my waist again and flipped me onto my back. Moving down a couple steps, he pushed my thighs apart and buried his face between them, using his tongue the way he had last night, greedily, mercilessly, relentlessly, until my body convulsed with pleasure beneath him.

Somehow we made it from the stairs into my bedroom—a haze of clothing being torn off and flung wherever, of tripping up the steps and scrambling down the hallway, of hands that wouldn't stop clutching, mouths that wouldn't stop claiming, and hearts that wouldn't stop pounding.

Then finally—*finally*—his huge, hard cock was easing inside me, his broad chest was hovering over mine, and his scent filled my head. I raked my nails across his skin, gasping as he plunged in so deep it hurt, yet desperately wishing I could take him even deeper. Wishing he didn't have to leave tomorrow. Wishing I could stop time and stay wrapped up in him this way, even as we raced toward the inevitable finish, our bodies unwilling to slow down, to savor the moment or make it last.

My need for him shocked me. I cried out with abandon, I bit his shoulder, I pulled his hair. I arched my back and rocked my hips and begged him not to stop. I let go completely, unashamed of the way I wanted him. And he wanted me just as badly—I felt it in the violent way he moved, heard it in his ragged breathing, knew it from the way he cursed and growled my name. We gave in to the rush together, spiraling higher and higher until we careened off the edge together, the world reduced to one blissful, rippling pulse shared between us.

Afterward, we lay on our sides, limbs tangled atop twisted sheets, hot and sweaty and panting.

That's when I thought I heard him say something crazy.

"What?" I whispered, struggling to hear him over my thundering heart.

"I don't want to leave here tomorrow." He pushed my hair back from my face. "I want to stay."

CHAPTER 13

Tyler

SHE PAUSED, like maybe she hadn't heard me right. "You want to *stay*?"

"Yeah. What do you think about that?" It was so dark I couldn't see her expression, even though our faces were only inches apart.

"Are you serious?"

"Yeah."

"Tyler, I'd love that." She sounded surprised. "Did you think I might say something else?"

"I wasn't sure."

She laughed. "What would give you any doubt? I spent last night in your hotel room. I gave you a blowjob in my office. I was ripping your clothes off the second we walked in the door tonight. I am currently naked in your arms—all these things are indications that I like being with you. A lot."

"Good. That's how I feel too, although right up until a few minutes ago, I was planning on getting on a flight tomorrow afternoon. Or is it today already?" I tugged a strand of her hair. "I lose track of time when I'm with you."

"I think it's today already. But I have the same problem." Another pause. "So . . . how long would you stay?"

"I'm not sure. Maybe the rest of the week." I hadn't thought it through at all—I just knew that I wasn't ready to leave yet. This place or her.

"What made you change your mind?"

"Well, I'd be lying if I said the sex wasn't part of it. Does that make me an asshole?"

"Hmmm. Let me think about that." She tapped her chin. "No, I don't think it does. Because it's sex with me. Unless, of course, you're having sex with other people in this town I don't know about."

I laughed. "Uh, no. I'm not having any other sex, in this town or any other town, frankly. And I haven't in a long time."

"Really?" She tucked both hands under her cheek. "Why?"

I wound the strand of her hair around my finger. "Just haven't felt like it."

"I thought pro athletes were supposed to be players. Women throwing themselves at you everywhere you go."

"Some guys are players," I told her. "And I'll admit, there were plenty of willing women everywhere we went, and I used to like the attention. But I wasn't really a player. The game was always my top priority. I never had sex in the three days leading up to a game I was starting, so that put a lot of days off limits."

"Why no sex for those days before a game?" She giggled. "Did it zap your manly strength? Or were you just super-stitious?"

"A little of both, actually. Some guys believe abstaining from sex keeps the testosterone pumping harder because you don't get that release. But I was also superstitious."

"I remember you telling me you always put your left sock and shoe on first."

"Always. I still do. It's a whole process."

She laughed. "What else?"

"Well, my number was eight, so on game days I used to do everything eight times. I'd swipe my deodorant on eight times, flip every light switch eight times, blink eight times at every stoplight on my way to the clubhouse."

"Wow. And you believed all those things helped?"

"I must have. I couldn't not do them." I thought back to the painful weeks after the first wild pitches. "When everything fell apart and I couldn't throw anymore, I was even worse for a while. I was doing it all the time, game day or not. I was completely compulsive, convinced that if I was better about it, my arm would come back."

"How'd you finally stop?" she asked, a little quieter.

"It wasn't working, for one. Therapy helped too. And then I finally just quit playing. It was sucking the life out of me, trying to be something I wasn't. I just couldn't do it anymore."

She snuggled closer to me, looping one arm around my back and resting her forehead against my chin. "Does it make you sad to talk about it?"

I wrapped one arm around her shoulders and put one hand beneath my head. "Usually. Sad or angry." I paused and realized something. "But I don't feel that way right now."

"You don't?"

"No. And you know what? I didn't feel like telling a single person to fuck off today. I actually had a really good day. Best one I've had in a long time." For a moment, I wondered about that. What had made today so much better? Was it because of the sex last night? Seeing my sister so happy? Being around baseball again? I wasn't sure.

When I'd arrived here, all I'd wanted was to get through Sadie's wedding and get the hell out of town again. Go back to my cabin in the mountains where no one could find me and I was free to brood in peace. Now I felt differently—at least for the moment.

April wriggled like a fish in my arms. "That makes me happy. And I think it's a perfect reason to stay a little longer."

Eventually we crawled beneath the covers, and this time, I held her close as we drifted off to sleep.

The next morning, I woke up to rain pounding against the windowpanes and thrumming on the roof. April was still sound asleep, and I decided to attempt something I'd never done before—make breakfast for someone.

I hadn't been lying when I told her I had zero skills in the kitchen (I was probably a better dancer than I was a cook), but I wanted to do something nice for her. She'd made last night perfect for Sadie—and it hadn't been too shabby for me, either. I had the feeling that she was always the one taking care of other people, and wanted to treat her for once.

I managed to get out of bed without waking her, found my boxer briefs on the floor, and tugged them on. Scratching my head, I looked around for my pants, but didn't see them. Where the hell had they landed? Quietly closing her bedroom door behind me, I headed for the stairs and spotted them on the second-floor landing. I grinned as I pulled them on, remembering last night's stairway striptease, and the grin widened as I made my way down the steps and saw the rest of our clothing tossed haphazardly to the floor—except for April's bra, which I'd somehow managed to throw high enough to snag the light fixture, from which it now hung.

Guess my arm was good for something.

I used the downstairs bathroom, checking out my reflection in the mirror. I wasn't sure what was more impressive, my messed-up hair or the scratches on my shoulders. Damn —the girl had gotten crazy with her hands. Actually, she was pretty unabashed in bed all the way around. Vocal and playful and not shy about letting me know when she liked something or wanted more, when she needed me to slow down or speed up, when she wanted it harder or a little less aggressive. It was the kind of thing you wouldn't guess just by looking at her, with her buttoned-up blouses and knee-length skirts—I liked that.

I liked knowing her secrets.

I wandered into her kitchen and looked around for things I recognized. Okay, single-serve coffeemaker over there, I could handle that. I found a Cloverleigh Farms mug in the cupboard and brewed a cup for myself, and while the machine heated up, I poked around in her fridge and freezer. She had eggs, and I was fairly certain I could manage to fry or maybe scramble some, but I wanted something sweeter for her. Cinnamon rolls were out of the question, but I could attempt something like waffles or pancakes, right?

I was hoping to see Eggos in her freezer, but since I didn't, I decided to try to make them myself. Pulling out my phone, I searched "easy pancake recipe" and clicked on the link for "Karina's Best Fluffy Pancakes" because it sounded like something April would like and it also included a video. I'd need all the help I could get. After checking to make sure she had all the ingredients I'd need—what the hell was the difference between baking powder and baking soda anyway?—I got to work.

It took me a while, since I didn't know where anything was and I was also trying to stay really quiet, but eventually I had a mixing bowl full of batter. I can't say it looked exactly like the batter in the photos—mine had a few more lumps than Karina's—but it was close. I found a pan that looked like the one in the video, took a guess that "low-medium heat" was maybe the number four on April's stove, and said a quick prayer I wouldn't ruin breakfast or set her condo on fire.

I tried to turn the first couple pancakes too soon, but after that I had a pretty good feel for it, and I was awesome at the wrist-flip maneuver it took to cleanly flip them. Eventually, I had a stack of (mostly) fluffy pancakes on a plate, and I'd managed to spill only minimum amounts of batter on the counter. And the stove. And maybe the floor.

I was rinsing off some strawberries I'd found in the fridge when April appeared in the kitchen doorway in tiny little gray shorts and what looked like my white undershirt from last night. Her hair was a mess just like mine, and I immediately wanted to bury my face in it.

"Good morning," she said, her expression adorably surprised. "What are you up to in here?"

"Making you breakfast." I opened the cupboard where I'd found the mug and took down one for her. "Want coffee?"

"Yes, please." She grinned as she looked me over. "Wow, a hot shirtless guy is in my kitchen cooking pancakes. Pinch me."

I went over and pinched her side, making her giggle. "Is this my shirt?"

"Yes. I hope you don't mind." She lifted the collar over her nose and inhaled. "It smells like you."

"I don't mind," I told her. "Where did you even find it?"

She grinned. "It was on the floor in my bedroom." Moving closer, she slipped her arms around my waist and kissed my chest. "Have I told you how much I adore your body?"

"I think so, but you know me—I'll never get tired of hearing it."

"How long have you been up?"

"I don't know. Maybe an hour?" I kissed the top of her head. "I was hoping you'd stay asleep until I had this all done, but I'm not very fast in the kitchen."

She leaned back and looked up at me. "Why didn't you wake me, silly? I could have helped you."

"I was trying to do something nice to surprise you." I glanced toward my workspace. "But I made a mess. Sorry."

"I don't mind. I thought you didn't cook."

"I don't. But I can read, so I just followed the recipe. And there may have been a video involved. Is that cheating?"

She smiled and shook her head. "Nope."

"These pancakes could still taste like leather. Be prepared."

"They smell amazing. And I don't care what they taste like —no one has ever made breakfast for me before. I'm grateful."

I kissed the tip of her nose. "Good. Do you have any maple syrup?"

"I think so. I don't use it much, but I'm pretty sure there's an unopened one up here." She went over to the cupboard above the fridge and reached for the handle, but couldn't quite grasp it, even up on her tiptoes. "Um. I can't reach in bare feet."

"Well, give it a few minutes. Maybe you'll grow."

"Very funny. Can you help me?"

Grinning, I took her by the hips and gently moved her aside. "I got it, babe." I opened the cupboard and grabbed the bottle of syrup.

She took it from me, fluttering her lashes. "My hero."

We sat at her dining table, ate deliciously fluffy pancakes (Karina would have been proud) and strawberries, drank coffee, and talked about the wedding.

"I can't believe this rain today!" she exclaimed, sitting on her heels just like she always did. "We got so lucky to have that sunny day in between two rainy ones."

"Did you arrange that?" I asked her, taking one more pancake from the stack.

She laughed. "God, I wish I could arrange the weather. As an event planner, it's the one superpower I could use most."

"I have a feeling the wedding would have been just as perfect even if it rained," I told her, pouring syrup over my plate. "You don't need any superpowers."

Her cheeks went pink. "Well, thank you. I do think rain can be romantic on a wedding day, but I'm glad Sadie got sunshine. She deserved it."

After breakfast, we cleaned up the kitchen together—she loaded the dishwasher while I wiped up all the batter I'd spilled. When we were done, she turned and gave me a big hug. "Thank you for breakfast," she said, pressing close. "I loved it."

"You're welcome." I ran my hands down her back. My dick was already responding to her chest against mine.

"So do you have to be anywhere this afternoon?" she asked, kissing my neck.

"Nope." I moved my hands down over her butt.

"I don't either. Want to stay a while?"

"Aren't you tired of me yet?"

"Nope."

"In that case . . ." I lifted her up, setting her up on the counter. "I have an idea how we can spend this rainy day."

She wrapped her legs around me. "I hope it's the same as mine."

"Does it involve me fucking you on the kitchen counter?"

A smile crept onto her lips. "It does now."

We spent the entire day together, most of it naked.

We took breaks from sex to eat, drink, and nap, and somehow I even let her talk me into a bubble bath.

"Can't we just shower?" I asked, watching her fill the tub and light candles along its perimeter.

"We could, but this will be so much more romantic and relaxing. Remember what we talked about at dinner the other night? We're looking for ways to help you be less grumpy." She poured in some stuff from a bottle labeled Vanilla Bergamot Dream.

I sniffed. "You're going to make me smell like a cupcake."

"Perfect. No one can be grumpy when they smell like a cupcake." She turned off the water, lowered herself into the tub, and crooked her finger at me. "Come hither, boy."

"I'm not even going to fit. I think you're forgetting I'm six foot five."

"I'll make room." She scooted all the way to one end and threw a handful of bubbles at me. "Come on, it'll be fun. I'll give you a massage and you can talk about your feelings. It will be like that scene in Pretty Woman."

Grumbling, I managed to get into the tub without spilling too much water over the side. I couldn't stretch my legs out all the way, but I was able to wedge myself in between April's.

She wrapped them around me, along with her arms. "There. Doesn't that feel nice?"

I had to admit it did.

"This tub was the thing that made me say yes to buying this place," she said, rubbing bubbles over my chest. That felt nice too.

"You take a lot of baths?"

"Yes. But not with other people."

"So I'm the first guest in your tub?"

"You are the first," she confirmed, crossing her ankles above my hips.

I grabbed one of her feet and pressed a hand to the bottom of it. "You have very small feet."

"You have very big hands."

"I know."

"Did that help you pitch better?"

"I don't know. Maybe." I rubbed the sole of her foot with my thumb. "The truth is, I don't know what made me so good. I mean, I worked hard, I had the physical size and strength, and I was intensely focused, but all of that was true right up to the day I couldn't throw strikes anymore. Nothing had changed. So what was it?"

"I don't know," she said softly.

"Sometimes I wonder if there was always a time limit on it. Like, did God say, 'Here you go, kid. You're gonna be one of the best in the game, but it's gonna be over before you know it. Enjoy it while it lasts.'"

She was quiet a minute while I kept rubbing her foot. "Let's say that's true. Let's even say God gave you the choice. Would you choose it?"

"What do you mean?"

"I mean, what if God, or whoever it is that hands out souls, came to you before you were born and said, 'In your next life, you'll be a rock star baseball pitcher—but only for a limited time, and you won't like the way it ends.' Would you take the talent? Or would you say 'no, thanks?'"

I didn't even have to think about it. "I'd take the talent."

"That's what I thought."

But for a few minutes, I wondered what I would have done with my life if I *hadn't* had the talent. If my dad had never taught me the game. If I hadn't grown up with a glove on one hand and a ball in the other. If I'd never swung a bat or heard that satisfying crack as it connected with the ball before sailing over the fence.

I couldn't imagine it.

"You just have to decide what you want *now*," she went on. "Because you can't go back."

"Like *right* now?"

She giggled. "Why do I feel like I know where this is going?"

I looked at her over one shoulder. "What I want right now is to do very bad things to you in this tub."

The dimples appeared. "Then it's definitely your lucky day."

Eventually, the rain stopped, the sky went dark, and I got dressed, reluctantly retrieving all the pieces of my suit from last night and pulling them on. It was crazy to me that I didn't want to leave.

Which was exactly why I made myself do it.

Spending the entire day with April had been a little too comfortable. The last thing I needed was to start getting confused about what this was—and I didn't want to do that to April either. Staying the rest of the week was fine, but when seven days were up, I was getting on that plane.

"What are you up to tomorrow?" I asked her at the door.

"Monday is usually my day off for errands and stuff," she said, "but I actually have to go over to Cloverleigh in the morning for a meeting with my sisters about our dad's retirement party."

"Oh, when is that?"

"End of the month. What will you do tomorrow?"

"Work out in the morning, most likely, and then head over to baseball practice in the afternoon. I'd like to stick around long enough to help that kid with his motion, watch him pitch a game or two."

She smiled. "Aha! So it's not only about sex, it's about baseball too."

"It's about baseball too," I confessed.

"Listen, I think that's great. Baseball is part of your soul, and you need to find a way to love it again. I think hating it is taking too much out of you."

"You're probably right," I said.

She opened the door for me. "Maybe I could come with you to a game this week."

"Sure."

"So is this kid as good as you were in high school?"

I gave her a look. "*No one* is that good, April."

Laughing, she pushed me out the door. "Get out of here. And take your giant ego with you."

I turned around and walked backward a few steps. "Still think it's the biggest thing about me?"

"Actually, you may have changed my mind about that," she said.

I nodded and gave her the grin. "It's about time."

CHAPTER 14

April

THE MORNING MEETING with my sisters was moved at the last minute to Frannie's house, because one of the girls was sick and home from school.

We sat around Mack and Frannie's dining room table drinking coffee and finalizing the details for the party.

"How many R.S.V.P. yeses did we end up with?" Meg asked.

"Two hundred thirty-eight," I answered, double-checking the count on my laptop. "Almost everyone invited is coming."

"Do you think we need a seating chart?" asked Sylvia.

I tilted my head this way and that. "I mean, we could—it *is* a lot of people. But I feel like we could get away without one too."

"Let's just let everyone sit where they want to," said Chloe. "Seating charts are a pain to make."

We all agreed, and moved on to the final menu, the wine list, and the timing of the evening. "Invites said cocktails at six, so I think we're safe with formal toast at seven, followed immediately by dinner, then dancing and dessert," I said.

"Sounds good to me," said Frannie.

"You're the expert," said Meg.

"So who wants to make the toast?" I looked around the table, and they all went silent.

"Syl?" Frannie said finally. "You're the oldest. Want to do it?"

Sylvia shook her head. "Last time I gave a public speech, I got drunk, stole a mic from Santa, used the word 'asshole' in front of children and elves, then *dropped the mic* before leaving the floor. You do not want me giving that toast."

"I'm not doing it either," Meg said.

"Not it." Chloe put a finger on her nose.

"Not it." Frannie did the same.

I sighed. "You guys. Really?"

"Come on, April, you're a natural at this stuff," Meg said. "You've got a degree in PR and you're definitely the most polished."

"What?" I gestured to Sylvia. "Before Breakfast with Santagate, Sylvia was the *definition* of polished!"

"But I'm pregnant now," Sylvia said. "Don't make me get up in front of two hundred people in a maternity dress. That's just cruel."

I rolled my eyes. "Okay, fine. I'll do it. But you guys have to help me think of what to say."

"It'll be easy." Chloe reached over and patted my arm. "Just say some sentimental shit about family."

"Make some jokes," suggested Frannie.

"Yes—be funny. People like that." Meg nodded.

"Just don't be boring," Sylvia put in. "Or too wordy."

I rolled my eyes. "Gee, thanks, you guys. That's really helpful."

Frannie laughed. "You'll figure it out. I have faith."

We finished up, and Meg left in a hurry for a ten o'clock arbitration. Chloe took off shortly after for Cloverleigh, and Sylvia said she had to cover a volunteer shift at the middle school clinic, so eventually it was just Frannie and me at the table.

"So?" she said, lifting her coffee cup to her lips. "How was the rest of your weekend?"

"Good," I said, reaching for a sliced strawberry out of the fruit salad bowl. It reminded me of the breakfast Tyler had made for me yesterday. "Sexy."

"More, please."

"Tyler came home with me Saturday night and stayed over. The next morning my bra was hanging from the chandelier."

Her eyebrows rose. "Do go on."

I laughed. "There's not much else to say. We had a lot of good sex. He made pancakes for me. We hung out all the next day. I made him take a bubble bath and talk about his feelings."

She nearly choked on her coffee. "You did?"

"Yes. Also . . ." I reached for another strawberry. "He's not leaving."

A pause. A smile. "What?"

"He decided not to fly home yesterday. He wants to stay longer."

"How much longer?"

"Maybe a week."

"Why?"

I shrugged. "He ran into his old coach at Coffee Darling when we were there. The coach asked him to stick around and help out this pitcher who's struggling with his motion a little bit."

Frannie sat back and folded her arms. "Right. And I suppose it had nothing to do with the way he can't stop staring at you across a room?"

"I'm not saying I had nothing to do with it. But I think it's a combination of things. He really does miss baseball, and I think coaching this young pitcher might be a good re-entry into the game. What happened to his career really messed him up—to the point where he started to hate baseball."

Frannie sighed. "We sort of tiptoed around it Saturday night. Mostly he and Mack talked about their old high school team, and the two of them just lit up remembering how awesome they were. They were like two peacocks strutting around the table."

I laughed. "Yeah, they were a pretty awesome team. But for Tyler, he thought that was a forever thing. In his mind, it was the only thing he was good at, it was what he was meant to do with his life, and he staked everything on it. What happened felt like a betrayal of his own mind, his own body —if not his faith. Baseball was a religion for him."

"Yeah, but he would have retired anyway, right? Nobody can play forever. What was his plan for after?"

I shook my head. "I'm telling you, he never even imagined it. It was baseball, then death."

Her expression was amused. "That's kinda dark."

"I know." I took another sip of coffee. "But I feel like coming back here was good for him. Between seeing his sister get married and taking an interest in coaching, I feel like he's getting to the point where he can see the sun rising."

"That's good." She was quiet a minute. "And what about you? Still doing okay with everything?"

"I'm fine," I said with more confidence than I felt. "Really. We're actually being very honest and open with each other. I know this is only temporary. He's not staying forever. I just like being with him."

"Okay. I'm only asking because I can tell you feel things for him, and now that I know what you went through, I just . . ." She shrugged. "You always put other people's feelings first, that's all."

I smiled. "I'm a big girl, and I'm learning a lot about taking care of myself."

"Promise?"

"I promise."

But it wasn't a promise I was certain I could keep.

I spent the rest of the day catching up on personal stuff and trying not to think too hard about anything—the fact that I'd been sleeping alone for years but had missed Tyler in my bed last night, that I still had no reply to my letter, that somehow I'd gotten saddled with giving a speech at my dad's retirement party. What on earth was I going to say that wouldn't bore everyone to tears?

I made a pot of spaghetti sauce, and while it was simmering, I sat down at the table to brainstorm some ideas. But the only thing I wrote down in my notebook was *Tyler Shaw*. I was still staring at his name when my phone buzzed.

Tyler Shaw calling.

I smiled and picked it up. "Hello?"

"Hey you. What's up?"

"Not much. I'm at home freaking out about the speech I have to give at my dad's retirement party."

"Now you know how I felt about the dancing. Have you eaten dinner yet?"

I looked over at the stove. "I just made spaghetti sauce. Want to come over?"

"Mmm, I could go for some spaghetti sauce. Can I pour it over your naked body and lick it off?"

"That sounds . . . like a hot mess."

"Hot messes in the kitchen are my specialty, remember?"

I laughed. "How could I forget?"

He arrived about twenty minutes later with a bottle of red wine and a smile that turned my bones to jelly. As soon as I shut the door behind him, he kissed me hello like he'd missed me.

"How was your day?" I asked as we moved into the kitchen.

"Great," he said. "God, it smells good in here."

"Thank you."

"Reminds me of old times when I'd come home from practice and you'd have dinner made."

"You definitely smell better tonight."

He hooked an arm around my neck and pretended to choke me. "Admit it. You secretly loved the way I smelled."

Laughing, I tried to get away but couldn't. "I did not! It was like a gym bag that had been left out in the sun all day to bake!"

"I showered when I got home, didn't I?"

"You did, thank God." He finally let me go, and I set the bottle of wine on the counter.

"Want me to open that?"

"Sure. Corkscrew is in there." I gestured toward the drawer and pulled down two glasses from the cupboard. "Did you go to practice this afternoon?"

"Yeah." He took out the corkscrew and closed the drawer with his hip.

"How'd it go?"

"I think it went well." After pulling the cork from the bottle, he poured us each a glass. "I worked with the lefty again. He's struggling with his balance point, and his stride length is a little off too."

"Can you help him?"

"I think so. He's all concerned about speed and power, but that's not gonna mean shit if he's got no accuracy. It's great to throw a ninety mile-per-hour pitch, but unless it goes where you want it to, it's not much use. Trust me."

I smiled sympathetically at him and turned on the gas beneath a large pot of water.

He picked up one of the glasses and took a sip. "Can I help you with something? I'm an expert in the kitchen now that I made pancakes."

Laughing, I handed him a knife and a loaf of Italian bread. "Here. Slice this up, but not your hands, please. I'm partial to them."

He gave me a kiss for that.

"Use the cutting board right there."

He washed his hands and got to work while I put together a spinach salad. "Have you heard from Sadie?" I asked.

"Yes. I called her this morning to tell her I was staying in town a little longer, and of course she begged me to please bring in their mail while they're away. And before you ask, *yes*, I did it today."

I smiled and tossed the spinach into a big round bowl. "They're in New Orleans, right? When are they back?"

"Yes. Thursday. I also have to take out their trash and recycling on Wednesday night."

"What a nice brother you are," I said, cutting up a tomato.

"I *am* a nice brother. I don't even take out my own trash and recycling," he complained.

"What? That is ridiculous. Who on earth takes out your trash and recycling?"

"My housekeeper. She's the only person I can tolerate in my house for long periods of time. She's awesome. Not only does she keep my house clean, but she shops and cooks for me too. And she'll put each meal in a container and label it with what it is and instructions for reheating it. Sometimes she even puts a little smiley face on the note."

"Oh my God," I said, laughing as I tossed the tomatoes on top of the lettuce. "You're like a fourth grader. Do you call her Mommy?"

"No, I call her Anna, and I pay her very, very well to put up with me. She has a good salary *and* benefits, and I also just bought her a car because hers wasn't reliable and she does so much driving for me. She comes to the cabin once a week too."

"Well, good." I started slicing a cucumber. "Does she get a vacation while you're here?"

"Yes, she does. I called her this morning and told her she could have the week off—paid, of course."

"Good man." I paused. "Did you book your return flight?"

"No. I kind of forgot about doing that."

I was glad my back was turned so he couldn't see my gigantic smile.

"Okay, the bread is sliced," he said. "What else can I do?"

"Want to taste the sauce?"

"Yes, please."

Over at the stove, I handed him the wooden spoon. "Here. Give it a stir, and then taste. Be careful, it's hot."

He took the lid off the pot, stirred, and tasted. Then he smiled. "So good. And it totally reminds me of you."

I laughed. "Oh, come on, you've had pasta sauce a billion times since high school."

"And every time, it reminded me of you."

My heart beat a little faster. "Liar."

"That's the truth, I swear," he said. "There were always certain things that reminded me of you."

"Like what?"

"Red hair, dimples, the smell of birthday cake. Weren't there things that reminded you of me?"

I thought about it while I took the spoon and tasted the sauce. "Baseball," I told him, reaching for the salt. I added a little to the sauce and stirred again. "And for a while, sex."

"Really?" He seemed pleased about it. "Sex?"

"Well, yes." I glanced at him. "But it was sort of terrifying."

He frowned. "That is not as hot as I wanted it to be."

Laughing, I set the spoon back on the rest. "Well, after

what happened my first time, I was scared of having sex again because I was worried about getting pregnant. So you were the only guy I ever had sex with for a pretty long time."

"How long?"

"About four years. And even then, I was a nervous wreck."

He looked contrite. "Jesus. I'm sorry."

"It's okay. I got over it. It's not like it was a mystery why I got pregnant, Tyler, or even bad luck—it was biology. We had unprotected sex. We were eighteen. It's like the most fertile time in a girl's life, which is just a cruel joke, but that's another issue."

"I still feel bad."

"Don't." I couldn't resist giving those lips a quick kiss before turning off the burner beneath the sauce. "I told you—I was glad you were my first."

He caught me around the waist from behind. "Me too."

Later, after we'd had dinner at the kitchen table, dessert on the couch in front of the television, and sex on my living room floor because we were too impatient to make it upstairs, we laughed that our pace was getting closer to what it had been in the back of his truck.

"I can't help it," he said, lying on his back next to the coffee table. "You just make me lose control."

I was straddling him, my hands braced above his shoulders, my hair dangling over his chest. "I'm not complaining. And I'll never get tired of hearing you say that. I won't even make any rifle jokes."

"Good." He squeezed my hips, then sighed. "I should probably go."

"You don't have to." Leaning forward, I rubbed my lips back and forth against his. "You can stay over again if you want."

"Are you sure?"

"Of course. I'll even give you a toothbrush." I grinned.

"But if you leave the cap off my toothpaste, I'm kicking your ass out."

He laughed. "Deal."

While I was at work Tuesday afternoon, Tyler called and asked if I wanted to go watch the high school baseball game with him. I did, but the game started at 4:30 p.m. at a neighboring school about thirty minutes away, and I had a meeting with a prospective bride at 5:30.

"I'm sorry, I can't," I told him. "This is potentially a big wedding. The bride is kind of a local celebrity. Is your lefty pitching?"

"Yeah, he's starting."

"Shoot, I wish I could be there."

"Dinner when I get back?" he asked.

"Sure. Want to come over again? Although I should warn you, I was just planning on leftover spaghetti tonight. Kind of boring."

"I'll take leftover spaghetti and being alone with you over a crowded restaurant any day. You know how I feel about *people*."

I laughed. "I do. Okay, just head over here when you're back."

He arrived around 7:30 with another bottle of wine, a grocery store bouquet of roses, and his luggage.

"Are you moving in?" I joked as he shut the door behind himself.

"I'm running out of clean clothes," he said with a guilty expression. "I only packed for a long weekend. Do you mind if I do some laundry?"

"Not at all," I said.

He handed me the flowers. "These are for you. Sorry they're not too fancy."

"They're beautiful, thank you." I put my nose in them and sniffed. "But what's the occasion?"

"No occasion. I'm just thankful you're putting up with me and my dirty laundry tonight."

I smiled. "You're sweet."

He put his finger on my lips. "Don't tell anybody."

"So tell me about the game," I said, watching as he stuffed an alarming amount of clothes into my washing machine, which was located in a utility closet off the kitchen. "Did they win?"

"They did," he said, shoving dark jeans, white T-shirts, and boxer briefs in all different colors into the drum. "They played really well."

"You know, you shouldn't put all that in together. You should do darks and lights separately."

"But I don't even have that much stuff. I can probably do this all in one load," he said proudly, like that was a good thing.

"Oh, for heaven's sake." I set my wine glass on the counter and pushed him aside. "Do not do it all in one load. Those T-shirts will never be white again." I started pulling out all the non-white stuff and dumping it into an empty laundry basket.

"But that's going to take longer."

"Do you have somewhere else to be tonight?" I glanced at him over one shoulder.

He shrugged, then gave me a wry grin. "No. But I've got things I'd rather do with you than laundry."

"We'll get to that. But let's not ruin your clothing in the process. Tell me about the game."

While he talked animatedly about baseball, I added some of my whites to the machine, poured in the soap, and turned it on. Then I separated the rest of his things into my three-bag sorter.

"I was really happy with the way that lefty applied my advice," he said. "I could see him slowing down, thinking through each pitch, breaking down the motion like we talked about."

"That's awesome," I said, happy to see him in such a good mood.

"I'm going to work on pick-off moves with him tomorrow. He's got balance issues there too."

"What's a pick-off move?" I pulled pasta bowls down from the cupboard, and Tyler shut the cupboard doors behind me.

"It's a throw from the pitcher to a fielder to prevent the runner from stealing a base."

"Ah. Got it."

While we ate, he continued talking about the game. "There was a scout there today watching the lefty. He's got interest from several really good schools."

"That's great," I said, pouring both of us a little more wine.

"It is, but David, the head coach—Virgil's son—is worried that he's not gonna take any of their offers."

"Why not?"

"Apparently, this kid's dad died last year, and he doesn't want to leave his mom and sister alone."

My heart ached a little. "Sounds like a sweet kid."

"I met his mom today too. She's got the same concern."

"She wants him to go?"

"Yeah. David asked me to talk to him about it, but I don't

know . . ." Tyler's voice trailed off as he took another bite of pasta. "Seems too personal."

"But you know he'll listen to you, right?"

Tyler shrugged. "He might."

"Then why not try?"

He picked up his wine glass and took a drink, his forehead furrowed.

"I mean, it's good that he's thinking about his mom and his sister and not just about himself," I said. "It means he has a good heart."

"Yeah. He's definitely not like I was at eighteen. I couldn't wait to get out of here and go be a big shot, and nothing was going to stop me. This kid is different. He's more like you."

I laughed. "Like me how?"

"He's not self-centered," he said. "His mom said he's always been that way. He puts other people first."

My heart melted a little more. "Well, this is one instance where I think he needs to be told it's okay to think about what *he* wants for his future. That putting himself first does not make him a bad person. I know I've certainly been in a spot where I had to make a tough choice, and it helped me to hear that."

Tyler was quiet for a moment, then he spoke with finality. "Okay," he said. "I'll talk to him."

CHAPTER 15

Tyler

WHEN THE DINNER dishes were done and the last load of laundry was in the dryer, we stretched out on the couch to watch TV. I practiced my sharing skills again by letting her control the remote, which was how I ended up watching something called Kids Baking Championship.

"What the hell is this?" I teased her. "Making cookies is now a competitive sport?"

"Yes, but don't worry, it's not mean. They've created a very supportive environment, and the kids can always get help or a hug when they need it."

"Oh good, because I was *very* concerned," I said, which earned me an elbow in the gut.

But I didn't even really mind watching the show, since it felt so good just to lie on her couch beneath a blanket, an arm curled over her stomach, her back against my chest. In fact, I got kind of into it and found myself rooting for this little kid with thick glasses and a huge smile, who'd tried out for the show three times before he made it.

"That's some serious determination," I told April. "I dig that."

She was all for this little dark-haired girl named Talia, the youngest contestant, but the one who spoke the most languages—her mom was Brazilian, her father was French, and she lived in Austin, Texas.

"Can you imagine speaking three languages?" she asked.

"No. One was hard enough. Remember how you used to have to write all my English papers for me?"

She clucked her tongue. "I didn't write them for you—I just helped you organize your thoughts."

"Um, I'm pretty sure it was more than that. School was never my thing. I hope our kid got your brains."

Holy shit. Had I just said that? I couldn't believe it—what the actual fuck? I'd never even *thought* anything like that before, let alone said it out loud.

Our kid?

April was silent, and her body seemed frozen.

"Sorry," I said. "That was a weird thing to say. I have no idea why I said it."

"It's fine."

But she was quiet after that, and I felt like I might have upset her. After a few more episodes, she turned off the TV and rolled to face me.

"I feel like I need to tell you something," she said, playing with the buttons on my shirt.

"Okay."

She looked at my chest while she talked. "I didn't tell you this the other night when we talked about—about the adoption, because it just seemed like a lot all at once, but I . . . I recently reached out to the parents."

"The mom?"

Her eyes met mine. "The people who adopted our son."

"Oh." My gut clenched, then turned over—again and again, just like it had the night she'd told me she was pregnant. "Why?"

"Because I want to meet him."

My pulse had started to race. The blanket was too hot. "You do?"

"Yes."

I had no idea what to say.

"It's okay if you don't," she said.

"I don't," I admitted, hoping it was better to be honest. "I'm sorry if that makes me sound like a dick. It's just not something I've ever wanted." Especially now that my name was synonymous with *choke* in major league baseball. The kid would just be embarrassed. The media would have a field day. My life would be upside down again—and I felt like I was just starting to right the ship.

April nodded. "I understand. And it doesn't really have anything to do with you. But for me, I think it's an important part of making my final peace with the decision to give him up. I think it will help me to be more open about it moving forward. And . . ." Her eyes filled. "Part of me just wants to see the person he's grown up to be. In my own way, I still love him. I always have. Does that make any sense?"

"Sure," I said, forcing myself to act like the man I wanted to be. I had no desire to come face to face with my biological son, but if she did, I'd support her. "And if it will make you feel better to meet him, I think you should do it."

"You do?" she asked, her voice full of surprise.

"Of course. You deserve to have that peace. And he deserves to know the woman who loved him so much she gave him up because she knew it was the best possible thing for him."

Her eyes closed, and she nodded. "It *was* the best thing. I know it was. And this isn't about second-guessing my decision. It's about owning it. Being proud of it. Letting it be a part of my life without feeling ashamed of it. And feeling like I still deserve to have a family in the future, even though I gave away a child."

It made my chest hurt to hear her talk about being

ashamed of what she'd done. "Of course you do. You're so fucking brave. Do you know that?"

She opened her eyes and laughed a little. "Thanks. Believe it or not, I actually feel brave."

"Good." I paused. "So when is this happening?"

"I don't know. I haven't heard back yet. I might not ever hear back, if he's not interested in meeting me."

"Would you be okay with that?"

She sighed. "Yes. I would be. I hope I get a different answer, but if that's the case, I'll be okay."

"And still be able to have peace and move on?"

"Yes."

"Good." I pulled her closer to me, wrapping her tightly in my embrace. My stomach was still not entirely okay, but this time around, I was determined to remember this wasn't only about me. In fact, it wasn't about me at all. This was something she needed to do for herself, and she wasn't asking me for anything—again.

The least I could do was be there for her this time.

Even if it was from a comfortable distance.

At practice on Wednesday, I worked with Chip Carswell for a solid hour on both his pitching motion and his pick-off throw. He was definitely the most talented pitcher on the team, but there were a few other kids that threw the ball fairly well, and David asked me if I might start working one-on-one with some of them too.

"They're asking," he said once practice was over. "And after seeing what you're doing with Carswell, I know they'd benefit from your lessons on mechanics. We haven't had a pitching coach really hammer those since my dad retired."

"Sure," I said. "I mean, I'm not sure how much longer I'm going to be around, but I can work with a few more guys."

"Some of the parents are calling too, inquiring about private coaching sessions, how much you'd charge and all that."

I shook my head. "I don't want their money. If what I'm saying helps them, I'm good with that."

"Oh, it'll help. I wish you didn't have to leave." He looked out across the field. "Any chance you'd consider staying longer?"

"How much longer?"

"Until the end of the season? Hell, how about permanently? Would you consider moving back home and coaching full-time?"

I laughed. "I don't think so."

"Why not? You could even split your time between here and California. Spend winter out there, spring and summer here."

"I don't know, David. Kinda seems like something an old man would do—letting the cold weather dictate his life. I'm not ready to be an old man yet."

He nodded, folded his arms over his chest. "You think you'll play again?"

I shook my head. "Nah. If it hasn't come back yet, it's not going to."

"So what's the plan? What are you gonna do for the next fifty years?"

Exhaling, I adjusted my cap and stared out at the field, thinking, *Right there is where I stood and struck out nineteen batters in a row. That fence over there in left field is the one my final home run sailed over. Those bleachers were where my sister and my dad and April sat and cheered me on while I stood on the mound staring down the next victim of my fastball.*

I did have a lot of good memories here.

But coming back after such a public failure to take a position as a high school assistant coach? It was the opposite of the triumphant return I'd envisioned myself making one day, where I might throw the opening pitch of the season's first game, sign autographs and baseballs in the stands, shake hands with fans who'd watched my whole career start to finish—the right finish. Coming back after what actually happened would just be embarrassing, wouldn't it? Instead of returning a hero, I'd return a disgrace.

"Look, just think about it, okay?" David clapped me on the shoulder. "You could do some real good here. I know the majority of these kids won't even go on to play college ball, but a good coach will give them things they take with them no matter where they end up in life—things they'll remember forever. And you've got something to give, Shaw."

"I'll think about it."

"That's all I'm asking."

We started walking toward the parking lot. "I didn't get a chance to do it today, but if I have the chance, I'll encourage Chip to take the Clemson scholarship. I think that's the best place for him," I said.

David nodded. "I like that for him too."

We said goodnight, and I drove over to Sadie's house to bring in the mail and put out her trash and recycling. While I was there, I noticed a box sitting on the floor in the dining room. It was the one from the attic that Sadie had rescued when she moved out of our old house. I'd gone up and gotten it the day I'd painted the bedroom and then forgotten to take it with me.

As expected, it appeared to contain mostly junk I didn't need or want—championship trophies, some ribbons and medals, old photos, stacks of papers. I hadn't gone through it yet, but I was ninety-nine percent sure it all belonged in the trash. Shaking my head, I picked up a framed eight by ten photo of me in uniform my first high school season. I'd played varsity, while all my freshmen friends had been stuck on the ninth-grade team. On my face was the cocky smile I'd already perfected. In my hands, a bat and glove. At my side was six-year-old Sadie in pigtails, looking up at me instead of the camera. We were standing in front of the crab apple tree at our old house. I wondered if that tree was still there.

Not wanting to hurt my sister's feelings, I took the box and tossed it in the back of my SUV, which Rental Car Steve had said I could rent for the week . . . not that I'd booked a new return ticket to San Diego yet. I really needed to get on that—it was already Wednesday. I'd been here a full week at this point. Wasn't it time to get back to my real life?

I thought about it as I drove back to the hotel—the long way, past our old house so I could see if that apple tree was still there . . . it was. Parked across the street, I stared at that damn tree and thought about the offer David Dean had made me this afternoon. I thought about the second act of my life, for which I'd made no Plan B.

I thought about returning to my big house with its security gate in San Diego and my little cabin in the mountains. Both offered the privacy and solitude I'd craved over the last year, but was that really what I wanted for the rest of my life?

On the way back to the hotel, I thought about buying a place on the water here, where Sadie and Josh could bring my nieces and nephews to go swimming or fishing or boating. I thought about having an influence over the next generation of players, of passing on the wisdom that had been given to me, not because they were going to make millions of dollars or become famous pro athletes, but for the love of the game. And I thought about the woman who, within the space of one week, seemed to know and understand and accept me better than anyone ever had.

All of it was making me wonder *what if.*

What if I stayed more than a little longer? What if my worth didn't have to be measured in balls and strikes? What if the way my life had veered off course wasn't a punishment, but an opportunity?

What if this place started to feel like home to me?

Late that night I was lying in April's bed, my arms wrapped around her soft, warm body, when I realized it already had.

"Hey," I whispered. "Are you still awake?"

"Yes." Her voice was sleepy.

"I was thinking."

"I thought we weren't supposed to do that."

I laughed gently, nudging her hip. "Smartass."

"What were you thinking about?"

"About . . . staying. Maybe for good."

She rolled onto her back and looked up at me. "Really?"

"Yeah. David Dean offered me a permanent position on the coaching staff at the high school. I was thinking about maybe getting a place here."

"Like a house?"

"Yeah." I grinned at her in the dark. "Somewhere I can leave the cap off the toothpaste and not worry about it."

"I only scolded you about that *once* this week."

"Well, I feel like I've imposed on you long enough, with all my cover hogging and my dirty laundry. And I don't really want to live in a hotel—too many people around all the time. Earlier today I was picturing a big house on the water, maybe a boat. A place where we can hang out on the deck and drink good bourbon and I'll yell at kids to get off my beach."

Laughing, she shook her head. "Wow. That sounds amazing. But . . . that's a big decision. A big change."

"I know." I brushed the hair back from her face. "But I was thinking today about why I haven't booked a ticket back to San Diego yet. And I realized it's because I just don't want to go. Something about being here feels right to me, and I haven't felt that in a long time."

She looped her arms around my neck. "It makes me really happy to hear that."

"I'm happy too." I rolled on top of her. "Can you tell?"

"Yes. And I love when you're happy. In fact, making you happy is my new favorite sport."

"Better not skip practice then." I lowered my mouth to hers, my body igniting, my heart racing, my mind full of possibilities for the future.

CHAPTER 16

April

THURSDAY MORNING, I burst into Chloe's office without knocking. "He's staying!"

Seated at her desk, she looked up at me in surprise. "What?"

"Tyler. He's staying."

A grin broke out on her face. "You're kidding. For real? Like he's moving back?"

I nodded. "That's what he said last night. He's talking about buying a place on the water."

"Oh my God!"

I put a hand on my chest. "I swear, my heart has not stopped racing since he told me. It's so crazy!"

"So, what did he say, exactly?"

"He said he hadn't booked a ticket back to San Diego yet and when he thought about why, he realized it was because he didn't want to go. He said something about being here feels right to him." I paused and smiled. "And then we had sex again."

Chloe burst out laughing. "Listen to you! First you were all, 'Oh I'm totally not going to bang him, I'm just wearing perfume for fun,' then you were like 'Well, maybe I'll bang him, but first I'm going to overthink it,' and now you're head over heels in love!"

I rolled my eyes, even as my heart continued to gallop. "Stop it. I'm not *in love*. We're just spending time together. Getting to know each other. Having a *lot* of amazing sex. I'm just happy it doesn't have to come to an end before it even has a chance to begin."

My sister smiled sweetly. "You're cute when you're in denial. Frannie claims he never once took his eyes off you at the wedding and talked about you nonstop. Have you told her yet?"

"No, this just happened late last night! But I'll text her, and maybe we can all meet up for a drink this weekend."

"Sounds good. That way you don't have to tell the story four times." She grinned. "You look like you're on cloud nine."

"Do I? I'm trying not to let myself get too carried away—I mean, we haven't even talked about what this *is* yet—but something about it feels really good." I chewed my bottom lip. "Am I getting my hopes up too high? It's only been a week . . . a very intense week."

"Hey. Every happily ever after has to start somewhere, right?" She smiled. "Maybe this is your somewhere."

I thought about her words all day long and decided she was right. I'd waited so long to feel this for someone—the rush when he walked in the room, the butterflies in my stomach when he looked at me, the compulsion to get my hands anywhere and everywhere on his body, the unbelievable thrill I felt being close to him—why should I tamp down on that happiness? Opening your heart to someone was always a risk, wasn't it?

This was my chance to take it.

After work, I had an appointment with Prisha.

"How are you?" she asked, lowering herself into her chair.

"Great." I smiled from my usual spot on the couch. "A lot has happened in a week."

"Oh?" She returned the smile, tilting her head. "What's new?"

"Well, I did my homework—I told my sisters about the pregnancy and adoption—and you were right. It was a little scary, but I felt so much better afterward."

"Good." She typed something into her iPad. "I'm really glad to hear that."

"But wait, there's more." I laughed, tucking my hair behind one ear. "I reconnected with Tyler Shaw."

She glanced at her notes. "The baby's father?"

"Yes."

"And how did that go?"

"Actually . . . it's been incredible." I felt the bloom of warmth in my face. "Really and truly incredible."

"How so?"

"Well, we ran into each other sort of by accident. And I was prepared for it to be awkward, but it wasn't. It felt nice. So when he asked if I wanted to have dinner, I said yes, figuring it was the universe putting this opportunity in my lap."

"The opportunity for what?"

"To give that chapter an ending and close the book. Except that's not what happened."

"No?"

I shook my head. "We did more than just reconnect that night. We sort of rediscovered this chemistry we'd always had."

"I see." One eyebrow peaked. "Physical chemistry?"

"Yes, there's that," I confessed. "But it's more than that." I moved to the edge of the couch. "It's emotional chemistry too. I feel like I can really be myself around him. I hear myself telling him things I've never said out loud to anyone—deeply personal things. I trust him. He makes me feel beautiful and special and deserving of the things I want."

"Wow. That's certainly a powerful feeling. All that plus physical chemistry too?"

"Yes. The physical connection is . . ." I fell back and fanned my face. "Hot. He's still ridiculously gorgeous, and I find myself craving him all the time. And when we're together, it's like"—I stopped as the memory of his body on mine made my stomach tighten and the room spin—"it's like magic. I can't explain it. I don't feel self-conscious or ashamed or detached or any of the other things I used to feel during sex. It just feels good. So good that I was starting to worry."

Prisha sat back. "About what?"

I sat up again. "Well, about the fact that he was leaving. That all this good stuff I was feeling was just going to evaporate when he left. But then . . ." I grinned. "He decided not to leave."

"Oh?"

"He says he doesn't want to. At first, he thought he'd just stay the rest of the week and go home this weekend. But last night, he said he's thinking about moving back here for good. He was offered a coaching position at the high school."

"Wow. This is a lot to process."

"It is." I took a deep breath. "I also sent the letter."

Prisha crossed her legs in the other direction. "Did you?"

I nodded. "The day after I was last here, but . . . I haven't heard back."

"Well, that's only, what, a week?"

"Yeah." I had to laugh a little. "I guess so much has

happened for *me* in that week, it feels like it's been much longer."

My therapist smiled sympathetically. "Understandable."

"I actually told Tyler about the letter. About wanting to meet our son."

"And how did he react?"

"He was . . . supportive." I played with the hem of my top. "He said if it was something I felt I needed to move forward, I should do it. He made me feel good about the decision."

"Does Tyler want to meet him?"

"No," I admitted. "He was very clear about that, and I completely understand. He's never struggled with guilt over the adoption like I have. He was able to leave it behind more easily."

"Sounds like you two are communicating very well."

"I think we are." I met her eyes and smiled. "I really think we are."

CHAPTER 17

Tyler

AT PRACTICE THURSDAY AFTERNOON, I worked with a few more pitchers on their motion, ran double-play drills with the middle infield, and gave advice on different offensive situations during batting practice. For the most part, the guys were all eager to learn, receptive to criticism, and grateful for the feedback.

There was only one kid—a right-handed pitcher with the last name Brock—who acted like he knew everything already, and I sensed him bristling when I suggested he didn't have as solid a grasp on the mechanics as he should, but he wasn't openly antagonistic.

His father watched the last half of practice, though, and I didn't like the look he gave me, or the way he stood with his chest puffed out and his jaw jutting forward, or the way he yelled at his kid through the fence, basically telling him to do the opposite of what I was saying.

Virgil was there, sitting in the dugout, and when I was done, I sank down next to him while David finished up practice.

"Who's the asshole?" I asked, nodding toward the guy.

"Brock? He's nobody. Just one of those guys who thinks

he's better than everybody else because he's bigger and louder. Ignore him."

"He was interfering while I tried to work with his kid."

"Yeah, he does that all the time. Always huffing and puffing about the lineup and where his son should be in it. He was on the team here way back when, long before your time. But he wasn't good enough to be scouted for college ball and he's still mad about it."

"Oh." I took some satisfaction in that.

"I hear David offered you a position."

"He did."

Virgil side-eyed me. "Gonna take it?"

"I said I'd think about it."

"You should take it."

I chuckled. "And why's that?"

"Because it's where you belong. And if your dad was around, he'd say the same thing."

I looked out at the mound and decided to give a voice to a feeling I'd kept buried far from the surface. "You don't think he'd call me a quitter for leaving the game? He wouldn't think I'd been weak?"

Virgil didn't answer right away. "Is that what you think? That your pop would've called you a quitter?"

I shrugged. "Maybe. It was my choice to get out. I wasn't fired or anything. I could have stayed and kept working on it."

He remained silent.

"Maybe he'd think my real failure was giving in to the fear that nothing would land where I threw it ever again. There's no room for fear on the ballfield. You tough it out. You try harder. You beat it. Or you don't deserve to be there."

Virgil looked at me, but I didn't meet his eyes.

"You deserved to be there, son," he said. "What happened wasn't your fault."

"What if it was? What if I was too sure of myself? Too

convinced that the game owed me, rather than the other way around? What if God or the universe or whatever is out there decided I was just an asshole like everyone else and didn't deserve the arm?"

My old coach had no answer ready, but he let me talk, which was maybe all I needed. These were things I'd never said to anyone. Only another ball player would understand it, but admitting this kind of stuff was not acceptable in pro sports. It showed weakness, and you had to be tough.

"My dad was a good man, Coach. The best. Why did I get the chance to prove myself in the majors, but he didn't? And what would he say to me now that I blew it? I can't stop feeling like I let him down."

Virgil scratched his head. Shifted on the bench.

I closed my eyes and exhaled. "Sorry. Didn't mean to unload all that on you. But lately I've been trying not to keep so much shit bottled up."

"Yeah, that happens when there's a girl involved."

I had to laugh. "Right."

Practice ended, and I rose to my feet. "I should take off. I wanted to try to talk to Chip Carswell about his offer from Clemson before he goes home."

"Good. Good." Virgil nodded.

I'd already started to walk away when he spoke again.

"I know what he'd have said, Shaw."

"Huh?" I turned around.

"Your dad. You asked what he'd have said to you. I know what he'd have said."

"What's that?"

"He'd have said, 'Get up, son. Dust your ass off. The game's not over.'"

I wasn't sure what he meant. "What game? My pitching career?"

He shook his head slightly. "Your life. You're not done

showing 'em what you got, kid. But you gotta quit hiding. That's what he'd say."

I thought about that for a minute. Was he right? Would my dad have been more ashamed that I'd been hiding out than the way I'd failed on the mound? But baseball had been *everything* to him. What could I ever do that would even come close? "I'll think about it. Thanks, Coach."

"Have a good night, son."

Just for the hell of it, I treated the Brock's asshole dad to my best menacing glare before catching up with Chip on his way to the parking lot.

"Hey, Carswell, wait up!"

He turned, shifting his bag higher on his shoulder. "Hey."

"Nice job today. Your motion is already improving."

He smiled. "Thanks. I really appreciate the help."

"You talk to the scout from Clemson yesterday?"

"Yeah. A little." He hesitated. "They made me a pretty good offer."

"You gonna take it?"

"I don't know." He looked back toward the field. "My mom wants me to."

"It's a great place to play."

"Yeah." He chewed on his bottom lip for a second. "South Carolina is just kind of far."

"It's not that far."

"Yeah, but . . . my mom's on her own since my dad died. It doesn't feel right to go so far from her and my sister."

I nodded, folding my arms over my chest. "I get that. My mom died when I was young. When I left, I had to leave my dad and my little sister too."

"You did?" He looked at me in surprise, and it struck me that he didn't have to look *up*—he was almost as tall as I was.

"Yeah. I can't say that I felt as guilty as you do at the thought, but—"

"But you got *drafted*." He shook his head, a smile tugging

at his lips. "In the first round. You *had* to go."

"I did, because I felt in my gut that it was what I was supposed to do," I said. "A good pitcher trusts his gut."

He nodded, chewing on his lip again.

"What's your gut telling you?"

"To play baseball," he admitted. "To go. To take the chance, because I might not get another one."

"Then you should go, not because your mom or your coach or even I tell you to, but because your instincts are telling you to—you start ignoring that voice, it's gonna stop talking to you."

"Yeah. I hear you." His eyes dropped to the ground. "I think my dad would've wanted me to go too."

"I'm sure he would have, especially if he liked baseball."

Chip smiled. "He loved baseball."

"There you go." I clapped him on the shoulder. "Think it over. I know it's a big decision. I'm around if you need someone to talk to."

"Thanks, Coach."

Coach. It was the first time anyone had called me that—and I liked it.

"You're welcome, Carswell. You're a really fucking talented player. Oh, shit—sorry." I grimaced. "I'm not used to being around kids."

A crooked grin appeared on his face. "Don't worry about it. I'm eighteen anyway."

"Eighteen." I shook my head. "It's a good age to be. And in that case, I meant what I said—you're really fucking talented."

The grin widened, and a dimple appeared in his cheek. "Thanks."

Sadie had asked me if I'd stop by after practice, so I swung by her house before heading back to my hotel.

"You're still here!" she squealed when I walked into her kitchen, rushing over to give me a hug. "I don't believe it!"

"I'm still here." I hugged her back, let her go, and mussed her hair. "Who else would have brought in your mail or taken out your trash?"

She swatted my hand away. "Thank you for doing that. We appreciate it."

"No big deal." I leaned back against the counter. "How was your trip?"

She sighed. "Over too fast. But New Orleans is always a good time."

"You flew in this afternoon?"

"Yes. And I'm so tired. I wish I had tomorrow off too, but I already took six full days off for this wedding." She pulled a bottle of water from the fridge. "Want one?"

"Sure, thanks." I took the bottle she offered and twisted off the cap.

With her back to me, she reached into the fridge again for a second bottle. "Josh went out to grab some groceries. I have no idea what we're doing for dinner, but you're welcome to stay."

I hesitated. Took a sip of water. "I'll probably eat with April."

She shut the fridge door and spun around. "You will?"

"Yeah. We've been hanging out."

Her eyes narrowed. "And by hanging out, you mean . . ."

I shrugged.

Her mouth fell open. She uncapped her water bottle and took several big swallows. "Come on. Let's go sit on the porch and you can fill me in. I have a feeling I've missed a lot since the wedding."

We went out her front door and sat on the front porch steps. It was a warm, mild evening, and the sun was just starting to slip behind the houses across the street. "Remind me to buy you guys some chairs for out here," I said, lowering myself onto the cement.

"Josh wants to put a patio in the back. This porch isn't even big enough for furniture. This is more of a slab." She sipped her water and sighed. "Although the patio will probably be put on hold with the baby coming."

"See? Kids ruin everything."

She kicked me with one foot. "So tell me about you and April. Is that why you're still here?"

"No," I said quickly. "Not entirely."

"But partially?"

"You could say that." I took another drink of water.

"What's the other part?"

"I've been working with the baseball team over at the high school. David and Virgil Dean kind of guilted me into it, but it's actually been a pretty good time." I sipped again, remembering the talk I'd had with Virgil today.

"That's great."

I watched a few kids go by on their bicycles. "I wasn't sure how I'd feel getting back into baseball without playing the game myself. I thought I might hate it."

"But you don't?"

"Not really. I mean, I'm always going to be angry that my career ended the way it did. It's never going to make sense or seem fair to me. But . . . I guess I shouldn't let it dictate the rest of my life."

"No. You shouldn't."

I tipped up the water bottle, finishing it. "April has been on me this week about how I need to stop wallowing in the past and decide what I want the future to look like."

"You mean she wants you to stop being a grumpy old man? Stop living like a hermit? Admit there's life worth living off the pitcher's mound?" My sister poked my shoulder. "Gee, where have you heard that before?"

"Yeah, well, you don't have long red hair and dimples."

She laughed. "Okay, fine. I guess it doesn't matter who got through to you as long as someone did. I was getting worried about you. And you live so far away, I can't check up on you like a sister should. You make it hard to meddle."

"Well, guess what? I'm about to make your life easier—and mine harder."

She looked at me. "What do you mean?"

I readjusted my cap. "I'm thinking of moving back."

"*Here?*"

"Yeah."

Her spine straightened. "Are you serious?"

"Yeah." I laughed. "Are you glad to hear it or not?"

"Yes, I'm glad! I'm just shocked."

"You're not the only one." I shook my head. "A week ago, I wouldn't have considered it for a minute."

"That's because you were too busy wallowing." She poked my shoulder again. "So what changed your mind? Wait, let me guess—red hair and dimples."

I laughed a little. "She's part of it. I like being around her. But also . . . I guess being back here isn't as painful as I thought it was going to be. I mean, I still don't like when people come up to me and ask me what the fuck went wrong, but I suppose they're going to do that no matter where I am."

"That's true," she said. "It's not like bad manners are limited by state lines."

I remembered something Virgil had said. "And hiding out was only going to work for so long. It's not like I'm eighty. I'm not even forty. I don't want to spend the next half of my life obsessing over the first half, wondering what the hell went wrong."

"That sounds like a lonely, miserable way to live," she said softly. The kids on the bikes rode by again, and this time they waved at us. We both waved back.

"And this thing with April," I said, but then I couldn't

think of a way to finish the sentence. "I don't know. It feels good."

Sadie said nothing but out of the corner of my eye I could see her smile.

"What?" I said accusingly.

"Nothing. It's just a smile. It means I'm happy."

"Oh."

"But I have questions."

I groaned.

"First, where are you going to live?"

"No idea. I haven't even looked yet, since I just started thinking about this last night."

"When would this happen?"

"Don't know that either. Summer? Maybe I can check out some listings over the weekend."

"Perfect. Finally, this thing with April. . . is it serious?"

"Why do you need to know?"

She sighed in exasperation. "Because I need to know how excited to be on a scale of one to ten that you actually might, for once in your life, have an honest-to-goodness adult relationship." She clutched her heart. "A—gasp—girlfriend."

I rolled my eyes, but I thought about it. "Seven."

"Seven?"

"Maybe eight. I might even go as high as nine, but remember, it's only been a week."

"Romeo and Juliet met on a Sunday, got married on a Monday."

"And weren't they dead by Tuesday or something?"

"*No*," she said, as if she were offended. Then she quietly added, "It was *Thursday*."

Laughing, I shook my head. "We will not be getting married—or dying, I hope—anytime soon. But yes. I might have a girlfriend."

She swooned, tipping back on her cement porch and shouting at the sky. "You hear that, Dad? It's a miracle!"

Later, I took April out for dinner, and we talked more about everything—when I'd move, where I might look for houses, how much I'd miss Anna, what else I might do once I was back for good.

"What about owning a business?" she suggested. "A sporting goods store? A sports bar? Batting cages?"

"I don't know anything about running a business."

"Well, you could hire people to run it. You could be the silent investor. Or the loud investor, whatever you prefer. You could be as involved or as uninvolved as you chose."

"I'll give it some thought." I took a bite of my New York Strip. "I talked to the lefty about his scholarship."

"Did you get through to him?"

"Maybe? Hard to say for sure, but—"

"Excuse me for interrupting."

Even before I saw who was standing there, I recognized the smooth feminine voice dripping insincerity—it was that fucking reporter, Bethany Bloomstar. "I told you before," I said without looking up from my New York Strip. "No comment."

"I was hoping maybe you'd changed your mind," she said. "The piece is running tomorrow, and there's still time for changes. Are you aware that some local parents have a problem with you coaching their children?"

"Fuck off."

"And hello, April. We meet again," she said.

I looked up. *Again?* What the hell?

"Yes. Hello." April cleared her throat and met my eyes.

"You two have met?" I asked.

"Bethany and I had a meeting earlier in the week about

having her wedding at Cloverleigh," April said, her face flushed. "I didn't realize you knew each other."

"We don't." I glared at Bethany, knowing a game player when I saw one. "Are you even planning a wedding? Or were you just digging around for dirt on me?"

Bethany laughed and tossed her hair. "I'm *practically* engaged. And a woman needs to be prepared, right?"

"I'm sorry, I'm confused." April shook her head. "You're not really getting married? That meeting was just an excuse to talk to me?"

"Let's just say I was killing two birds with one stone."

"Let's just say you get the fuck away from us right now," I told her, keeping my tone under control. The last thing I wanted was a scene.

"Are you threatening me?" she asked loudly.

A murmur rippled through the crowd, and I knew without even looking around, there were now phone cameras aimed at us.

"Of course not," April said, rising to her feet. "Why don't we just—"

"Because I'm only trying to do my job!" Bethany whined. "And I don't appreciate being threatened by a man!"

"Bethany, he's not threatening you. He's only—"

"Forget it, April." I stood up, grabbed my wallet from my pocket, and threw more than enough cash to cover the meal on the table. "Let's just go."

Without another word, we grabbed our jackets and headed for the door, and just as I suspected, plenty of people took a video of us moving through the dining room toward the exit.

In the car on the ride home, April took my hand. "I'm sorry, Tyler."

"Don't be. Not your fault."

"It really stinks that people are so rude to you. They don't respect your privacy at all."

I shrugged. "I can take it. I'm sorry your dinner was ruined."

She was quiet for a minute. "I feel so stupid about that meeting. I honestly thought she was getting married and wanted her wedding at Cloverleigh. But she asked me to please be discreet because she didn't want anyone to know."

"Of course she didn't."

"God, I'm so *gullible*. She went on and on about all the good things she'd heard about me, how incredible the place was, how it was exactly what she wanted."

I harrumphed. "What she wanted was dirt on me."

She slapped her hands over her face. "She asked about Sadie's wedding and said she was a huge fan of yours, so I answered all her questions. I'm so sorry, Tyler."

"It's okay."

"No, it isn't. I should have known something was off when she kept trying to bring you up. But I swear, I never said anything personal."

"She's not worth getting upset over," I said, even though I was upset too. When would people leave me the fuck alone? Now April was being dragged into this—and the last thing she needed was a reporter digging around in her life.

"Do you think she'll try to make it sound like you threatened her in there?"

"Yeah. And she'll have video to *prove* it," I said sarcastically.

"How? You didn't do anything except ask her to leave!"

"Doesn't matter. People will see and hear what they want to."

She took my hand again. "I'm sorry. People suck."

I lifted her hand and kissed the back of it. "Told you so. But let's forget about her, okay? I'm still hungry, so what do you say we go back to my hotel room, order room service, and shut out the rest of the world tonight?"

"Perfect."

CHAPTER 18

April

I **WOKE** up in the middle of the night in an empty bed. The room was so dark I could hardly tell whether my eyes were open or shut. I heard a noise and sat up. "Tyler?"

"Go back to sleep."

"What are you doing?"

"Nothing."

I reached over and switched on the bedside lamp. Blinking in the light, I saw Tyler standing as far back as possible from the full-length mirror, sideways, eyeing himself in the glass. He wore a pair of sweatpants, and his hands were balled at his chest, as if he were on the mound, about to throw a pitch.

And then he did it—went through his entire motion, from windup to release, and I gasped, expecting the mirror to shatter when the ball struck it.

But he hadn't thrown a ball. He'd thrown . . . socks?

"Hey," I said, watching him retrieve the socks and go back to where he'd stood. "What's going on?"

"Nothing. I do this when I can't sleep sometimes."

I bit my lip. "Why can't you sleep?"

He shrugged, getting into position again. "I don't know. I just can't."

"Is it because of that reporter?"

"I don't know."

"Or the asshole dad you told me about? The one at practice?"

"I told you. I don't know." He wound up and threw again, and even though I knew it was only socks, I still winced when they hit the glass.

"Is it me?"

He went over and picked up the socks. "It's not you."

I didn't believe him for some reason. Not entirely. "Come talk to me."

"I don't feel like talking, okay? Just turn off the light and go back to sleep."

In my head, I went over the last couple hours before we'd gone to bed. Had I missed something? We'd gone up to his room, ordered dinner, watched a movie, and gotten naked before the credits even rolled. The sex had been incredible, as usual—maybe a little less loud and playful than usual, but he'd seemed fine afterward. Or had I fallen asleep so quickly, I hadn't noticed that he wasn't?

Naked, I slipped out from beneath the covers and went up behind him, wrapping my arms around his waist and pressing my cheek against his bare back. "If you don't come talk to me, I won't be able to sleep either."

"Then I guess we'll both be up," he snapped. We stood there for a minute, then he exhaled. "Sorry. I had a bad dream. One I used to have all the time after I couldn't pitch anymore."

"What's it about?"

"Being buried alive."

"Oh."

"By a cement mixer."

"Yikes."

"And the wet cement starts to harden right away, so I can't move. Can't save myself. My arms and legs and hands are just . . . stuck. Useless." He rolled his shoulders. "So I had to get out of bed and move. Remind myself I'm in control."

"Of course." I kissed his spine. "Do you have bad dreams a lot?"

"I used to. Since I quit baseball, not so much anymore."

"So what brought the dream back tonight?"

"I'm not sure. Could have been that reporter, I guess. Or Brock, the asshole dad." He paused. "Could have been the talk I had with Virgil this afternoon."

"About what?"

"Just some stuff about my father."

"Yeah?" I wouldn't press. Instead, I gave him space to tell me about it if he wanted to.

A beat went by before he spoke. "I asked Virgil if he thought my dad would've called me a quitter. If he thought my dad would've thought less of me for giving up the game."

"And what did he say?"

"He said no, of course. That's what he had to say."

"You don't think that's true?"

"I can't decide. I want it to be true, but . . . baseball was the only thing I ever did that made my dad proud. Without it, what's left?"

I swallowed hard. "How about the rest of your life? All the amazing things you're going to do and be? Maybe you can't see them yet, but I can."

He turned around and looked at me. Took my face in his hands. "No one has ever seen me the way you do."

I smiled. "Maybe no one ever bothered to look beyond the surface—I mean, you're Tyler Shaw. The surface is pretty nice to look at."

He kissed me hard then, and deep, his tongue penetrating my lips, his hands sliding into my hair. The kiss grew hotter as he moved me backward toward the bed, shoving his pants down, and lifting me onto the sheets.

"God, April," he whispered as his mouth traveled down my throat and his hands roamed over my skin. "I want you so much. I want you so much it scares me."

"Why?" I arched beneath his lips and tongue and teeth and palms and fingers as they moved over my body. I put my hands in his hair.

"Because I keep imagining this life with you, this life full of things I've never wanted before."

"What kinds of things?" As much as I loved his dirty mouth, his sweet words were just as thrilling, and I wanted to hear them all.

"I want to share a bed with you every night. And wake up to you every morning. I want to make breakfast for you, see you in the stands at Central High baseball games, reach all the stuff in the high cupboards in the kitchen. I want to be the one you come home to."

I smiled. "Don't be scared. I want all those things too."

"But what if I fuck it up?" He kissed his way up the center of my chest and braced himself above me. "What if I'm not good at it? What if I don't deserve it?"

"Tyler." I took his face in my hands. "You deserve it. Do you hear me? You deserve to be loved the way I'm going to love you."

Then his mouth was crushing mine and we were pressed chest to chest, rolling sideways with our arms and legs tangled as we tried to get under each other's skin. I reached low between us, sheathing his cock with my hand, desperate to feel him deep inside me, to let him take control, to show him I trusted him—and that he was safe with me.

He left my side only for the twenty seconds it took to put a condom on, and then he was back, easing into my body. When he was buried deep, he stopped and looked down at me. "I don't know what the second act of my life is going to look like, but I know you're the best part of it."

My heart, already beating hard, threatened to burst right out of my chest. "Really?"

"Yes."

Tell me again, I wanted to say, even as his mouth possessed mine once more and he began rocking into me with deep, steady strokes. *Let me hear those words again*, because they meant I didn't have to be alone anymore. They meant the risk was worth it.

They meant that finally I could say to myself . . . *This is what it feels like to fall in love.*

The following morning, Tyler got up early. Like, it-was-still-dark-outside early.

"You okay?" I asked as he pulled on sweats. I'd fallen asleep right after our round two in the middle of the night, so I had no idea if he'd been up all night or managed to get some rest.

"Yeah. I'm just gonna go down and get a workout in."

I bit my lip. "Did you sleep?"

"I slept some."

"Okay. I think I'll sleep in a little more. I have to be at work late tonight for a wedding."

He came over and kissed my forehead. "Sleep as long as you want. I like you in my bed."

Wiggling my toes, I snuggled down deeper into the covers, and I didn't wake up until I heard the door open and shut again. "Hey," I said, stretching. "How was your workout?"

"It was okay. A little sluggish."

"I bet." I patted the spot next to me. "Why don't you come back to bed?"

He peeled off his shirt. "Because I am a sweaty fucking mess. I need a shower before I even get near you."

The sight of his bare chest and arms made my heart beat faster and my core muscles clench. "Okay, but hurry. Your muscles are doing things to my insides."

I caught a glimpse of his old grin as he walked naked to the bathroom, and I had to stop myself from following him in there. My phone was dead, so to distract myself, I grabbed the remote and turned on the television, flipping through channels and listening to the shower run. I watched about five minutes of one morning show and ten minutes of another, and I'd just switched to a local news channel when I heard Tyler's name.

And there we were onscreen.

The clip of us hurrying out of the restaurant last night.

Baseball's Hottest Headcase Behaving Badly, read the chyron.

"I asked Shaw several times if he wanted to comment for this story, but I can't repeat his answer," Bethany Bloomstar was saying in a voiceover. The camera cut to her, and I was shocked to see that she was standing on the grounds at Cloverleigh Farms, the inn clearly visible in the background behind her.

"Now, do I have this right?" the news desk correspondent said, glancing at something in front of her. "Sources are saying he got belligerent when you approached him?"

She nodded. "That's right, Heather."

"And who's the woman with him? Do we know anything about her?"

"We do. Her name is April Sawyer." She gestured toward the inn. "I'm here at Cloverleigh Farms, which is run by the Sawyer family. April Sawyer is the event planner here. Last week I interviewed April off the record, and she confirmed that she and Tyler Shaw are old friends, but I have to tell you, it definitely looks like more than that to me."

The bathroom door opened, and Tyler walked out with a towel around his waist. Quickly I snapped the television off.

But not quickly enough.

"What the fuck was that?" Tyler demanded.

"It was nothing." I hid the remote behind my back, under a pillow.

He gave me the glare.

"Okay, fine. It was that stupid Bethany Bloomstar," I said.

"Talking about *you*?"

"Well, about both of us." And because he looked like he might be thinking about going down to the TV station and taking someone's head off with a fastball, I added, "It wasn't anything bad. Just that we looked like more than friends."

He frowned. "That's it?"

"Um, there might have been something about you getting belligerent with her at the restaurant."

"Christ," he muttered. "That wasn't belligerent. I could show them belligerent. That wasn't it."

I put my hands over my mouth.

"Are you laughing at me?" he asked, shifting his weight to one foot.

"I'm sorry," I said, unable to stop myself. "But you're standing there in a towel being belligerent, and I know it's not supposed to be funny, but it is."

"Oh, that's it. You're in trouble now." Ditching his towel, he launched himself onto the bed and came after me. Squealing, I did my best to scramble out of his reach, but he was much bigger and stronger, and had me pinned down on my stomach in seconds, his body flattened on top of mine.

"How much trouble am I in?" I asked, gasping for breath. I felt the hard length of his cock against my ass.

"A lot." He bit the back of my neck.

"A lot like you're going to make me run sprints? Eat snails? Watch golf? All of which I hate, by the way."

"A lot like I'm going to spank you."

"What?" I shrieked.

"You heard me. Now don't move." He let go of my arms and slid down on my body, straddling my thighs. "Damn, your ass is adorable. I can't wait to put my handprints on it."

I gasped. "You wouldn't!"

His response was a great big slap across one cheek, which stung like crazy, although I liked when he put his palm over it and held it there for a moment.

"Is that it?" I asked, panting.

He laughed and spanked the other cheek just as hard, making me cry out—but not just from the pain. Not that it didn't hurt—believe me, those massive hands were no joke—but it hurt in a way I *liked*, which surprised me.

"Are you sorry for laughing now?" he asked, rubbing both his hands over my ass.

"Yes!"

"Are you lying to me?"

I hesitated. "Yes."

He laughed again, but instead of delivering another spanking, he rubbed the tip of his cock over my stinging flesh. "I never knew about this naughty side of yours, April Sawyer. I like it."

"I don't think it existed before you."

He reached beneath me and hitched up my hips, then grabbed a fistful of my hair, pulling it tight. "I like that even better."

"Come on, slowpoke," I scolded him two hours later, watching him get dressed. "I'm going to be late for work."

"Okay, okay. I'm hurrying." He sat down on the bed and pulled on his socks and shoes—first the left, then the right.

I walked over to the mirror and fussed with my hair. Behind me I heard him laugh.

"Hey, you're walking kind of funny there."

Bending down, I picked up the pair of socks he'd been pitching at the mirror last night and lobbed them at his head —I missed.

He laughed harder. "Remind me to teach you how to throw."

"Can you just hurry up please? And if I'm walking funny, it's your fault. I probably won't even be able to sit down today without pain."

"Sorry."

But I could see his face in the mirror, and that grin told me he wasn't sorry at all. I didn't even mind—it was good to see him laugh and smile.

"Just give me one minute," he said, rising to his feet. As he passed me on the way to the bathroom, he kissed my shoulder. "I wish you didn't have to work today. I could spend all day in bed with you and be completely happy."

I turned and gave him a hug. "Do you feel better?"

"Yes. I do." He went into the bathroom and closed the door, and a minute later, he opened it and came out again.

But first, I saw the strip of light at the bottom of the door flash on and off eight times.

CHAPTER 19
April

I THOUGHT about mentioning the light switch thing on the way home, but never seemed to find the right words. It worried me, though. Was he okay?

He pulled up at my place and put the SUV in park. "Can I see you tonight?"

"Sure. Want to come over after I'm done at work?"

"Yes." He yawned. "Sorry. I'm so fucking tired today."

"I know. And I'll be late tonight," I said apologetically. "Why don't I give you my spare key, and you can wait for me here? That way, you can just fall asleep if you're exhausted."

He shrugged. "Okay."

"Let's do that. Then I won't feel so bad. Give me a minute." Getting out of the car, I hurried to the front door and let myself in, stepping over a pile of mail. I scooped it up and set it on the table before grabbing my spare key from a kitchen drawer and taking it back out to Tyler.

"Thanks." He tucked it into his pocket. "The team has a home game tonight, so I'll head over after that."

"Perfect. I'll text you and let you know what time to expect me." I leaned over and kissed his cheek. "You okay, babe?"

"I'm fine."

"I'm sorry again about the Bethany Bloomstar thing."

He yawned again. "It's okay. I'm more mad that she dragged your name into it. And Cloverleigh's."

"Don't worry about that. I bet no one even saw it."

He shook his head and gave me a look.

"Okay, well, even if people did see it, the people who matter to us know the truth, right?"

"Right."

"Hey." I took his hand. "I can tell you're upset. And I saw the light switching on and off eight times in the bathroom."

He shrugged. "Don't worry about it. It's just a thing I do sometimes. A habit."

"Are you sure?"

"Yes. Look, I'm tired, I'm not thinking straight, and my brain is all muddled. I promise—it was just a reflex. I'm okay. I'm going to go back to the hotel and take a nap."

"Good idea." I leaned over and kissed his cheek. "I'll see you tonight."

I went into the house, plugged in my phone, and headed upstairs to take a shower and get ready for work. When I came down an hour later, I had a ton of text messages—some from my sisters, one from my mom, a few from friends I hadn't seen in a while. All of them were about the same thing: the news story about Tyler and me. Many of them had sent me the link to the online video.

Knowing it was a bad idea, I clicked on it.

"Few major league baseball careers have imploded as spectacularly as hometown hero Tyler Shaw's." Bethany Bloomstar's voice accompanied a series of photos of Tyler, starting with one from high school, in which he appeared cocky and grinning.

"A first-round draft pick right out of high school, Shaw rocketed to fame within a few years, making millions, breaking hearts, and winning game after game, thanks in large part to his phenomenal fastball and supreme confidence." Now the photos showed Tyler in his San Diego uniform—on the mound looking fierce, signing autographs after a game, celebrating a win in the clubhouse.

"But you know what they say—pride goeth before destruction, and a haughty spirit before a fall—and Shaw's fall from grace was huge, it was public, and it was enough to kill his career for good." Video footage showed Tyler throwing wild pitches one after the other, sometimes hitting a batter, sometimes sailing wide, sometimes hitting the dirt just ten feet from the mound. I cringed with every throw, knowing how it was killing Tyler inside.

"What caused Shaw to go from hero to head case was a phenomenon widely known as the yips, a sudden loss of ability in pro athletes. While it's not well understood, most experts agree it's not due to a physical problem—the issue is entirely in the athlete's head." A photo of Tyler sitting on the bench with his head in his hands put a lump in my throat.

"Most of them never recover, and Tyler Shaw was no exception. His career tanked. His endorsement deals ended. His dreams shattered. Once famously charming, Shaw became reclusive and angry, refusing all interview requests. Within three years, he retired from baseball and retreated to a cabin in the San Bernardino Mountains to avoid the media maelstrom." Video footage of a small, secluded cabin in the woods appeared, although there was no sign of him, and I wondered if it was even his place.

"But interest in the former superstar has never waned, and Shaw featured prominently in a recent sports documentary about careers cut short by the yips." The shot cut to a clip from the documentary in which some crusty old coach was shaking his head and referring to Tyler as a "poor bastard." My hands clenched into fists.

"Shaw hasn't been home since his career ended, but last weekend, he was seen at Cherry Capital Airport." Cell phone footage played of a stern-faced, square-shouldered Tyler moving through the airport, cap low, sunglasses on. "He was home for his sister's wedding, but don't be surprised if you see him around town a little more often now—with a brand new girlfriend on his arm." My jaw dropped as amateur footage of Tyler and me appeared—chatting on the track at the high school, having breakfast at Coffee Darling, walking down Main Street.

"April Sawyer, a hometown honey, is a high school friend of Shaw's." A slightly out-of-focus photo of Tyler and me from senior year appeared, the other faces blurred out. "But someone might want to warn her about Shaw's dark side."

Now the video footage was of a clearly frustrated Tyler yelling obscenities at photographers, cameramen, and reporters, getting in their faces, going so far as to shove one away from him as he tried to leave his house. "He might have lost his arm, but he obviously gained a violent temper. Last night the two were spotted having dinner in a local establishment, and when he was approached for an autograph, things got ugly fast."

Outraged, I watched the clip of us leaving the restaurant again. "You lying bitch! You didn't ask him for an autograph! You just wanted dirt!" Huffing and puffing, I felt my face getting hot as I yelled at my phone. "And what about the way you tricked me into talking to you?"

"I asked Shaw several times if he wanted to comment for this story, but I can't repeat his answer," Bethany was saying, but at that point I turned it off. I'd already seen the rest anyway, and if I had to look at her phony-concerned face anymore, I was going to lose it.

My phone vibrated in my hand, and I saw it was my mom calling. "Shit," I said, not in the mood to talk but knowing I had to.

I accepted the call. "Hi, Mom."

"April! Are you okay?"

"I'm fine." I gritted my teeth.

"Have you seen it?"

"I've seen it."

"I can't believe we didn't notice the cameras out on the lawn. When your father realized they were out there, he and Mack went right out and kicked them off the grounds."

"Good."

A pause. "I didn't realize you and Tyler were in touch."

"We weren't. I mean, we haven't been." My head began to ache, and I touched two fingers to my temple, closing my eyes. "We reconnected right before Sadie's wedding."

"Oh. And is it . . . how's it going?"

"It's actually going great, Mom," I said with a little more venom than necessary. "We have fun together. That news story was bullshit, okay? Don't believe it."

"Okay, darling. I didn't mean to upset you. I just wanted to check in."

I sighed. "Sorry. I'm just—my head is pounding right now. I'm not upset with you. I'm just angry at that story."

"Of course you are. Can I do anything for you?"

I took a deep breath. "Not right now. But thanks for checking in."

"I'm always here, honey."

After we hung up, I called Chloe.

"Hey," she said as soon as she picked up. "I saw it. Fucking Bethany Bloomstar. I hope she gets a big wart on her face."

I almost laughed. "Yeah, she deserves it."

"You okay?"

"Yes. But I'm worried about Tyler. He's trying so hard to move on from everything, and the media attention doesn't help."

"I know."

"Why can't they just leave him alone?" I asked angrily. "He's not even playing anymore."

"Because he's still a story, especially around here. People are still interested."

I frowned. "He's going to hate that. He doesn't want to be a story. He just wants to be himself. But it's like the public only has one version of him they want, and if he can't be that, they won't accept it."

"Well, that's why it's good he has you," she said. "And soon he'll realize he has the rest of the Sawyer clan too. We're a package deal."

That made me smile. "Yeah."

"Hey, want to get together this weekend? Maybe we can all hang out at Sylvia's. Or even at Mom and Dad's for Sunday dinner. You skipped it last weekend."

"I was busy," I said.

She laughed. "Yeah, I know what you were busy doing. But now that he's staying for good, you guys don't have to be so precious about your time. You can spare a few hours for the rest of us."

"I guess we could. Actually, I like that idea a lot."

"Perfect. And don't worry about that stupid news thing. It'll blow over and Bethany Bloomfart will be on to the next fake scandal."

"Thanks. I appreciate it. And I was just snippy to Mom. I'll call her and apologize, then I'll ask if I can bring him to dinner."

After ending the call with Chloe, I reached out to my mom and asked about bringing Tyler to Sunday dinner.

"Of course, darling," she said brightly. "Your friends are always welcome here."

I took a deep breath. "Mom, I need to ask you something. Did you ever tell Dad about the baby and adoption?"

She didn't answer right away. "I did. I'm sorry if I

betrayed your confidence, but I didn't feel it was something I should keep from him. Plus, I was struggling too—it's not easy to see your child in pain, and I knew how hard that was for you to go through. Also . . . it was our grandchild. I had to mourn a little bit."

I swallowed hard. "I understand."

"If it makes you feel better, he was very understanding. He wanted to respect your privacy, so he never mentioned it, but he knew, and he was so proud of you."

My throat tightened, and I had to take another deep breath before speaking. "Thanks, Mom."

"Would it be okay to tell him you're aware that he knows now?"

"Sure," I said, feeling oddly good that the air would be cleared once and for all. "I recently told Meg, Chloe, and Frannie as well."

"Did you?" She sounded surprised.

"Yes. My therapist encouraged me to be more open about it, starting with people I trust. And there's no one I trust more than family."

"That's wonderful, darling," she said warmly. "I'm so happy to hear it."

I thought about telling her I'd written a letter to the adoptive mom, but decided against it. One thing at a time. I could wait until I heard back—if I heard back—to share that news.

"I better go, Mom. I have to get to work, and I'm running a little late."

"Okay, darling. I'm glad you called."

We hung up and I glanced around for my bag.

That's when I looked over at the table, where I'd tossed the stack of mail.

Gooseflesh blanketed my arms, and a strange shiver moved up my spine. Slowly, I walked over to the table and picked up the letter on top. It was addressed to me in black cursive lettering. I picked it up, knowing what it was before I even checked the return address.

My legs trembled, and I sat down. Holding my breath, I slipped my finger beneath the seal and tore open the envelope. With shaking fingers, I pulled out the letter.

A photograph dropped onto the table, and I gasped. There he was—in a *baseball uniform*. With Tyler's signature grin plus my dimples. Tyler's dark eyes and the Sawyer family ears sticking out from under his cap. He was tall and lanky, like Tyler at that age, and his hands looked almost too big for his body. Before I knew it, tears were streaming down my face, but I was smiling too.

Reluctantly I tore my eyes off the picture and unfolded the letter.

Dear April,

Thank you so much for reaching out. I have thought of you often over the years, and I'm glad to hear you are doing well. Chip would very much like to meet you.

At this, I put a hand over my stomach and allowed myself a couple sobs of relief. Of joy. Of anticipation.

I want to apologize for the delay in getting back to you—we moved to Michigan last year, so your letter did not reach me right away. But in fact, we live quite close to each other, as you will see from the return address.

I quickly checked it and discovered—my jaw dropping— that not only had the family moved from Ohio to Michigan, but they'd moved to within fifteen miles of me. My head began to spin . . . had I seen my son already and not even known it?

It has been a difficult couple of years for us, as we lost my husband Chuck last year very suddenly to a heart attack. We moved here to be closer to my mother. The loss of Chuck has been very tough on all of us, but particularly on Chip, who was very close to his father and feels a lot of responsibility to be the man in the house now that his dad is gone (we adopted a baby girl several years after adopting Chip).

We have always been open with Chip and Cecily about the fact that they were adopted, and in fact, Cecily (who is twelve) enjoys a nice relationship with her birth mom—much like an aunt or older cousin. While Chip has never asked many questions about his birth parents (boys are less inquisitive than girls, I suppose), he seemed intrigued when I mentioned that I'd heard from you. Upon learning you'd like to meet him, he thought about it for a minute and asked me how I felt about it. That is the kind of person Chip is—considerate and sensitive to other people's feelings. When I told him the decision was his, he said he'd like to meet you. In the wake of his loss, I think he is searching for additional family ties, and I truly believe it will be good for him.

His schedule is fairly busy these days with school and baseball—he is an honor student and a very talented pitcher with scholarship offers from multiple schools—but perhaps you'd like to come to our house sometime?

My email address and cell phone number are at the bottom of this letter. Please feel free to use it and we can set up a meeting. In addition, if you'd like to see him play, he is a starting pitcher for the varsity team at Central High School.

We look forward to hearing from you.

Sincerely,

Robin Carswell

I could hardly breathe—I was bursting with something like pride, which was ridiculous, wasn't it? I hadn't raised him. But he was handsome! And smart! And talented! And considerate of other people's feelings! It seemed like he'd gotten all the best things about Tyler and me, and had been raised exactly right. A rush of gratitude for Robin and her husband flooded me, as well as sympathy for the loss of Chuck.

God, what a morning this had been—my emotions were all over the place. And I was totally going to be late for work if I didn't get out of here. I'd have to repair my ruined eye makeup in the car. I stuck the letter in my bag, grabbed my keys and phone, and hurried out the door.

I was halfway to work when it hit me.

Chip was a starting pitcher for Central High School, where Tyler had been coaching the team all week long.

Which meant he'd already met his son.

CHAPTER 20

Tyler

AFTER DROPPING APRIL OFF, I decided to head downtown. There were several real estate offices along Main Street with listings in their front windows, and I figured I could check them out without having to go in and talk to anyone. If I saw something I was really interested in, I'd take a picture of it and make a phone call.

But I wasn't standing there for sixty seconds before someone poked his head out. "Tyler Shaw, right?"

Fucking great. "Yeah."

The guy held out his hand. He looked kind of familiar, but I couldn't place him. He wore a suit, an excited grin, and a lot of cologne. "Bob Dennis. Huge fan."

Reluctantly I took the guy's hand. "Hey."

"Come on in."

I glanced up the street toward where I'd parked, tempted to make a run for it, but decided to go in. If April were here, she'd want me to. And maybe this weekend, if she had time, we could check out a few places together.

Bob led the way to his desk, which was right near the front of the room. He gestured toward the chairs across from it before taking his seat. "So what can I do for you? You thinking of buying a place around here? I saw the news this morning."

I'd just sat down, but I stood right back up again. "Sorry. I changed my mind."

"No, wait!" he said, also rising to his feet. "I've got some great listings. You like privacy, right? I have one that's perfect. Right on the water, boat dock, deck with jacuzzi, gourmet kitchen, master suite. Everything top-notch."

Slowly, I sank into the chair again. "I'm listening."

But instead of telling me more about the house, he went in the other direction. "Tyler fucking Shaw. I can't believe it. You probably get asked this a lot, but what the hell happened? I was in that documentary they made about you, did you see me? I was the guy in the barber shop. The one that said the thing about the tight underwear." He laughed as if he'd made a great joke. "People loved that line. I hear it all the time."

That's why he looked familiar.

I stood up again, put both hands on his desk, and leaned forward. "Yeah, well I didn't."

He looked slightly alarmed. "Hey, take it easy. I was just making a joke."

I cracked my knuckles. "That was my fucking career you were joking about, asshole."

The room, which had been humming with quiet conversation, quieted. Heads turned in my direction.

Bob held up his palms. "Look, I'm sorry. It seemed funny at the time."

"I'm sure it did." And then, because I knew someone probably already had a phone camera aimed at me, I resisted the urge to knock over the chair I'd been sitting in before storming out of the office.

Back in my car, I made the mistake of checking my text messages. I had one from Sadie that said, **Have you seen this? WTF is wrong with people?** She included a link to the

Bethany Bloomstar story, which I clicked on, because I was already having a shitty day.

I watched the entire thing, growing more furious every minute. How *dare* these assholes take video of April and me! How *dare* they drag her family's name and business into this! How dare they suggest I'd flown off the handle because of an autograph request rather than a rude invasion of privacy! I was plenty familiar with the way gossip "journalism" worked, so it shouldn't have surprised me, but somehow it did.

And the last thing April needed was someone prying into her personal life—or her past.

It was all my fault.

Spewing curses, I drove back to the hotel, figuring I'd just go up to my room and hole up before the game and cool my temper. But there was a fucking photographer waiting for me in the lobby, and as soon as I started for the elevators, he was following me, snapping away. Every instinct in my body was to take the guy's camera and smash it on the marble floor, but I managed to hold back, and lucky for him the elevator doors opened quickly. When he attempted to follow me and one other female guest in, I shoved him back. "Don't even fucking think about it."

The doors closed, and I turned to the woman, who had a hand over her chest and a terrified look on her face. "Sorry," I muttered.

She didn't say anything, but she got out on the first floor she could.

Back in my room, I fell forward onto the bed, burying my face in the pillow. Since I'd hung the Do Not Disturb sign on the door, the sheets hadn't been changed and the pillowcase smelled faintly of April's perfume. I breathed it in and tried to relax. My body grew heavy. My head grew foggy.

The next thing I knew, I was lying on my back watching television. The remote was in my hand, so it had to have been me who'd turned it on, but I had no memory of it. Even stranger, I was watching that damn documentary, but instead of the usual talking heads, it was April and her sisters discussing me. At least, I assumed they were her sisters. They all looked almost exactly like her and every single one of them had her red hair, even Frannie—whose hair, I knew, was not that color at all.

But I recognized the names that flashed on the screen as they spoke.

SYLVIA: He was never good enough for her. Not then, and especially not now.

MEG: I mean, even if she forgave him for abandoning her when she was pregnant with his child, I can't.

CHLOE: I can't get over the way he fooled everyone into believing he was something he isn't. You just can't trust a guy like that.

FRANNIE: I really thought he would change, you know? I thought he really cared about her.

SYLVIA: A guy like that only cares about himself. He'd make a terrible husband and father.

MEG: Oh, totally. I can't even believe they're letting him coach those kids. Especially now that we know about his secret dark side.

CHLOE: Which doesn't surprise me at all.

FRANNIE: I'm so sad for April. I wish he'd never come back.

Then my own sister Sadie appeared, but even she had April's red hair. And she was wearing my Central High School jersey.

SADIE: Growing up, I thought the sun rose and set on Tyler. He was my hero. Now I don't know who he is.

I woke up with a sudden jerk of my head, soaked in sweat. When I looked around, I discovered I was still lying exactly as I had been when I'd flopped onto the bed—on my stomach, face down, arms and legs splayed like a starfish. The room was light, but the television was off.

It was just a dream, I realized, rolling onto my back and throwing an arm over my forehead. Jesus. I needed to get a grip. What the hell was wrong with me today?

I lay there for a few more minutes, then decided I needed food. I picked up the phone and ordered room service, and while I waited for it, I scrolled through some real estate listings on my phone.

But I wasn't in the right mood, so I ended up tossing my phone aside and watching a stupid car chase movie. Might have been a mistake because I felt even more amped up and pissed off than I did before I watched it. I did manage to take another nap—dream-free this time—before I had to go over to the field, but even that didn't take the edge off.

I just couldn't shake the feeling that no matter what I did, I couldn't win.

Speaking of not winning, the game that afternoon did not go well.

Chip's motion was off, and no matter what I said, he couldn't seem to get his stride length right. We took him out of the game, and I knew exactly how he felt when he sank onto the bench, head down.

We sent in a relief pitcher—Brock—but he didn't fare any better. The other team was playing a great offensive game, and it didn't help that Brock's dad was screaming at the umpire through the fence the entire time, arguing with the calls. Finally, I went over to him and tapped his shoulder.

He turned to me and puffed out his chest. Admittedly, I did the same.

Mine was bigger.

"You need to stop," I said.

"I need to stop what, you fucking has-been?" he asked, jerking his chin at me.

I shrugged, feeling my temper spark but trying hard not to let it catch fire. "Stop being an asshole, and go sit down."

He stuck a meaty finger in my face. "Who are you calling an asshole?"

"You. You're making the entire team look bad, and you're not doing your son any favors. The ump is less likely to give us the close calls if he's pissed off."

"What the fuck do you know about it? I don't even get why you're here—you suck, Shaw! You couldn't throw a strike if you tried!"

People were watching, I reminded myself. Players were watching. Kids were watching. "Look, let's not argue here. This isn't about me, or even about you."

"The hell it isn't. You're telling me I can't support my son. And I'm telling *you* to go to hell."

My hands curled into fists, and at that point I realized I had to remove myself from the situation or it was going to get ugly. So instead of smashing the guy's jaw like I wanted to, I turned around and went back to the dugout.

His voice followed me. "That's right, get the hell out of here, you head case. You don't know shit."

Seething, I stood with my arms crossed over my chest. Virgil, who was also in the dugout, shuffled over to me. "Brush it off. There will always be overbearing parents."

"That guy is more than overbearing," I snapped.

Virgil shrugged. "Part of the game. Let it go."

But I couldn't. The team lost, the players were dejected, and Chip seemed especially down. He came over to me after the game, cap pulled low. "Sorry, Coach. I couldn't get it right."

I put a hand on his shoulder. "We'll work on it. Rest that arm."

He nodded and walked off toward the locker room with a couple buddies. I rubbed my face, feeling exhausted and good-for-nothing and craving a drink. Pulling my phone from my pocket, I texted Mack, who'd given me his number and said to reach out if I ever wanted to grab a beer.

Me: Hey. You busy? Could use that beer.

Mack: Sounds good. Give me a minute to check with F.

I was starting my car when he texted back.

Mack: I'm good for a beer. Jolly Pumpkin has great brew.

Me: Sounds good. I'll meet you there.

I walked into the bar with my head low and took a seat way down at the end of the bar, hoping no one would recognize me. I'd just ordered a beer when I felt a hand on my shoulder.

"Hey." Mack slid onto the stool next to me.

"Hey."

"Were you at the game? How was it?"

I shook my head. "Rough."

"What happened?"

I gave Mack a rundown of the game over a couple beers apiece. Since I was hungry, I ordered a burger and fries, and Mack ordered two pizzas, which he said he needed to bring home for Friday night movie night. The order was complicated, since in a house with four females, nobody ever wanted the same thing on their pizza.

"And I'm sorry I don't have more time," he said. "I wish I did. I could sit here and talk baseball all night."

"No big deal. You should go home to your family." I tipped up my glass.

Mack rubbed his jaw. "This might not be my place to ask, but is everything okay?"

I shrugged. "I had an off day. Nothing seemed to go right."

He nodded. "I saw the news story. Fuckers."

I signaled the bartender for another beer. "Yeah, well. I'm used to it. But I don't like that April's name was dragged into it. I don't want them going after her because of me."

"I get it." He paused. "Frannie said you might be moving back here for good? Taking a permanent coaching position?"

I looked at him. "News travels fast."

He shrugged. "I think Chloe might have told her. But the Sawyer sisters have some kind of psychic network, I swear to God. They know everything about each other within minutes. So it's true?"

The bartender brought my beer, and I took a sip. "I was thinking about it. But today was the kind of day that just makes me want to go back to my cabin in the mountains and say to hell with it. People don't want to give anybody room to make mistakes. They just want perfection."

His pizzas arrived, and after he paid the bill, he stood up. "I don't know, man. Everybody loves a good comeback story."

I tried to smile. "Thanks."

Clapping a hand on my shoulder, he grabbed his pizza boxes off the bar. "Take care. Let's do this again—I'll get out of movie night next time."

"Don't worry about it." I waved him off, fighting a small pang of envy, which surprised me. I'd never wanted a family at all, let alone a family tradition taking up my Friday night. But watching him walk out of the bar with dinner for his wife and kids while I sat there by myself was pretty fucking depressing.

I paid my bill but I was still sitting there finishing my beer when I heard a loud voice behind me.

"And then that asshole head case Shaw had the nerve to tell me to sit down."

My jaw clenched. My gut tightened. Bad things were about to go down—I could feel it in my bones.

"I don't even know why they let that guy near the team. He just fucked up their winning streak with his goddamn yips. There was a college scout there too. He probably blew my kid's chances at being noticed."

I got off the stool, went over to Brock's table, and stood right behind him. "The only thing blowing your kid's chances of being scouted is you. I guarantee he was noticed—for the wrong fucking reason. Your big mouth."

The guy got out of his chair and stood chest to chest with me. I had at least five inches on him, and I was in way better shape, but that didn't mean this idiot wouldn't throw a punch. Actually, I was hoping he would.

"You need to mind your own business, Shaw."

"I heard my name. My name is my business."

He poked my chest. "You jinxed my kid, you fucking loser! You jinxed the whole team! And you need to get the fuck out of here before I show you with my fist how I feel about that!"

I smirked. "Go ahead and show me, if you think you can."

The guy immediately took a swing at my face, but I blocked it easily and delivered a quick, hard jab to his solar plexus that knocked the wind out of him and sent him sprawling back across the table. It was clear he was not going to get up and fight back.

At that point, the manager of the place came rushing over, but I was already on my way out. "Sorry," I said to him as I took off for the door.

Adrenaline pumping, I stormed down the street to where I'd parked, got in my car, and slammed the door shut.

Motherfucker. I'd just punched a parent.

He'd deserved it, but still. David was going to kill me. Virgil was going to be disappointed. And given the media attention to my "dark side," the school board was probably going to ban me from all future events.

Angrily, I banged the heel of my sore hand on the steering wheel and started the engine.

Why couldn't I get anything right?

I drove over to April's, stopping on the way to pick up a bottle of whiskey. My anger and self-loathing were at an all-time high, and I needed something to numb it. Using the key she'd given me this morning, I let myself into her condo and went straight to the kitchen, pulling a glass from the cupboard and pouring myself a shot of Templeton Rye.

After tossing it back, I poured another, and I was just lifting it to my mouth when I noticed a photograph on the floor by the kitchen table. Carrying the glass with me, I went over and picked it up.

Right away I recognized Chip Carswell and wondered why the hell April would have a photograph of him. I turned the picture over. On the back was written *Charles Andrew, age 17.*

Huh, his real name was Charles. I hadn't realized that. I tossed back the second shot and looked at the front again.

Wait a fucking minute.

I froze and stared at the kid in the photograph.

At his dark eyes. And his long arms and legs. And his big hands. And his cocky grin, complete with dimple.

It was a boy. They named him Charles, after his father and grandfather.

The floor quaked beneath my feet. Sirens went off in my head. My vision clouded over.

My empty glass clattered to the floor. I grabbed the back of a kitchen chair to keep my body from going down next.

I couldn't believe it. It was too crazy, too out there. Real life couldn't be this fucked up, could it?

But the proof was right there in front of me.

Chip Carswell was my son.

CHAPTER 21

April

ALL DAY LONG, I'd been in a state of panic.

What should I do? Tell Tyler right away? Wait until I saw him? Say nothing at all?

No. I *had* to tell him. But how was he going to take it? Would the realization throw him too far off balance? Would he panic and retreat? Or was I overreacting? Maybe once he got over the shock, he'd see the blessing in knowing his son. After all, he'd matured a lot since the day he'd asked me not to put his name on the birth certificate. He wasn't that freaked-out kid anymore. Maybe he'd see it as a sign from the universe that it was time to unlock that box and own that part of his identity.

Was it too much to hope for?

As Coco and I set up for that evening's huge wedding reception, I fretted endlessly. Picked up my phone a thousand times and set it down again without calling or messaging him. Imagined every possible response on his part, from shock and denial to pride and acceptance.

"You're sure you're okay?" Coco would ask every now and again, looking at me suspiciously.

"I'm fine," I lied.

But I wasn't. The knowledge was burning a hole in my brain, and it was growing bigger with every passing hour. The reception began, but I was distracted and withdrawn all night. People would come to me with easy questions or requests, and I'd stare at them blankly like they'd spoken a foreign language. Coco had to pick up a lot of the slack.

Eventually, she just sent me home.

"Look, I can handle this," she assured me. "You're not yourself tonight. Go home and get some rest."

"Are you sure?" I asked.

"Yes. Go."

"Thanks. I owe you one." But as I packed up to go, part of me dreaded the conversation ahead. As I drove home, the knots in my stomach pulled tighter. As I walked up to my own front door, I couldn't remember the last time I'd been so nervous. Actually, maybe I could—it felt a lot like going over to Tyler's house the night I told him I was pregnant.

That night had ended with me crying alone in my bed.

Please, God, let this one be different.

I let myself in, and the first thing I noticed was the silence. "Tyler?" I called, heading for the kitchen.

That's when I saw him sitting alone at the table, staring morosely at the surface.

No, not at the surface—at the photograph of Chip.

My stomach dropped, and I sucked in my breath, grabbing the wall for support. I'd thought the picture was in my bag with the letter. It must have slipped out when I'd tucked the envelope in my bag. I closed my eyes and swallowed.

"How long have you known?" he asked angrily.

I looked at him and took a breath. "Just today."

"Why didn't you tell me?"

"I was going to." I moved closer and set my bag on the table. "But I didn't want to do it over the phone, and I had to go to work."

"I feel like I've been hit head-on by a fucking freight

train." He shook his head. "You realize this is the lefty? The one I've been working with?"

"Oh, God." My stomach turned over again. "No, I didn't realize that. You never mentioned him by name, Tyler."

"Well, it's him."

I took the letter from my purse, telling myself to be patient. Of course he was going to be upset. "I opened this right before I left for work," I said, sliding the handwritten pages across the table. "The photo was inside."

He started to read, but then pushed them aside and stood up. "No," he snapped. "I don't want to know this. I don't want to know any of it. I don't want to know *him*, and I sure as hell don't want him to know me."

"I'm sorry," I said helplessly, my throat growing tight. "I didn't mean for you to find out this way, but Tyler—I didn't know! I had no idea he lived so close, or attended Central, or played baseball!"

"I'm not saying it's your fault."

"What *are* you saying?"

Agitated, he began to pace, one hand on the back of his neck. "I don't know what I'm saying. I just know I don't want to be Chip's father. He doesn't need me fucking up his life."

"Tyler, what are you talking about? You don't have to be his father!"

"Are you planning to keep it a secret, who you are to him?"

"No. That's kind of the point—I don't want to keep it buried anymore. But your name never has to come up."

He stopped moving and turned to face me, his expression incredulous. "And you think people won't figure it out? You think the media won't have a fucking field day with this? You think they'll *respect our privacy*?"

"How would anyone find out? The only people who know you're the biological father are my family, and I trust them."

"April, use your head! This is a small town. You're already

the subject of speculation because of me. As soon as people realize you're his birth mother, they'll immediately start doing the math and guessing at who the father was. The timeline works. They know we were friends." He pointed at the picture of Chip. "The kid looks exactly fucking like me. He's a lefty pitcher. It's not rocket science. It's third grade shit."

"What do you want me to do?" I cried, tears starting to fall. "I've worked so hard to get to this point, where I don't feel ashamed of this. Knowing him is important to me, I don't want to go backward!"

"I'm not saying you have to go backward," he said defensively. "I'm saying that I can't stay here. It's for his own good —and for yours. I've already booked a flight out."

"What? No! Tyler, don't go." Fighting tears, I went to him and placed my hands on his chest. "Let's talk about this. I know you're upset—I am too. But we can figure it out together."

"There's nothing to figure out. I'm leaving."

"But . . . but what about your coaching job?"

His expression was grim. "I already blew it."

"How?"

"I got into a fight with the asshole dad. I'm sure I'm already fired."

"Can they do that? Just because of an argument?"

"It was more than an argument, April. I punched the guy. In a public place. Yet another embarrassment. I don't even know why you'd *want* me to stay."

I felt like I was in quicksand. "Don't run away from this. We'll get through it, Tyler. I don't care what people say. Let them talk."

"You think that now, but I promise you, it wears you down until you hate getting up in the morning." He exhaled through his nose, jaw clenched tight. "And eventually you'll hate me for it."

"No, I won't! Can't we at least—"

"I'm sorry, April. This is all my fault." With that, he shouldered by me and headed for the door.

I followed him on trembling legs. "So that's it? You're just going to leave?"

"I've got no choice."

"But . . . what about us? What about all those things you imagined sharing with me? What about that life you envisioned?" Catching up with him, I grabbed his arm and yanked him around. "Don't you feel something for me?"

He swallowed, his expression tortured. "You know I do," he whispered. "I've never felt for *anyone* the things I feel for you."

I shook his arm. "Then look at me, Tyler. Look me in the eye and admit you *do* have a choice, and you're choosing to run away out of fear of what some stupid jerks will say. You're choosing them over me."

He shook his head, his eyes full of pain and longing. "I'm choosing to leave in order to spare you and Chip a lot of pain. I'm not who you think I am."

Tears streamed down my cheeks. "You know what? Maybe you're right. Maybe I have been seeing you all wrong. Because the man I see isn't a coward. He's not afraid to face whatever life throws at him. He's braver and stronger and better than this."

He struggled for words, his neck muscles taut. "I ruin everything, April. I don't live up to expectations. I'm doing this to protect you."

"Bullshit." I let go of his arm. "You're doing this to protect *you*—because you don't think you deserve to be loved. You're leaving because you don't want me or Chip or anyone else to see the real, flawed, imperfect version of you. You think all you had to offer anyone was a million-dollar arm, and since that's gone, you've got nothing to give. But you're wrong."

He was silent, his hands flexing.

"And you know what else? Never, not once in eighteen

years, did I feel you had betrayed or abandoned me when I was pregnant. You had to go after the life you wanted, and I understood. I wasn't part of it." I lifted my chin. "This time is different."

I saw his shoulders tense up, his jaw tic. For a moment, I thought he was going to take me in his arms, tell me I was right, kiss me and hold me and say he wasn't leaving. Say he would stay and face his fears. Say he would forgive himself and stop caring about what other people would say, because he was falling for me, and this time *was* different—this time he wanted me in his life. This time he would stay.

But he didn't. He turned away from me, opened the door, and stormed out, yanking it shut behind him.

CHAPTER 22

Tyler

I **LEFT** April's with her words lodged in my chest like arrows.

How could she think I didn't care for her or want her in my life? She was the best thing to happen to me in years. She'd made me laugh and smile and feel alive again. She'd given me hope.

But dammit—she didn't understand! She had no idea what it was like to fail, to disappoint people who believed in you, to be forced day after day to confront the fact that *this wasn't the life I was promised.*

And wouldn't that be exactly what she said to me when she discovered the truth about me? That I wasn't just flawed, I was defective? I wasn't just imperfect, I was broken?

I drove straight from April's to the airport, since I'd already gone to the hotel and packed up my bags after discovering the photo on her kitchen floor. My gut instinct had been to get the fuck out of this town *fast*, but once I'd booked a flight and checked out of my hotel, I realized I couldn't do it. I owed her a goodbye, at least. Even though I'd known it would be gut-wrenching to tell her I was leaving, I wanted to see her one last time.

Maybe someday she wouldn't hate me for it.

What happened wasn't your fault, Virgil had said yesterday in the dugout—not that I believed him. But if it wasn't, did that mean there was some other force working against me? Was it fate? The universe? God? Whatever it was, it was powerful enough that it had taken me down at the top of my game. It had beaten the unbeatable. Sunk the unsinkable. And it continued to work against me even now—the sleepless nights. The tireless media. The assholes in every corner bar and barber shop. I'd never be able to escape it. Why would she want to take that on?

And Chip. Jesus Christ. That poor kid had been through enough. There was no way I could handle him knowing who I was, and there was no way for me to act like everything was normal. I couldn't face him. I didn't want to. Staying out of his life had been the right decision the first time around, hadn't it? That's why leaving now was the right choice too.

But goddamn, it hurt like hell thinking I'd never see April smile at me again. Or hear her laugh. Or kiss her lips or smell her skin or put my hands in her hair. And I'd never forget the way she looked at me—like I'd ripped her heart out and crushed it—before I walked out the door.

I knew how she felt.

My heart was crushed too.

CHAPTER 23

April

HOW HAD I not seen this coming?

Devastated, I stood crying at the front door, waiting for my tears to run dry, but they refused. Eventually I turned off all the lights, locked the door, and dragged myself upstairs.

If you've never cried after a breakup while brushing your teeth, let me tell you—it's horrible. You're watching yourself in the mirror, blubbering with a mouth full of foamy toothpaste, thinking that this is the worst you've ever looked and it's no wonder he doesn't want you.

I put on my pajamas and curled up in my bed, going over the last ten days again and again in my head. What had I missed? Where had I gone wrong?

At first, I was convinced it had come out of nowhere, but the more I sifted through the events of the previous week—or at least the last twenty-four hours—the more I could see that it hadn't.

The restaurant debacle. The nightmare. The news story. Losing his coaching offer. Discovering Chip—his lefty—was his son.

Admittedly, it was a lot.

But he didn't have to run away! And he wouldn't have, not if he felt for me what I felt for him.

That was the sad truth of it. He hadn't felt what I felt. He hadn't imagined a future for us, not really. He'd just been playing with an idea. Playing with my heart. He'd told me right from the start he wasn't interested in a serious relationship, hadn't he? Nothing that would lead to love, marriage, a family.

And I'd been so blinded by the idea of him wanting me, by the seductive notion that I was enough to change his mind, to break through his walls, to show him his best was yet to come . . . well, it wasn't the first time I'd been irresponsible with Tyler Shaw.

But it would be the last.

I'd taken a risk opening my heart to him, and when it was time for him to take a risk for me, he'd bolted.

I deserved more.

The truth of it was right there in front of me, and yet . . . I cried for him all night.

In the morning, I texted my sisters.

Hey. Sorry for the 6 a.m. text, but I need a hug. Anyone who can come over for coffee this morning is encouraged to bring tissues.

Within minutes, responses were coming in.

Meg: OMG I will be there as soon as I can.

Frannie: Shoot! I'm at work already! Are you okay?

Me: I don't know.

Chloe: OMW.

Sylvia: I have to get Whitney from her sleepover at 8 and then I'll come over!

Forty-five minutes later, I was sitting across from Meg and Chloe at my kitchen table, telling them the entire story. When I got to the part about the letter and the photograph, they both gasped.

"Can we see it?" Chloe asked.

Nodding, I got up from my chair and went over to the kitchen counter where I'd placed the envelope, letter and picture tucked back inside. I placed it on the table in front of them, then went and poured myself another cup of coffee.

A second later I heard one of them gasp. "Oh my God! It's Tyler in high school! But with your skin!" Meg exclaimed.

"And Dad's ears!" added Chloe.

I would have smiled if I could. "Yep."

They were silent as they read the letter, and I made my way back to the table. I studied their faces as they read—Meg's brow furrowed and serious, Chloe's jaw hanging open in disbelief.

When they finished, they looked up at me. "Wow," breathed Meg. "That's . . . a lot to take in."

"God, April. You must be just—I don't even know what you must feel." Chloe shook her head. "He's been right here. For months. At our old school. Playing for Tyler's old team."

"And Tyler has been working with him one-on-one," I told them.

Meg sucked in her breath. "Jesus. Does he know yet?"

I nodded, plucking a tissue from the box on the table. "Yes. This is the part where I might have screwed up. I opened the letter right before going to work. I was already kind of upset because of that stupid news story. Not so much for me, but for Tyler, and because Cloverleigh and our family had been dragged into it. But learning about Chip was a whole other level of *holy shit, what is my life?*"

"I bet," Chloe said.

"I sort of gave myself the day to figure out how to tell him," I went on. "I knew he was going to freak out—he'd already made it clear he was not into meeting his biological son, although he was supportive of me wanting to establish contact. He understood why it was important to me."

"Chloe said he'd made the decision to move back?" Meg asked.

"Yeah. It's been so crazy I haven't really had time to update you guys. But yes—he was planning to move back." I felt the tears coming again. "Until last night."

"What happened?" Chloe sat up taller in her seat.

"I'd given him a key to my place so he could come over while I was at work. I knew I'd be late, and I didn't want him to have to wait up if he was tired. I'd taken the letter with me to work, but apparently the photograph fell out, and he saw it on the kitchen floor when he got here. On the back is Chip's full name—he figured it out."

"Wow," Meg said again. "That had to be a shock."

"What did he do?" Chloe asked.

"Exactly what I feared. Freaked out. Went back to his hotel and packed his bags. Booked a flight back to California."

"He left without even saying good*bye*?" Meg looked shocked.

"No, he was here when I got home. He said goodbye." The memory of it had my tears spilling over, and I blew my nose. "He said a lot of things."

Chloe reached across the table and rubbed my arm. "Like what?"

"He's scared. He thinks if he doesn't leave, people will put it together—if I don't hide the fact that I'm Chip's birth mother, he says people will do the math and figure out he's the father. We're all over the news together."

"In all honesty, he's probably right," Meg said gently, picking up the photograph again. "The resemblance is *really* strong. It's a small town. And everyone knows you guys were close back then."

"I guess you're right," I said, reaching for another tissue.

"And he just isn't ready for that. He doesn't want Chip to know. He says he'll just mess up Chip's life. He thinks he ruins everything he touches."

"And what do *you* think?" Chloe asked.

"I think he's using that fear as an excuse."

"How so?" Meg tilted her head.

I blew my nose again before going on. "Deep down, he's so scarred from the way his career ended, he thinks he's a failure as a man. As a human being. He thinks he can never live up to anyone's expectations of him, so he's refusing to even try. He thinks I don't see the real him. But I *do*, you guys," I wept. "I *do* see the real him. And he saw the real me. I thought he felt the way I did. I thought we had something worth fighting for. How could I have been so wrong?" I folded my arms on the table, dropped my head onto them, and cried.

Chloe rubbed my arm. "I'm sorry, honey. Relationships are so hard."

"You know, Noah and I went through this," Meg said softly. "When I first mentioned moving back from D.C., he freaked out. He tried to pretend it was because he didn't want to be in a serious relationship, but really, it was just fear."

"That's right," said Chloe. "Wasn't he worried about his brother?"

"Yes. He'd always felt guilty because Asher had cerebral palsy, and he didn't. They were twins, and he knew Asher's CP was likely caused by a lack of oxygen to the brain during birth. So anything that Asher struggled with that came easy to Noah—from walking to talking to girls—he felt guilty about. From a young age, he had it in his head that he didn't deserve things like becoming a husband and father. As if denying himself the things he wanted deep down was the right punishment for being born without CP."

"God, that's so sad," I said, picking up my head and grabbing another tissue.

"It *was* sad," Meg agreed. "He needed to work through it, and I had to give him the time and space to do it. Maybe Tyler just needs time to work through this."

"I don't know," I said miserably. "He seemed pretty determined when he left here last night. I got the feeling it was goodbye for good."

Sylvia showed up a little while later, and I went through it all again, complete with more tears and soggy tissues.

After two pots of coffee, my sisters said they had to get going, but each of them hugged me tightly before they left. "Don't give up," Sylvia whispered fiercely in my ear. "If you love him, don't give up."

Frannie called and said she was so sorry she'd been unable to get away, but she was dying to talk to me. "Can you meet up later?"

"Maybe," I said. "I do have tonight off."

"Then come over," she pleaded. "You shouldn't be alone."

"Okay," I said. "Thanks."

I spent the rest of the day doing laundry, cleaning my condo, and trying not to think about Tyler. But it was impossible—everything reminded me of him, from the scent of his cologne clinging to my sheets to the bottle of whiskey he'd left on my kitchen counter. The toothpaste tube. The Netflix remote. The stairs. The couch. The bathtub.

I racked my brain, wondering what, if anything, I could have done differently yesterday to prevent Tyler from leaving.

But no matter which way I pulled at the threads, the end result was always a knot I couldn't untangle. People *would* talk—it was a fact. And Tyler was still a hot news commodity. If people did figure it out, my life *would* be affected—and possibly Chip's too . . . I could see the headline now. *Baseball's Hottest Head Case Has Secret Son.*

We'd face social media blow-ups and news media scrutiny and judgment from people around town about the "scandal." People would stare. They would gossip. They might say ugly, hurtful things that made me feel bad about myself.

Had Tyler been right to leave?

At one point, I sat down at the kitchen table to work on the toast I had to give at the retirement party, but I ended up reading the letter from Robin Carswell over and over again. Staring at Chip's picture.

That grin of his took the edge off some of my sadness. If there was a silver lining in all this, it was that I'd still get to meet my son. I'd focus on that.

I opened my laptop and composed an email to Robin.

Dear Robin,

Thank you so much for writing me back. What a shock to realize we all live so close! I am very excited about meeting Chip, and I loved seeing his photograph and hearing about his interests. He's so handsome, and it sounds like he's also smart and kind and talented. You must be very proud.

I was so sorry to learn of Chuck's passing, and I'm sure the last year has been difficult. If this feels like the wrong time to add to your emotional burden by introducing me to your son, please let me know. I do not want to make things harder for you.

If you would like to discuss things over the phone, my number is below.

Sincerely,

April Sawyer

I hit send and closed my laptop.

CHAPTER 24

Tyler

AS SOON AS I got back to my house in San Diego, I took a sleeping pill, crashed into bed, and slept hard. When I woke up, it was already getting dark outside. I dug one of Anna's meal containers out of the freezer, microwaved it according to her instructions, and ate it sitting alone at my kitchen island.

When I was done, I took a shower, threw on some clean sweats, and fell onto my couch. I knew I should call my sister, and David Dean had been trying to get ahold of me too, but I couldn't handle talking to either one of them yet. They'd only make me feel worse.

I sent Sadie a text saying I was sorry for leaving so fast and telling her I'd call her in a day or so. I sent one to David Dean apologizing again for the incident at the Jolly Pumpkin and saying I'd decided to return to California after all, so the school didn't have to worry about their offer. I wished him well for the rest of the season and asked him to please tell the team how much I'd enjoyed working with them.

Every time I thought about Chip Carswell, I felt sick.

It wasn't that I didn't have, deep down, a kind of pride that he was my biological son. I did. I couldn't help it. He was a great kid—smart, talented, strong, respectful, popular. What more could any father ask for in a son? But I *wasn't* his father, and it felt wrong to think of myself that way. I'd forfeited that privilege when I'd walked away from him. From April. From the whole situation. I'd justified it the way I always justified everything back then—what mattered was my baseball career, and anything that threatened it had to be cut off at the source.

Including my feelings.

That wasn't being a coward, was it? That was being a man. At least, that's what I'd been raised to believe.

But what about now?

I reached for the remote and turned on the television. I needed a distraction. I'd go crazy if I let myself start rethinking everything. The bottom line was, they were better off without me.

Without even thinking about it, I searched for Kids Baking Championship and binged an entire season.

I missed April so much it hurt.

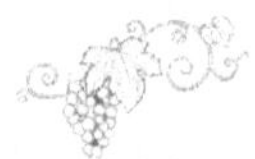

I stayed that way for eight straight days.

Alone. Miserable. Depressed.

I ignored my phone and never once checked email. I even told Anna not to come. I didn't want to see anyone, talk to anyone, or answer any questions. When I ran out of meals in the freezer, I had my groceries delivered, cooked my own food (okay, I mostly microwaved shitty frozen entrees), and did my own laundry. Of course, I turned a load of whites pink because I didn't realize a new red T-shirt had gotten in the washer with them, and I remembered the night April had scolded me about separating my colors. My first instinct was to take a picture of my new pink socks and undershirts and tell her she was right, but of course, I couldn't do that.

And I couldn't call her and tell her that the spaghetti sauce I made from a jar didn't taste right. And that my bed felt too big without her next to me. And that I'd heard that Stevie Wonder song and—swear to God—started air-dancing with an imaginary partner, turning her out and bringing her back in just like she'd taught me.

On Friday, one week after I left April, I went up to my cabin in the mountains, but the silence and solitude there no longer felt peaceful to me—they felt stifling. I couldn't stand being alone with my thoughts in such a small space. The voices in my head argued constantly.

You did the right thing. She's better off.

You're a dumbass. Go get her back.

You're a head case. Quit doubting your decisions.

You're a chickenshit. If she doesn't care what people say, why should you?

I left after just one night.

Back in San Diego Saturday afternoon, I swam fifty laps in my pool, and the physical activity helped a little. I was just pulling myself out of the water when I heard a voice.

"Good, you're alive. You asshole."

I straightened up to see my sister standing there on the patio. "Sadie?"

She ran straight for me, and threw her arms around my neck, soaking herself. "I was so worried about you. I thought maybe something had happened."

I hugged her back, amazed at how good the human contact felt after a week of isolation. "Sorry."

"You should be." She let me go and stood back. "Now that I know you're okay, I'm super pissed at you."

"Look, I can explain. I—"

"How could you leave without saying goodbye?"

I frowned and moved past her, grabbing my towel off a chair. "I had to get out fast."

"Why?"

I dried off and wrapped the towel around my hips. "It's complicated."

"Lucky for you, I've got all night."

"You flew all the way out here for *one night*?"

"How else was I supposed to make sure you were okay? You weren't answering texts or calls. I'm just glad I had the code to the privacy gate or I'd still be sitting out there in my rental car."

"I'm okay," I said. "I just needed some time by myself."

"You mean you needed time to mope," she clarified with a sniff. "What happened to your coaching job? What happened to a house on the water? What happened to red hair and dimples?"

"That was never going to work," I said. "It was a stupid idea."

"What happened to no more hiding out?" she pushed.

"What do you want me to say, Sadie?" I ran a hand through my wet hair. "I changed my mind about it. About all of it."

"But *why*? There must have been a reason."

"There was. There *is*."

"Well?" She put her hands behind her back like a patient teacher. "I'm waiting."

Exhaling, I shook my head. "Fine. I'll tell you. But I'm not going back there, okay? So don't try to convince me."

"Okay," she said. "I won't."

She followed me inside, and I went up to my room to throw on dry clothes. When I got back down, she was sitting at my kitchen island drinking a bottle of water. I grabbed a beer and sat next to her, spilling the entire story.

"Wow," she said. "So you knew him the whole time?"

"The whole time."

"That's so crazy. A lefty pitcher."

"And he looks just like me. I almost passed out when I saw that picture."

"I bet." She took a drink of water. "But I still don't see why you left."

I got off the stool and went to the pantry for a bag of chips. "Sadie, I just explained it. I left to protect them."

"Really?" Disbelief colored the word.

"Really." I opened the bag and leaned back against the counter.

"Protect them from what?"

I rolled my eyes. "From the media shitstorm. From gossip. From knowing what it's like to be stared at and whispered about."

"How do you know they care?"

I crunched on a chip while April's words echoed in my head. *I don't care what people say. Let them talk.* Would Chip have felt the same way?

No. What eighteen-year-old ball player wants to learn his biological father is a MLB pitcher . . . only to learn *oh, it's* that *one.* The fuckup. The has-been. The choke joke. He'd want nothing to do with me.

"They would care," I insisted. "Even if they thought they wouldn't, they would. It's embarrassing."

"Hmm. Because I don't think you left to protect them. *I* think," she went on, "you left to avoid dealing with your feelings."

"What feelings?" I snapped.

"The same ones you shut out your entire life. The ones you felt you could never show because they were a detriment to your macho reputation. Shit, there's probably a little of everything in there by now. Love? Fear? Compassion? Vulnerability? Shame? A secret longing to be a dad?"

I squinted at her. "Are you fucking crazy? I don't want to be a dad."

"Maybe not." She shrugged. "But you were the one who told me what an expert you were at shutting out anything you didn't want to feel for thirty-odd years. And I'm not saying I blame you—that habit served you well in baseball, maybe even in life. And it isn't just going to go away. You have to consciously decide to grapple with those feelings."

"I have no idea what you're talking about." Although part of me was afraid she was making a little too much sense.

"I suppose I could be wrong. I mean, maybe you don't really care for April."

"I do care for her!" I shouted, gesturing so wildly that chips flew out of the bag. "I care a lot, that's why I left!"

"You broke her heart to show her how much you care?" Sadie blinked at me. "Sorry. Maybe it's the pregnancy hormones, but something about that is not making sense."

I reached into the bag and grabbed another handful of chips. "You said you weren't going to argue with me."

"No, I didn't. I said I wasn't going to try to convince you to come back, but my fingers were crossed anyway, so it doesn't count."

I spoke slowly through clenched teeth. "I'm not going back, Sadie. I can't. And I don't want to talk about it anymore." She was making me second-guess myself. I hated that feeling.

She sighed. "Okay. Fine. You can stay out here eating chips in your castle with its fancy gate and high walls and security cameras and never have to let anyone in ever again. But it seems like an awfully lonely way to spend the rest of your life."

"It's my decision," I said stubbornly, shoving the chips in my mouth.

Her smile was sad. "Yes. It is."

We ordered dinner in, and after Sadie closed the door behind the delivery guy, she gestured to a large cardboard box sitting in the front hall. "Is that the box from my attic?"

"Oh yeah. I forgot about it."

"How'd you get it here?" she asked.

"Actually, this is kind of funny. I forgot it was in the back of my rental car until I got to the airport to turn it in. The guy at the desk happened to be the same one who was there when I rented it. Steve."

"Oh?"

"He offered to ship it to me, and I said okay. Gave him a big tip."

She laughed. "Nice. Did it just get here today?"

"A few days ago. After we eat, we can look through it if you want." *Anything* was better than listening to her analyze my feelings—even looking at plastic trophies.

But actually, it turned out the box held some neat things. Notes my dad had taken during early coaching sessions with Virgil—things I'd internalized and had repeated to Chip. *There's an art to the mechanics. Focus on the process and not the result. You have to trust your pitches.* A few of my favorite baseball cards, some of which were signed by the players.

"If you have a boy and he's into baseball, he can have these," I said to Sadie, who was kneeling next to me in the living room, looking through old photos.

"What if I have a *girl* who's into baseball?"

I flicked her earlobe with a card. "She can have them too."

"Hey, look at this one! I think I took it."

I leaned over and saw a picture of April and me at the kitchen table. "Let me see that." Grabbing it out of her hands, I studied it more closely. April was sitting how she always did, on her knees, her feet bare, her elbows on the table. She had a pen in her hand and her lower lip caught between her teeth, like she was concentrating hard on whatever she was writing. I, on the other hand, was looking directly at the camera, tilting the chair back on two legs and wearing my usual confident smirk. My hair was wet, as if I'd just gotten out of the shower.

"Here's another one." Sadie handed me a second photo, which looked as if it had been taken right after the first. I appeared exactly the same, but in this one, April was looking at me with undisguised adoration, still biting her bottom lip. Sadie giggled. "Her crush on you is pretty obvious there."

"Yeah." God, I missed her. She was never going to look at me that way ever again, and it was all my fault.

"Oh, look at this one of you, Dad, and Virgil Dean!" She showed me the picture she'd found, and I had to smile.

"That was the day of the draft. I don't know who was more excited, Dad or Virgil."

"I heard he's in the hospital. Any word on how he's doing?"

My gut clenched. "What?"

"Something about his heart maybe?"

"Why didn't you tell me?" I jumped to my feet and started looking for my phone.

"I'm sorry, I thought you knew. Don't you talk to his son?"

"I haven't. Not since I left." I found my phone and started scrolling through my texts. Of course, there were a bunch from David, which I'd ignored because I'd thought he was contacting me about the incident. God, how self-centered could I be?

He'd left a voicemail too, which I immediately listened to. "Hey Tyler, it's David Dean. It's, uh, Wednesday. I just wanted to let you know that Dad's in the hospital after a bad fall. We think he had some mini strokes earlier in the week, but they're still running tests. He's doing okay, but they're worried about a bigger stroke in the near future, so they want to keep him here. Anyway, he's in and out of consciousness, but he was asking for you at one point. I know you already went back to California, but maybe you could call him or something. Well, just wanted to let you know. Give me a call if you'd like an update."

"Shit," I said aloud.

"What is it?"

"It's Virgil. He had some mini strokes, and they're worried about a bigger one. He's in the hospital, and he's doing okay —at least, he was on Wednesday when David called me." But it was Saturday already, and a lot could happen in four days. "I need to call him back."

"Definitely. But it's late out there. Almost eleven."

"You're right. Crap." I grimaced. "It'll have to wait until tomorrow."

Sadie continued pawing through the box for a few minutes, but before long she was yawning. "I guess I'll go to bed. Is my room free?"

"Of course." I showed her to the guest room, which Anna always kept perfectly made up, even though the only person who ever came to see me was Sadie, and she hadn't visited in nearly a year. "Need anything?"

"Nope." She set her shoulder bag on the floor and gave me a hug. "Just this."

I didn't sleep well, and before Sadie was even up, I went down to the kitchen, made a cup of coffee, took it out by the pool and called David Dean. He picked up right away.

"Hello?"

"David, it's Tyler Shaw."

"Tyler. Good to hear from you."

"How's your dad?"

"He's okay. Had a decent day yesterday."

"Just decent?"

"Well, he's ornery as hell about being in the hospital. Wants to be at home."

"Sure." I took a sip of coffee. "You said he asked for me?"

"Yeah, he did. He was a little incoherent that day, but we clearly heard him saying your name and requesting—not too politely—that you get your ass to practice."

I had to laugh. "Sounds like Coach."

"We think he was confused about what year it was, but he was definitely looking for you." He paused. "If you were thinking of paying him a visit, I'd make it sooner rather than later."

My heart lurched. "Is it that serious?"

"Yes. He's got congestive heart failure."

"Oh. I didn't realize." I made my decision in a snap. "Of course I'll come. I'll be there as soon as I can."

"Thanks. I think it would mean a lot to him." Another pause. "You know, Tyler, I'm not sure what happened before you left, but the team was really disappointed to find out you'd gone."

I stiffened. "Sorry. I just . . . wanted to get out fast after what happened. I never should have thrown a punch at Brock."

"Nah, you shouldn't have, but he deserved it. Nearly every other parent on the team reached out to me and said they fully support you. Even a couple of them who were there when you hit him."

"Seriously?"

"Yeah. They'd like you to come back. The offer's still there if you're interested."

"That's . . . that's really cool of those parents. I had the impression some of them were talking to the press because they didn't want me there."

"As far as I know, only one gave an interview like that. And I bet you can guess which one."

"Brock?"

"Yep."

I wavered for a second, then came to my senses. "I appreciate the offer, but I have to decline. I'm going to jump on a plane as soon as I can to come visit though."

"Okay. Safe travels."

We hung up and I lay down in one of the chairs overlooking my pool, bare feet crossed at the ankles. I wondered what April was doing right now, if she was walking at the track or getting ready for work, or maybe having breakfast at her sister's café. Was she mad at me? Did she miss me like I missed her? Did she think about how close we'd come to being happy together and feel like I'd let her down?

How long would it be before thoughts of her didn't fill my every waking moment?

A few minutes later, Sadie came out in sweatpants and a T-shirt and stretched out on the chair next to me, a cup of tea in her hands. "Morning."

"Morning."

"Did you talk to David?"

"Yeah."

"How's Virgil?"

"Not good."

"I'm sorry to hear it." She looked over at me. "You've got some seriously dark circles under those eyes. Did you sleep at all?"

"Not really." I hesitated. "But it's not all about Virgil. I'm fucking miserable, Sadie."

"I'm sorry."

"I miss her. I really fucking miss her."

"I know. I can tell. Why don't you—"

"Because I can't, Sadie. I don't know what possessed me to think I could in the first place. I'm not the guy who stays. I'm the guy who leaves."

She sighed and looked out at the pool again. "Well, it's beautiful here. I can see why you like it so much."

"I don't like it that much."

She looked at me again. "So why are you still here?"

I shook my head, feeling more lost than ever. "I don't know."

Prepared for another psychoanalysis or lecture about repression or even just a good shaming about how I wasn't the person she wished I was, I was surprised when all she did was reach over and take my hand.

Surprised and grateful.

"I'll fly back with you if I can," I said after a while.

"Really?"

"Yes, but don't get too excited. I'm only going to see Virgil."

She smiled sweetly. "Of course you are."

I rolled my eyes. "Sadie."

"What?"

"It's temporary."

"I know."

"I'm not staying."

"I didn't say anything."

"I haven't changed my mind."

"I never said you did."

"Okay. Just so you understand."

She sipped her tea and looked out at the pool, that grin still on her lips. "I understand completely."

Turned out I couldn't get on a flight until Tuesday, but I checked in with David each day, relieved to hear there was no turn for the worse.

Seated in first class, ignoring the woman next to me trying to flirt, I put on some headphones and watched a few TED talks, then gave in and watched Bull Durham for probably the five hundredth time. The funny thing was, it's my favorite baseball movie ever, but I hadn't seen it in a long time—maybe ten years. In the past, I'd always identified with Nuke, the hotshot minor-league rookie pitcher who needs to learn discipline and control before he's called up to the majors. But this time around, I saw myself in Crash, the mentor. He's a catcher, not a pitcher, but he sees the game differently than Nuke does, because he's been around it so long. And when he's let go because the team wants to bring up "some young catcher," I felt the sad punch to the gut as much as Crash did. I knew what it was like to feel you weren't worth anything anymore.

Even funnier, I used to hate the ending—the cheesy porch scene with the stupid eighties background music, the fucking dancing in the living room—but now I found myself watching with new eyes, listening with new ears. When Crash says, "I just want to *be*," I fucking got it.

But the dancing still made me cringe.

I hadn't checked a bag, so once my flight landed, I went straight to the rental car desk.

"Shaw!" Steve said happily. "You're back!"

"I'm back." And I was actually kind of glad to see him.

What the hell was happening to me?

I called David, and he said the sooner I could get to the hospital, the better, because visiting hours were nearly over. He texted me the room number as soon as we hung up, and I went straight there.

I'd been expecting Coach to look weak, but he was even frailer than I'd imagined. He looked shriveled and pale, and his breathing was labored. His eyes were closed. He wore a hospital gown, which was embarrassing, but the covers were pulled up high on his chest. David was sitting in a chair by the side of the bed and stood when I entered the room.

"Hey," he said, extending his hand.

"Hey." I shook it and glanced at his father. "How's he doing?"

David shrugged. "He's okay today. A little confused here and there, but physically okay. My mom finally left to get some decent food and rest."

"Tell her to bring *me* some decent food," grumbled Virgil. His eyes were open now but a little unfocused. "The food is awful here. I'm not confused about *that*."

"Hey, Coach," I said, glad to see some of his spirit was intact.

"That you, Shaw?"

"It's me."

"You been skipping practice."

"Sorry, Coach. I'm here now."

"Good. I need a word."

"I'll give you guys some time," David said. "Tyler, want anything from the coffee shop?"

"No, thanks." I gave him a wave and sat down in the chair he'd vacated. "What can I do for you, Coach?"

"Can you spring me?"

I grinned. "Nope."

He sighed heavily, closing his eyes. "Figures."

"You doing okay?"

One eye popped open again. "I look okay to you?"

"I've seen you look better," I admitted.

"Yuh." His eyes closed again, and he was silent for so long that I thought he might have fallen asleep. I was almost about to doze off myself when he spoke. "I was talking to your dad about you."

I was about to ask when, but realized A, he might not even be able to answer that, and B, it really didn't matter. "Oh yeah? What did he have to say?"

"He's worried."

Present tense. Interesting. I shifted in my chair. "About what?"

"He thinks maybe he pushed you too hard to be the best."

"Nah."

That one eye opened again. "You gonna let me talk?"

"Yes. Sorry."

"He said he didn't want you to feel like baseball was the only thing that mattered. Because even the best careers only last so long. There are things that matter more and last longer."

"Yeah, we never really got a chance to have that conversation."

"We're having it now, aren't we?"

"I guess."

He appeared to go back to sleep, and I felt restless. A couple minutes later he spoke again. "You asked me why you got the chance to prove yourself and he didn't."

"Huh?"

"The last time you came to practice. You asked me that. About your dad."

"Oh. Right."

"But he did prove himself, didn't he?"

My first thought was that Virgil was confused again. What I'd *meant* was that my father had loved baseball like I did, but he hadn't gotten the chance to prove himself where it really mattered—*on the field,* in front of thousands of screaming fans and television cameras and the best players in the game. But before I opened my mouth, I realized what he meant.

My dad had proved himself where it really mattered—*as a dad*.

On his own, with two children. Working his fingers to the bone. Making sure we were housed and fed and clothed, and beyond that, loved. I'd always felt loved. It had given me the confidence to chase my dreams.

"Holy shit," I whispered. "Holy shit! You're right, Coach. He did prove himself when and where and how it mattered most."

Virgil said nothing, but he nodded. Closed his eyes.

"It's not just about the ballfield. It's not about strikeouts or home runs or the speed of a fastball. In the end, it's about who's there for you, and why. Through the highs and lows, the wins and the losses. It's about the people who love and support you through anything because of who you *are*, not what you do. It's about family."

Virgil began to snore.

I stood up. "Sorry, Coach. I have to go."

On my way down the hall, I nearly crashed into David, who was carrying a cardboard cup of coffee. "Hey," he said. "Did he insult you?"

"No, just the opposite. He gave me the best advice he's ever given me!" I shouted as I raced for the elevator.

David laughed. "Well, good!"

I punched the down button until the doors opened, barreled into the elevator, and hit L.

As it began to descend, I prayed that who I was would be enough to make up for what I'd done.

CHAPTER 25

April

AT MY NEXT THERAPY APPOINTMENT, I told Prisha about everything. By the time I got to the end, I was pretty sure she was going to need to call her own therapist.

"Well. That is a lot to handle in a very short amount of time," she said. "How are you doing?"

"Better," I said. It had been ten days since Tyler had left my house, and I'd managed to get through yesterday without any tears. That was better, right?

"Are you really? Or are you saying that to please me?"

I winced. "Probably a little of both. I'm still really sad, to be honest. I know he was only here a short time, but we came so far so fast—at least it felt like it to me. We were so open with each other, and it just felt so right. When he said he wanted to move here, I guess I got carried away. I envisioned this whole future for us."

"It's natural to be excited about a new relationship."

"Yeah, but in my case I definitely stopped listening to anything I didn't want to hear. He was up front right from the start that he didn't want a serious relationship. He never lied to me. He just sort of . . ." I shrugged as Tyler's words echoed through my head. "Led me to believe he was ready for something he wasn't."

Prisha nodded.

"And I've been so hard on myself, wondering how I could have gotten him so wrong. But the thing is . . . I know what I felt. I know we had that connection. And I know we could have been good together if he could get over his fear."

"What's he afraid of?"

I'd thought this through a million times. "What it comes down to, I think, is that he grew up believing baseball was all he had to offer the world. And when he suddenly couldn't offer it anymore, he shut down. He couldn't forgive himself. It's like he believes deep down he needs to be punished for failing the game or his fans or his father—even the media! He hates the headlines and the speculation about him, but the *reason* it bothers him so much is that *he believes it*. So he's afraid to let himself be happy. Find love. Find acceptance. He doesn't think he deserves it. And I couldn't convince him otherwise."

"April, it wasn't your job to convince him otherwise. He has to reach that place on his own."

"I know." I felt a deluge of tears coming. "I just wanted to be able to help."

"Of course. You care for him."

I nodded, fighting the sob trying to get out. "And it's hard for me to accept that he's gone, but I have to."

Prisha waited for me to compose myself, nudging the tissue box closer to me. I thanked her, took a few deep breaths, and blew my nose. "Sorry. I'm okay. I think."

Smiling sympathetically, she checked her notes. "Tell me how things are moving along with your biological son."

"Chip." My stomach jumped, and I put a hand over it. "We're meeting on Saturday at his house. Three o'clock."

"Are you scared? Excited? All of the above?"

"All of the above, definitely," I said, laughing nervously.

"But I have realistic expectations. I know that meeting him might not provide immediate relief from all my adoption guilt or solve all my intimacy issues, but I'm hoping that over time, knowing him is part of my journey to being happy."

She smiled. "I have a feeling you're going to meet those expectations, and then some. You should be very proud of yourself, April. You've shown a lot of courage and strength. You took exactly the kind of risk that's necessary for real intimacy, and I think you experienced it, even if it didn't end the way you'd hoped."

I sniffed and smiled sadly. "Yeah."

"And was it worth the risk?"

I was tempted to say no. To say I wished Tyler Shaw had never set foot back in this town. To say I'd have been better off if I could just erase the last month from my life. But deep down, I didn't feel that way.

He might have let me down hard, but Tyler Shaw had shown me I was capable of letting someone in.

"Yes," I said. "It was worth the risk."

I walked out of Prisha's office feeling a little better. She always asked the tough questions and could sometimes make harsh observations when I was trying to avoid something, but she gave beautiful compliments too. She strengthened my courage, my confidence, and my compassion.

And in the next five minutes, I'd need all three.

Because when I pulled up at home, sitting there on my front porch was none other than Tyler Shaw.

I knew it was him right away. Besides the ridiculously tall and commanding body, who else put those butterflies in my belly? Made my breath get stuck in my lungs? Set my pulse on high alert? He watched me put the car in park and came to open the driver's side door.

My heart was hammering away, and I was almost afraid to stand up for fear my legs would buckle. But then I remembered what Prisha had said. I could do this.

I got out of the car and looked up at him. The sun hadn't quite set yet, but he wasn't wearing his sunglasses for once. Or a hat. I could see his eyes and his expression clearly, and he looked . . . happy?

"What are you doing here?" I asked.

He pushed the car door shut behind me. "Can I come in?"

"I don't think so."

"Please, April." He went to take my hand, but I pulled it away. "Sorry. I get it—I won't touch you, I promise. I just want to talk."

"About what?" I said. "You made your point ten days ago. I heard it loud and clear when you walked out the door."

He nodded. "I know. But I think I was wrong."

My eyebrows jerked up. "You *think*?" Immediately I started walking toward my front door.

"April, wait!" He ran ahead of me, hopping up onto my porch and spreading his arms out, like I wasn't allowed on it. "I'm sorry. You were always better than me at putting my thoughts into words. And I'm still working things out in my head. But I—I have something I need to say to you." He frowned. "I just don't know exactly what it is yet."

I stayed where I was, two steps below him. "Okay."

"Okay, what?"

I shifted my weight to one hip, wishing I didn't find his frown so adorable. "I'll give you a few minutes."

He looked relieved. "Thanks."

"So what are you trying to work out?"

"Well, it starts with Virgil. He's in the hospital."

"Oh, no! Is he okay?"

"Yes and no. He's got congestive heart failure, and they're

worried about a stroke, but he was able to have a conversation with me—sort of."

"Is that why you're back in town?"

He hesitated. "Also yes and no. It's the reason my *head* told me to get on a plane, but I think there were other reasons too. Reasons I wasn't ready to admit."

Gooseflesh swept across my back, but I held my tongue. I wasn't going to put words in his mouth tonight. He was on his own.

"Aren't you going to ask what the other reasons are?"

I shook my head. "Nope."

"Okay. Shit." He ran a hand through his hair. "This is hard. Words are *hard*."

"Yep."

"The other reasons are about you. And kind of about Sadie and maybe even about my dad and David and possibly the Central High School baseball team—"

"Okay, focus." I held up one hand. I couldn't help it. "What do all those people mean? What do they have in common?"

He came down the steps and took me by the shoulders. "They're family to me. They feel like family." His hands slid into my hair. "You feel like family to me."

Oh, how I loved his words. They were like hot chocolate sauce over vanilla ice cream, and they melted something inside me. But I had to be tough. "So what? So you've realized family is more than blood. What now?"

He frowned again, taking his hands off me. "Okay, give me a second. Maybe it's not just that I've realized you feel like family. Because Sadie has always been family, and I've lived apart from her since I was eighteen. It's something more."

My pulse kicked up. I bit my lip.

He struggled with what he wanted to say for a full fifteen seconds, so long that I was tempted to prompt him with words. Had he missed me? Was that it?

"It's home," he blurted.

"Home?"

"Yes." He looked relieved to have found the right words. "That night at dinner, you said this thing, and I guess it must have stayed in the back of my mind. You said home wasn't a place."

"I did?" I tilted my head. "I don't remember that."

"Well, maybe you didn't say it wasn't a place. But you said something about it being the feeling that you know you belong somewhere. You miss it when you're gone. You're the most *you* at home."

"Okay . . ."

He took me by the shoulders again. "Sorry, I'm bad at the no-touching thing. But that's what it is. When I'm with you, I know where I belong. I never want to be anywhere else. I miss you when you're not there. I'm the most *me* when I'm with you—because you're the only one who sees the real me." He took a breath. "Wherever you are is home to me. And I don't want to leave home again."

My throat had been tight ever since he'd started talking, and now it threatened to close completely. Which was fine because I didn't know what to say anyway. Thank goodness I was holding onto my keys and bag, because if I hadn't had something to clutch, I might have thrown my arms around him or let him kiss me—and I needed to take it easy this time.

"Did I say it wrong?" Tyler's expression was concerned.

I smiled and shook my head, trying to swallow.

"What's the matter? Why aren't you talking?"

I fanned my face as my eyes teared up.

"Oh." He looked relieved as he squeezed my upper arms. "I wish I could hug you."

"A hug might be okay," I whispered, desperately trying to avoid melting down in front of him. Or blowing up. Or giving in.

He wrapped me up in his warm, strong embrace, and I

pressed my cheek against his chest, allowing myself a small moment of comfort. Maybe he meant it this time. Maybe it would be okay. Maybe he would stay.

But he'd have to work to win back my trust—and *this* time, we were taking it slow.

When I felt certain a breakdown of some sort was not forthcoming, I stepped back from him, pushing against his chest. "Okay. I need to say a few things. I've missed you too— so much I've cried more in the last ten days than I did in all of middle school, and I cried *a lot* in middle school."

He pressed his lips together and braced himself, like he knew what was coming.

"I beat myself up every single night, wondering if I'd imagined the things you said, the plans we'd made, the way you looked at me. The things you said to me right before you left stuck—I thought maybe I made up this idealized version of you in my head. But I didn't, Tyler."

He shook his head. "You didn't. Everything was real. It's always been real between us."

I felt the ground giving way beneath my feet and stood taller. "But I don't trust you yet. If you're serious about what you're saying here tonight, you're going to have to prove it to me."

"Of course. Tell me what to do, and I'll do it."

I shook my head. "Nope. It can't work like that. I'm no longer writing your essays, Tyler. You have to figure this out."

Inhaling, he squared his shoulders. "Okay, I can do that. I think."

"I think you can too." I softened a little.

"Sadie flew out to see me over the weekend. Surprised the hell out of me."

"Why'd she do that?"

"She claimed she was worried about me, because I hadn't answered any of her calls or texts, but I think it was mostly to tell me I was being an idiot."

"Sisters are good for that."

"Well, she was right. I left here thinking it was the right decision for everyone, but I was more miserable and lonely each day. And I don't want that to be the rest of my life—not when so much more is possible. Anyway, I went right to the hospital after I arrived, but something Virgil said made my brain explode, and I realized I needed to see you right away."

"What did he say?"

"It was something simple, but it reminded me that the things I loved and respected most about my dad weren't about baseball. They were about family."

I smiled. "Virgil is wise."

"Virgil is wise."

We stood looking at each other for a moment, and I knew I'd better get inside—alone—before my resolve not to kiss him weakened. "I should go in."

"Okay." His expression was crestfallen, but he stepped aside and let me walk up the steps. "Can I see you tomorrow?"

Up on my porch, I turned to face him, wondering what was safe to agree to. Dinner seemed too much like a date, and a drink meant my decision-making abilities would suffer. I bit my lip. "I have to work, but I could meet you for lunch."

"I'll take it." He grinned, making my heart flutter.

"What?" I asked.

"I love it when you bite your lip. I just found an old picture of us at my dad's kitchen table, and you were chewing on it."

I laughed self-consciously. "I'm surprised I haven't chewed it right off."

"Don't do that. I love your lips. I've missed them."

My face got hot, and I smiled. "Get out of here, Tyler Shaw, before I lose my mind and invite you in."

He laughed. "God, I missed you. Goodnight, April."

"Goodnight." Then I unlocked the door, went inside, and leaned back against it, exhaling with relief.

I'd managed to resist him.

If that wasn't proof that I was stronger than I thought, I wasn't sure what was.

We agreed by text to meet for lunch at a restaurant downtown, and I arrived first. When I saw him walking toward me, my heart jumped around in my chest.

He sat down across from me in the booth. "Hey. How was your morning?"

"Good. Yours?"

"Excellent. Virgil is doing better, I accepted the school's offer for a coaching position, and I have an appointment with a realtor this afternoon to look at some listings on the water."

"Wow. You've been busy."

"I'm focused, that's all. It's easy when you know what you want." His eyes held mine over the table, and heat bloomed at my center. "And I know what I want."

I cleared my throat and picked up my ice water. "How did you sleep last night?"

He shrugged, giving me a rueful grin. "Not at all."

"Jet lag?"

"No. I was thinking about . . . a lot of things."

"Want to tell me about them?"

"Yes. Because most of them involve you—at least, I hope they do."

The server came over and we ordered drinks and sandwiches. When we were alone again, Tyler said, "We should talk about Chip."

I nodded. "I'm meeting him on Saturday."

Tyler's expression was momentarily alarmed, but he recovered and cleared his throat. "Okay. I was hoping for a little more time, but it's okay."

"*What's* okay?"

"So I was up all night asking myself how I could earn your trust again. How I can show you that I meant what I said last night—I want you in my life for good."

My entire body warmed, but I tried to stay cool. "And?"

"I came up with something that involves Chip, and I'll admit it scares the shit out of me, like every time I think about it I am *not* okay, and I get this horrible pit in my stomach, and my intestines are all twisted, and it feels like this one time I pitched against this one team full of—"

"Tyler." I raised my eyebrows. "I get it. It's scary. I'm scared too."

"Right." He took a breath. "So I still think people are going to find out I'm his biological father, or at least speculate out loud. And I think it could make things really hard on everyone if we have to waste a lot of time and energy issuing denials and refusing to comment and telling what we know are lies. So I've made a decision."

I couldn't even breathe. "What?"

"Let's get out ahead of it. I'll meet him too. I'll admit the truth, and we'll go to a news outlet we trust with the real story—*if* it's okay with him and his mom."

The room began to spin. "Oh my God, Tyler. Are you sure?"

"I'm sure."

Picking up my ice water again, I took several big gulps. "So . . . what does this look like?"

"I'd go with you on Saturday."

"You would?"

"Yes. Unless you think that would unfairly blindside them."

"It's going to blindside them no matter what." I paused

to think about it. "But I think it's a good thing. Robin's letter said in the wake of losing his father, she felt like Chip was searching for family ties. And we know he admires you."

"It's still going to be a huge shock." He frowned. "And they could say no. They could say they want no part of a media story."

"How *are* we going to handle that part of it?"

"I'd contact a local reporter Sadie and Josh know and give her the scoop. I think that's probably the best way to shut down gossip."

"When did you talk to Sadie about it?"

"This morning. I invited myself to their house for breakfast before they left for work."

My jaw dropped. "You're really serious about this."

"I am." He squeezed my hand. "I want to do right by you, and by Chip. I'm not gonna lie and say I'm ready to be his father, but I feel protective of you both. And I'll do whatever it takes to make this easier, no matter how uncomfortable it is for me."

My eyes filled, and I had to let go of his hand to fish a tissue out of my purse. "Really?" I said, dabbing at the corners of my eyes.

"Yes. Running away from this wasn't going to solve anything. It was me taking the easy out." He paused. "I'll be honest—if you'd never wanted to meet him or put our past out in the open, I might have been fine with it. But you know what? I keep thinking about this—I've enjoyed every single minute of the time I've spent with Chip. I'm not sorry he turned out to be my biological son. In fact, I'm proud of it. I just don't feel much like his father."

I reached out for his hand again. "It's okay. I don't feel like his mother either. It's not going to be that kind of relationship. But maybe we can get to a place where we feel . . . something like family to each other."

He turned his palm to mine and laced our fingers. "I'd like that."

Something occurred to me. "Will you see him at practice before Saturday?"

"I've decided to stay away from the team for the time being. I've got enough to do here, and I think this situation is awkward enough. I told David I'd officially start next season."

"Okay." I suddenly pictured Tyler and I standing on the Carswells' doorstep with a ticking bomb in our hands that was going to explode in their living room. Did I owe them a warning? Was this the right thing?

As if he knew I was nervous about what was coming, he squeezed my hand. "Hey. Look at me."

I met his eyes.

"Everything is going to be okay," he said, and his grin wasn't the cocky smirk of a hotshot teenager, but a genuine, reassuring smile. "We've got this."

My heart soared—he believed in me. He believed in *us*.

The next day, I texted him an invite to dinner at my house. He messaged me back saying he'd only come if I sent him a grocery list for making spaghetti sauce and allowed him to cook for me, which I did.

It took much, *much* longer than necessary.

He made a gigantic mess in the kitchen.

He put in too many red pepper flakes.

He didn't cook the pasta long enough.

He burned the garlic bread.

He made me close my eyes, then he surprised me with a

bowl of cherry ice cream topped with amaretto sauce for dessert.

"How did you get this?" I asked after one taste. "It's from Cloverleigh Farms, isn't it?"

"Well, I had to buy the ice cream from the grocery store," he confessed. "But the sauce I picked up from the restaurant. I know it's your favorite, and I wanted to watch you lick the spoon again."

I licked more than the spoon that night.

Apparently, *taking it slow* with Tyler Shaw was not a thing I could do.

He just did something to me.

Always had, always would.

CHAPTER 26
Tyler

ON FRIDAY, I crossed several things off my seemingly endless to-do list. Met with a realtor and looked at several properties for sale in the area, broke the news to Anna that I was moving back to Michigan (I may have shed a tear), and contacted my real estate agent in San Diego about putting my house up for sale.

I also hit a car dealership to test drive some new SUVs, opened up a bank account, and stopped at my sister Sadie's house to let her know what April and I had decided to do.

We were sitting out on her front porch when I told her.

"Are you serious?" she said, sitting up and clasping her hands under her chin.

"I'm serious. She loved your idea about contacting a reporter on our own and breaking the story ourselves."

"It's the only way to own the narrative. I really think it's the best plan."

I nudged her foot with mine. "Of course you do. Because it was yours."

She raised her chin in smug satisfaction. "You're welcome." Then she leaned back on her hands again. "So when will it happen?"

"Well, we're going over to their house tomorrow. If they go for the idea, I guess I'll need that reporter's contact information right away. What's her name?"

"Victoria Nelson. I'll give it to you before you go," she promised. We were silent then, watching the two girls across the street turn cartwheels on their front lawn. "You nervous?"

"Yeah," I admitted. "But this isn't about me. It's about being there for April and Chip. And it's about . . . what Dad would have done."

She looked at me. "You're right," she said softly. "It is what Dad would have done."

I didn't trust my voice not to crack, so I said nothing.

Later, as I was leaving, she said, "Give me a minute. I'll get Victoria's number for you. I just have to go upstairs and find it on the computer."

"Okay, but hurry up. I'm supposed to meet April over at Cloverleigh to talk to her parents."

Her brows shot up. "Oooh, facing the parents. Are you scared?"

"Fuck yes, I am. But she asked me to be there, so I'll be there."

She smiled. "I'll be right back."

I waited by the back door, checking my watch impatiently every thirty seconds. She was taking much longer than necessary to go find one phone number. Couldn't I just look the woman up online?

Five minutes later, she came rushing into the kitchen again, her hands behind her back. "Sorry," she said. "My helpers got a little carried away."

"Helpers?"

"Yes." She handed me a slip of paper. "This is Victoria's email and cell phone. And these..." Bringing the other hand from behind her back, she held out a handful of clovers. "These are for luck."

I stared at them in her palm, little shamrocks plucked from the lawn just like she used to give me before a game.

"Come on, take them." She wiggled her hand. "Put them in your pocket."

I did as she said, my heart swelling in my chest. Then I grabbed her in a huge bear hug. "Thank you."

"You're welcome. Although the twins did most of the work. I get dizzy bending down now. And their lawn had more of them anyway."

I laughed. "I'll thank them."

"Let me know how everything goes," she said as I went out the door. "I love you. And I'm so proud of you."

"I love you too," I said. "Thanks for everything."

As I walked to my car, which was parked on the street, I saw the little girls watching me. I gave them a wave, and they waved back.

"Did you get the lucky clovers?" one of them called.

"I did," I called back. "Thank you!"

"We picked the luckiest ones we could find!" hollered the other one.

"I appreciate it," I told them, thinking a little girl might not be so bad one day. "I need all the luck I can get."

CHAPTER 27

April

ON SATURDAY AFTERNOON, Tyler and I stood side by side at the Carswells' front door.

He looked at me, his hand poised to knock. "Ready?"

"I don't know." I looked up at him and grabbed his fist in both my hands. "I'm scared."

"Don't be scared. It's going to be okay."

"How do you know?"

"Because I just do. Listen—close your eyes."

"What?"

"Come on, do it."

I closed my eyes and he took me by the shoulders, turning me to face him.

"Now hold out your hands."

I peeked with one eye. "Why?"

"Hey. No cheating."

Sighing, I closed them both again and held out my hands. A moment later I felt him place something light and feathery on my palms. "Okay, you can look."

I opened my eyes and looked down —my hands were full of bright green clovers. I gasped. "Oh my gosh! Where did you get these?"

"From Sadie," he said. "They'll be right in my pocket. Feel better?"

Laughing, I nodded. "Yes. But let me keep one."

He took one from the little pile and tucked it into my purse. Then he took the rest of the pile and stuck them back in the pocket of his jeans. "Should I knock?"

I took one more deep breath. "Yes."

He knocked three times then took my hand.

A moment later, the door opened, and my pulse skittered.

"Hello." Robin Carswell smiled, looking back and forth between Tyler and me. "Well, this is a surprise."

"Hi, Robin." My stomach was flipping wildly. "I brought a friend. I hope that's okay."

"Of course. I understand," she said, although there was no way she could. "Come on in. It's nice to see you both again. I didn't realize you two knew each other."

We stepped into the front hall, my heart pounding so loud I was sure she could hear it. "Thank you. Yes, we've—we've been friends a long time." My voice sounded weird to me. High-pitched and quivery.

Robin shut the door behind us and smiled sympathetically. "I know you must be nervous, April. But I think it's wonderful what you've decided to do. Chip is anxious to know you."

I swallowed, exchanging a glance with Tyler, who looked astonishingly calm. "I think I'm a little of everything right now. But I'm anxious to know him too."

"Why don't you sit down in the living room?" She gestured toward a room on the left. "Chip's upstairs. I'll go get him. He'll be thrilled to see you again, Tyler. He was disappointed to hear you'd gone back to California and wouldn't be coaching anymore. He learned so much from you."

"He's an excellent student and a talented pitcher. I'd be glad to work with him again."

She beamed. "That would be wonderful. And I can't thank you enough for encouraging him to take the Clemson scholarship. I don't know what you said, but it got through to him. He accepted it last week."

"I'm happy to hear it."

We entered the living room and took a seat on a gingham-covered sofa. I felt like I had no idea what to do with my hands and clasped them anxiously in my lap. I couldn't believe how at ease Tyler seemed. Was it an act?

"Make yourselves comfortable," Robin said, heading up the stairs. "I'll be right back."

"Okay." As soon as she walked out, I looked at Tyler. "How are you so calm right now?" I whispered. "I'm dying."

"I'm not calm, babe. But I've had a lot of practice keeping cool under pressure while on the mound."

"Oh. Right." I moved a little closer to him, hoping some of his never-let-them-see-you-sweat would rub off on me. To distract myself from my nerves, I looked around at the room. It was comfortably furnished with a beautifully polished wood floor, a rug beneath the coffee table with fresh vacuum lines, and a vase full of fresh tulips on top of it. An upright piano stood against one wall, and I wondered if Chip or his sister played.

Footsteps coming down the stairs had me jumping to my feet, and Tyler stood slowly, placing a hand on my lower back.

For a second, I panicked. What if this was the wrong decision? What if we should just leave this kid alone? What if the decision to meet him was just selfish on my part—something I needed in order to move forward, but he didn't? After all, the situation was potentially going to get publicly messy with Tyler, and—

Then he walked into the room—that beautiful baby whose eyes I'd looked into so long ago—and his handsome smile melted my heart. "Hey," he said, extending his hand. "I'm Chip."

"I'm April," I said, taking his hand and returning his smile as my heart fluttered with happiness. "It's so nice to meet you."

"Hey, Coach," he said, shaking hands with Tyler too. "My mom said you were here."

"Good to see you again, Chip."

A little girl came sliding down the banister into the front hall, where she jumped off before coming to stand next to her brother.

"Cecily!" Robin scolded. "How many times have I asked you not to do that? And I thought you were going to stay in your room."

"I changed my mind," she said with a shrug. "I had FOMO."

"This is Chip's sister, Cecily," Robin said, giving her daughter a stern look. "She's eleven."

"Eleven and three-quarters," Cecily clarified.

Chip poked her on the shoulder. "No one cares about the three-quarters, CeCe."

She gave him a dirty look. "*I* do."

"Why don't we all sit down?" Robin suggested. "If you'll just give me one minute, I've got some cookies and coffee made."

"Of course," I said, barely able to take my eyes off Chip. He was so like Tyler at that age, from his coloring to the height to the way he stood. But I could see the Sawyer in him too.

While Robin was in the kitchen, Tyler asked Chip about the team's last few games, and I was grateful I could just listen for a few minutes. When she returned, I was glad to take a warm coffee cup in my hands, which felt twitchy. It was Chip who put me at ease.

"So I hear you went to Central High too," he said, meeting

my eyes. It was apparent within minutes that he was not only handsome but also confident, humble, good-natured, and mature.

He was naturally curious and asked a lot of questions about growing up at Cloverleigh Farms, wondering if he could see it sometime, expressing astonishment at the number of siblings I had.

"Four sisters?" he asked, glancing at Cecily, who grinned impishly from her perch on the piano bench. "I wouldn't survive."

I laughed. "It was a crowded house, but a nice way to grow up. I'd be glad to show you around sometime. All of you. My family would love that."

"Does your mom know about Chip?" asked Cecily, taking a bite of her cookie.

"Cecily," Robin said, giving her daughter a look.

"It's okay," I said, smiling at the precocious little girl. She reminded me of Chloe at that age—no filter. "She does. And she'd really like to meet him—and you too."

Cecily grinned. "Are there horses at your farm?"

"There are," I told her.

"Could I ride one?"

"Sure."

Her face lit up.

"So I hear you took the offer from Clemson," said Tyler.

"I did." Chip smiled. "Thanks again for all the advice."

"Any idea what you might study there?" I asked.

"I'm not sure yet, but maybe environmental engineering."

"Hey, who is Chip's biological dad?" asked Cecily, out of nowhere.

"Cecily!" This time Robin's tone was sharper.

"What, I'm just curious. You said you never knew, but *she's* got to know. Right?"

There was an awkward silence during which I wasn't sure what to say—Robin appeared mortified, and Chip looked like he sort of wished the earth would open up and swallow him. But rather than panic, I took it as an invitation from the universe to speak up. I exchanged a quick glance with Tyler, who gave me a nod and took my hand.

"Actually," I said, sitting up a little straighter, "I do know." I met Robin's eyes and then Chip's. "This wasn't something I ever planned on sharing, but I'm at a point in my life where I'd like to be more open about . . . everything."

Crickets.

Their faces were a mixture of confusion and expectancy, but I saw hope and excitement too—or at least that's what I chose to believe.

I cleared my throat. "Okay, so, as you know, Chip, I was very young when I had you. Just eighteen. And your, um, biological dad was young too. We were just good friends, and the pregnancy was a bit of a shock for both of us."

"You didn't use protection," stated Cecily matter-of-factly, swinging her feet below the piano bench. "We learned about that in sex ed this year. They call it *Adolescent Health*"—she made air quotes around the words—"but we all know what it is."

"Oh, my Lord." Robin shook her head. "Cecily Carswell, could you please button your lip? I'm so sorry, April. We do not have to discuss this."

"It's okay." I laughed nervously, suddenly grateful for Cecily's presence. "She's right. We weren't careful. And by the time I realized I was pregnant, I was already away at college, and he'd been drafted."

"To the Army?" asked Robin with some confusion.

I shook my head. "To the major leagues," I said, watching the shock overtake Chip's face. "He was a baseball player. In fact, he was a lefty pitcher."

Chip's jaw hung wide open as he looked back and forth between Tyler and me, putting it together. "Oh my God. It's you, isn't it?"

Tyler nodded and swallowed. "Yes."

"What?" Robin's voice was shocked.

"Holy shit. Holy *shit*." Chip glanced at Robin. "Sorry, Mom."

"It's okay." She looked at us, her face a jumble of emotions. Mostly shock. "I'm just—I can't quite—*Tyler* is Chip's biological father?"

"He is. But he didn't know that when they met," I said quickly. "Tyler and I lost touch after my pregnancy. For reasons that are too complicated to go into here, we never talked about the birth or the adoption. We only reconnected a few weeks ago, when he came back to town for his sister's wedding."

"I had no idea who you were when I started working with you," Tyler said to Chip, leaning forward, elbows on his knees. "I only realized it after April got the letter from your mom with a photograph. I was totally shocked."

"I know the feeling," Robin said, hands covering her cheeks. "This is—this is—"

"It's a lot to digest all at once," I said. "And I'm sorry to blindside you. We're still processing it too. But . . ." I looked at Tyler. "We felt it was better to get the truth out right from the start."

"That's why you left, isn't it?" Chip asked Tyler. "Because you found out about me."

Tyler's expression was grim. "At the time, I thought that was the best decision. I was trying to protect you."

"From what?" Chip looked confused.

"From media attention." I squeezed Tyler's hand. "Tyler is still a hot topic, and the stories are not always kind. He was concerned that if it got out he was your biological father, you'd find yourself the subject of a lot of tabloid gossip. He didn't want to embarrass you."

"I'm not embarrassed to be your biological son," Chip

said, as if he was surprised anyone would even think it. "Not at all. I think it's really cool."

"You really think media will care that much?" Robin glanced at Chip with maternal concern.

"Unfortunately, I think we have to plan for that," I told her. "I wouldn't have guessed it before, but after seeing first-hand how they manipulate and distort things to grab eyeballs, I believe he's right to be concerned."

"Grab eyeballs!" repeated Cecily. "Ew!"

"She doesn't mean grabbing actual eyeballs," Chip explained. "She means get people's attention."

"Oh." Her feet began swinging again. "I think it would be kinda cool to be in the news."

I smiled ruefully at her. "It would be, for the right reasons."

Tyler spoke up. "This is completely up to you, Robin. April and I are willing to handle it whichever way you think is best for your family. We could try to keep completely silent and hope for the best, or we could try to get out ahead of it."

"How would we do that?" Chip asked.

"Tyler's family knows a local reporter we could go to with the story," I explained. "That way we could go public with it on our terms."

"I'm thinking . . ." Robin rose to her feet and paced back and forth. "I used to work in PR. I think Tyler is right. What if we made this a story about family ties, about how adoption can create all kinds of wonderful nontraditional family relationships? You see all those stories now about DNA testing and how people are discovering their roots and connecting with people they didn't even know they were related to. Those are uplifting stories that make people feel good, don't you think? This could be that kind of story."

"I agree completely," I said. "That's a great idea. I love the idea of a pro-adoption story. Tyler?" I looked over at him.

"I'm all in, whatever you guys decide."

Robin looked at Chip. "How do you feel about this, honey?"

"About being related to one of the greatest pitchers in the game? I think it's awesome."

"I don't know about that," Tyler said, but I could tell he'd liked hearing it. "And maybe you should take some time as a family to talk it over. There will be reporters calling, possibly knocking on your door. People at school will talk."

"I'm okay with it," he insisted. "I'm more than okay with it."

Robin looked at us and smiled. "I think we have a plan."

"Good." I rose to my feet, and Tyler followed suit. "We should go—I have to get over to Cloverleigh for an event tonight—but we'll be in touch soon."

"Sounds good." Robin shook her head. "I'm still trying to wrap my brain around this. Life never stops throwing you curveballs, does it?"

"Nope," Tyler said. "I can attest to that."

Chip rose to his full height, and it struck me again how much he took after Tyler—even the way he got up from a chair. I wondered if there were other similar idiosyncrasies they'd discover over time. "Is it okay to tell my friends?" he asked.

"It's okay with me," Tyler said with a shrug. "My family already knows."

"And we told my parents last night," I added. My parents had reacted the same way we all had—with shock and disbelief giving way to joy and excitement. They couldn't wait to meet Chip, their bonus grandson, they called him, and my heart had filled with love and pride at the way they treated Tyler. He'd been so nervous, but they'd welcomed him with a hug and a handshake, and made him feel at home.

"Did you really?" Robin smiled and shook her head. "I remember your mother very fondly. How is she?"

"She's great. Both she and my dad are so excited to meet

you all. And everyone is invited to my dad's retirement party, which is also a huge celebration for Cloverleigh's fortieth anniversary. It's happening a week from tonight. And maybe before that, sometime this week, we could all get together for an introduction."

"Thank you," said Robin. "That sounds nice, if you think it won't be too much."

"Not at all," I assured her. "They understand why it took so long for this to happen, but now they don't want to waste any more time being strangers. They're really into family."

"I am too," said Robin. "And I couldn't agree more."

"Can I come to the party too?" Cecily asked.

"You sure can," I told her. "There will definitely be some kids there your age. I have lots of nieces and even a nephew. I'll introduce you. They'll be like bonus cousins!"

The young girl smiled. "Awesome."

Finally, I turned to Chip. I wanted to hug him, but I didn't want to be too forward, so I shook his hand instead. "It was so nice to meet you."

"You too," he said.

Tyler shook his hand as well. "Maybe I'll see you at practice next week."

"I'd really like that." He looked worried for a second. "Should I still call you Coach?"

Tyler laughed a little. "Uh, no. You can call me Tyler."

Chip grinned. "Sounds good."

The kids both went up to their rooms, and Robin saw us to the door.

"I'm sorry if this was unnecessarily traumatic," I said.

"No, no. It's okay. I think deep down Chip always wondered about *both* his birth parents." She laughed and shrugged. "He's sort of getting a twofer here."

I laughed too, placing my hand on her arm. "Thank you for everything—inviting us into your home, being so gracious, and . . . having the wherewithal to make something beautiful out of something awkward and difficult."

She exhaled. "You know, I wanted children more than anything. I tried so hard to get pregnant and stay pregnant, and it just never took. I had miscarriage after miscarriage. So when we turned to adoption and even *that* seemed to be taking forever, I made sort of a bargain with God."

"You did?"

"Yes. I promised that if He would send us a child that needed us as much as we needed him or her, that I would let love and compassion be my guide for the rest of my life. The very next day the agency contacted me, and said you'd chosen us to adopt your baby."

A lump formed in my throat and tears filled my eyes. Impulsively, I threw my arms around her. "It was meant to be."

She hugged me back, then hugged Tyler. "It was meant to be. It was all meant to be."

Much later that night, Tyler was waiting for me in my bed. It was so late, he'd already fallen asleep, and I undressed in the dark, kicking off my heels, peeling off my dress, tiptoeing into the bathroom to take off my makeup and brush my teeth.

He woke up when I slipped beneath the covers, immediately reaching for me. "Come here, you. How was the wedding?"

"Good. Long." I snuggled up against his warm, strong body. "How was your night?"

"Fine. I went and saw three houses."

"Did you like any of them?"

"They were all nice, but I definitely had a favorite. Maybe

you can come see it with me this week. It's not right on the water, but it's close. You can see it through the windows."

"I'd love that." I kissed his chest. "So are you okay? We've hardly had a chance to talk about how things went today."

"Yes. I feel good actually."

"I do too." I wrapped my arm around him and squeezed him tightly. "Thank you."

"For what?"

"For changing your mind. For coming back. For being there with me today."

"Well, how else was I going to win you back? Clearly my biceps were no longer enough. I had to get a little more dramatic."

I giggled. "It worked."

He kissed my head. "I'll never stop trying to win you, April. I promise."

Every part of me hummed with warmth—I felt so lucky. "He's so much like you. Isn't he?"

"In some ways, maybe. But much smarter. With a much bigger heart."

"You've got a big heart. You just never showed it."

He rolled on top of me, settling his hips between my thighs. "What a difference red hair and dimples can make."

Laughing, I wrapped my legs around him. "Everything's gonna be okay, right?"

"It's going to be more than okay," he said, brushing my cheekbones with his thumbs. "You know, I never imagined I could fall in love with anything the way I fell in love with baseball. But now . . . "

"Now?" I asked hopefully, my heart pounding.

He pressed his lips to mine, and his kiss tasted like forever. "Now there's you."

A week later, I crossed the band platform at my father's retirement party, hoping my voice wouldn't sound as shaky as my legs felt. Carrying a glass of sparkling wine in one hand, I moved to the vocalist's microphone stand and switched the mic on. "Excuse me everyone. Could I please have your attention?"

It took a minute for the roughly two-hundred-fifty people in the room to quiet down, during which I scanned the crowd for familiar, supportive faces.

They were all here—my parents, seated next to one another, their joined hands resting on the table. Sylvia and Henry. Meg and Noah. Chloe and Oliver. Frannie, Mack, and the three girls, who giggled along with Sylvia's two kids and Cecily Carswell over their plastic flutes of sparkling juice. It turned out that Cecily went to the same middle school as Sylvia's daughter Whitney and Mack's oldest, Millie. I'd asked Whitney if she could make sure Cecily was included since she might not know anyone else, and she'd said of course. I'd never felt more grateful for my family, who always stepped up when I needed them.

Robin Carswell, her mother, and Chip were seated with Tyler, Sadie, and Josh, who'd also been added to the guest list at my mother's insistence. She'd hand-delivered the invitation herself, and insisted they attend. "You're family now," she told them all. "You have to come."

When the room was nearly silent, I locked eyes with Tyler one more time. He was so gorgeous in his suit and tie, he took my breath away. His smile reassured me—I could do this.

"Good evening, everyone. For those of you wondering which Sawyer sister I am, I'm April—the second one."

Polite laughter echoed through the room.

"On behalf of my parents, my older sister Sylvia, and my younger sisters, Meg, Chloe, and Frannie, I want to welcome you and thank you for being here tonight to celebrate my father's retirement, as well as the fortieth anniversary of Cloverleigh Farms. It means so much to all of us." I paused for a breath, and saw my mom wiping her eyes. "As many of you know, my father was somewhat reluctant to retire."

More laughter from the crowd, and I laughed too.

"But who could blame him? I might be biased, but I truly believe Cloverleigh Farms is the most beautiful place in the world. Like all of us Sawyer sisters, it has grown in so many ways over the years. It's had its share of tough seasons—winter blizzards and bitter-cold frosts, too-wet springs and too-dry summers—but we have also seen hundreds of couples get married in the orchard, we've seen graduation parties and four-generation family reunions on our lawn, and we've even had a baby born at the inn, although it was not planned and my dad always said that's the night his hair turned white."

A murmur of amusement rippled through the room, and I paused a moment.

"But that's what Cloverleigh Farms has always been about—family. Milestones. Growth. Love. Celebration. Memories. And you're all a part of that." I took another breath. "My parents have taught us that this is a place where family means more than just DNA. It means opening our doors and our hearts to strangers. It means showing up for our neighbors. It means reaching out when you know someone needs it. It means forgiveness, acceptance, compassion, joy . . ." I locked eyes with Tyler again. "And it's that feeling you get when you know you're home."

"Hear, hear!" my father yelled, lifting his glass to me.

I smiled at him. "Dad, Mom, you've spent four decades making this place into something extraordinary, and tonight we honor your hard work and sacrifice, as well as your dedication to each other and to all of us." I raised my glass and looked out at the room. "So please join me in a toast to John and Daphne Sawyer, in wishing happy birthday to Cloverleigh Farms, and in celebrating all the life and love yet to blossom for us all. Cheers!"

"Cheers!" shouted the crowd.

I took a sip of my wine, made from grapes grown on the hillside right outside, and tasted in its sweetness all the beauty of the past and the promise of the future. Then I made my way to the side of the stage, where Tyler was waiting to help me down, his expression full of pride and affection.

I took his hand and stepped down into his embrace.

Life was good.

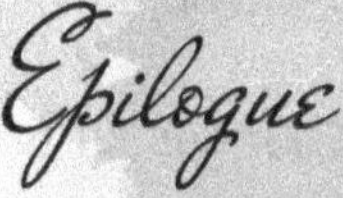

Epilogue

"YOUR CAR BROKE DOWN? Are you serious?" I checked the clock on my nightstand. It was barely seven a.m.

"Sorry, babe. I think it's the battery. Must be shoddy."

"The battery? Tyler, you drive a ridiculously expensive SUV. It has four-zone climate control. But the *battery* is shoddy?"

"Must be. Mind coming to rescue me? You've got jumper cables in your car."

I put a hand on my forehead. "I do?"

"Yes. I put them in there."

"When?"

"I don't remember exactly. But they're in there."

"Okay, I'm coming." I sat up and swung my legs over the side of the mattress. "But it will be a little bit. I'm still in bed."

"Sorry."

"It's my birthday, after all," I grumped. "And a Saturday."

"I know, I know. This is such bad timing."

"I didn't know you were going for a run this morning. I thought we were going to go get breakfast together." I walked toward the huge master bathroom Tyler and I shared.

"Yeah, I wasn't planning on it, but I had trouble sleeping last night. I thought the workout would relax me."

"Oh. I'm sorry." Immediately, I felt bad. "I didn't know you'd had a tough night. It's been a while."

"Yeah."

"Are you at the high school?"

"Yes."

"I have to get dressed, but I'll be there in about fifteen minutes."

"Thanks, babe. I'll make it up to you, I promise. I love you."

"I love you too."

After I got out of the bathroom, I quickly threw on sweatpants and a hoodie and shoved my feet into sneakers. I felt guilty about the way I'd whined on the phone. After all, it wasn't Tyler's fault his car broke down. And last month, when I'd gotten a flat tire on my way home from work, he'd jumped in the car and driven at warp speed to reach me. Then he'd changed my tire, drove behind me the entire way home, and gave me his SUV to go to work the following day while he got my car in for service.

But that wasn't unusual. For a guy who'd originally claimed he "wasn't good at that stuff," Tyler was beyond chivalrous—always opening doors for me, pulling out my chair at restaurants, never even letting me *look* at a bill let alone pay one. Some people might have found all that too old-fashioned, but not me. Because it didn't come along with any outdated bullshit about women being inferior to men. Sure, he loved it when I cooked dinner for him, but he liked cooking for me too.

And if I had to put up with the occasional ego trip or how loud he got while watching sports (especially if Mack or Noah was over, my God) or his leaving the cap off the toothpaste *again*, it was a small price to pay for how happy he made me. I grabbed my phone off the dresser in our bedroom

—*our bedroom*, that was just bananas—and hurried down the stairs.

The view from our huge picture windows never failed to leave me breathless and shaking my head with wonder. It wasn't directly on the bay, but it was close enough that we could see it from our perch in the trees. It had everything else that Tyler had wanted—privacy, luxury, plenty of space, and it was close enough to Cloverleigh that it was convenient for me to stay over.

He'd asked me to move in almost immediately. I was still trying not to rush things, but damn, he made it difficult. I'd never forget the July night he brought a blanket out onto the deck and we lay on it looking up at the stars.

"Remind you of anything?" he'd asked, rolling onto his side and propping his head on his hand.

"Of course it does." I looked at him and grinned. "Do you remember your line?"

"I've got a better one." He reached out and slipped his hand into my hair, but this time, instead of *come here*, what he said was, "I love you. And I never want you to leave. Stay with me."

I'd moved in the following day.

I hurried through the kitchen and out to the garage, where I jumped into my car and hit the button on the remote to open the door. I was about to back out when I heard my phone ping with a text.

Tyler: I'm not at the track. Meet me at the ballfield.
Me: Okay!

Smiling, I put my car in reverse. Lately, Tyler had been throwing again. Not in public—he wouldn't even let *me* watch him—so he always had to go super early in the morning or very late at night and just pitch balls at the back-stop, but it felt like progress to me. Whenever I asked how it had gone, he'd have a different answer.

"Fucking great," he'd say one day, the old grin on his face.

"Don't ask," he'd say the next.

I'd give him a kiss either way and tell him I was proud.

I left our gated neighborhood and drove over to the high school. Tyler's was the only car in the lot—not surprising, since it was barely seven a.m. on a Saturday morning. I was about to get out of the car when my phone pinged again.

Chip: Happy birthday!

I smiled, deciding to take a minute and text him back. I knew Tyler would understand.

Me: Thanks! How's everything going? Why are you up so early???

Chip: Haha good. I'm about to go work out.

Me: How'd the econ test go?

Chip: Don't ask.

I grinned.

Me: How about the essay for Freshman Comp?

Chip: A

Me: That's awesome. Have a good weekend!

Chip: You too. Say hi to Tyler for me. Can't believe his battery is dead.

Me: OMG I know. Thanks for the birthday text!

As I got out of the car, it struck me as a little odd that he knew about the dead battery already. Had Tyler texted him too? It was possible, since they were in touch all the time, and we couldn't wait to see him when he came home for Thanksgiving next month. We were also looking forward to going down to Clemson for some baseball games next spring.

For the millionth time, I marveled at how our plan to handle the media where Chip was concerned had worked. Tyler had been right—getting out ahead was key. And Robin's idea to make it a positive story about adoption had been brilliant. For the first time in my life, this thing that I'd kept in the dark was thrust into the spotlight, but it felt good. Social media had jumped on the positivity of it, and we'd been astonished with all the incredible feedback. Tons of people had reached out to us, coming forward with their own stories, saying we'd given them the courage to decide on adoption, or reach out to a birth parent, or stop seeing their own adoption as a rejection and start seeing it as a decision made from love. Even Bethany Bloomstar reached out with an apology and an offer to make things right with a more positive story.

We'd politely declined. (And secretly I still hoped she'd get a wart on her face, or even just a really bad zit.)

Was there judgey hate mail too? Sure. But we didn't let it take away from what we'd won—a relationship with Chip and his family, the certainty we'd done the right thing, and each other.

Always and forever, each other.

"Hey, handsome. You need a ride?" I approached the backstop and grinned at him through the chain links.

He grinned. "Actually, what I need is a catcher."

I laughed. "You're funny."

"No, I'm serious." He jogged over to the home team dugout. "Come here."

I made my way over slowly. "You *can't* be serious."

He was on one knee, rummaging in a big duffel bag. "Actually, I am. Could you just put this on?"

"What?" I stared at the catcher's mask and mitt he held up. "No."

"Please, honey? I feel like I'm on the verge of this major breakthrough."

I groaned, even as I let him put the mask over my face. "Tyler. Don't do this to me. I love you, but this is, like, a lot to ask."

"Why?"

"Why?" I gaped at him through the mask's cage. "I am not athletic! You throw ninety miles per hour! Don't you like my face?"

"You're wearing the mask. And you'll have this." He scooped something out of the bag that looked like a turtle shell.

"What's that for?"

"To protect your chest." He moved closer and put it on me. It was so big it went on *over* the mask.

"Oh my God." I took the mitt from him and put it on. "I'm going to die."

"You won't. I promise." His expression was earnest. "Please, April. Please. You're the only one who can catch this pitch."

I narrowed my eyes at him. "Is that a sexual joke?"

"No. I swear." He held up his hands. "It's the truth."

Sighing heavily, feeling like I was wearing a hundred pounds of body armor, I waddled toward home plate. "How do I even stand?"

"Well, you have to sort of crouch down."

I glared at him. "Crouch?"

"Yeah. Like this." He dropped down so his butt was nearly on the ground.

"Oh, Jesus." I was probably going to pull a muscle. But I supposed I could try. After this, he'd have to get Mack or Noah or anyone else to practice with. But I made it to home plate and hunkered down, glad I'd chosen the ugly sweats and not the cute skinny jeans.

Tyler went out to the mound and assumed the badass pitcher stance, the one he'd perfected years ago with the downward tilt of his head and the menacing glare. I have to admit, it turned me on. But it also scared me a little.

He wound up, complete with the leg up and everything, and I called out.

"Hey, you're not really going to throw at me, are you? Like, not all the way, right?"

Stopping his motion, he hollered back, "I have to *mean* it when I throw it, April. Otherwise, it won't be real."

"Yeah, but—"

"Just relax, okay? You have to trust me."

"I *do* trust you, I'm just—"

"Do you? Trust me?" He started walking toward me.

"Of course I do."

"With anything?" Now he was within fifteen feet.

"Yes."

He stopped about ten feet from me and gave me the grin. "Catch."

Then he tossed the ball at me, and I squealed loudly, but I actually caught it inside the mitt, my right hand covering it protectively. "I caught it!" I shrieked, jumping to my feet. "I actually caught it!"

Tyler was laughing as he closed the distance between us. "You caught it."

I uncovered it with my hand—but it wasn't a ball at all.

It was a box.

A ring box.

I looked up at him. "Oh my God. Tyler, what is this?"

He pushed the catcher's mask up onto my forehead and took the box from the mitt. Turning it in my direction, he opened the box.

I gasped at the giant diamond winking back at me in the morning sun. It was almost blinding. "What is happening right now?"

Tyler got down on one knee. "April, I know I took the longest possible detour to get to this place, but believe me when I say there is nowhere else I'd rather be. You let me go when I needed to be free, and you pulled me in when I needed to belong. I never want to wake up another day in my life not knowing what it is to be loved by you."

A sob escaped me. Then another. "I love you so much."

"I love you too. And I'm about ready to get on with that second act. Let's fill that new house up. What do you think— will you marry me?"

"Yes," I said, weeping openly. "Yes."

He glanced at my left hand. "You know, this would be easier if you took that mitt off, babe."

"Oh! Sorry." I dropped the mitt and held out my hand, fingers spread. He slipped the ring on—a perfect fit. "I can't believe it. How?"

"You can thank your sisters for that," he confessed, rising to his feet. "They helped me choose it and told me your ring size."

"I will," I said, throwing my arms around his neck. That stupid turtle thing was between our chests, and I still had that damn catcher's mask on my head, but I kissed him like he was the man I was gonna marry—because he was.

Suddenly I heard raucous cheering from the bleachers.

I pulled my lips off Tyler's and looked at the stands. It should not have surprised me at all to see my entire family there—and I mean my *entire* family, from my parents and sisters and their significant others, right down to Noah's dog Renzo, all three of Mack's girls, the Carswell clan, a very pregnant Sadie and Josh, and two little girls I didn't even recognize.

"That was awesome!" one of them hooted. "He did it much better than he did in rehearsal!"

I looked up at Tyler in surprise. "Who are they?"

"Sadie's across-the-street neighbors."

"The lemonade girls?"

He nodded sheepishly. "I practiced with them on their front lawn."

Laughing giddily, I threw my arms around him, and he picked me right up off my feet and swung me around. "I love it! I love you."

"I love you too," he said. "And this is just the beginning."

Maybe he sat me down after that, and maybe he didn't. I couldn't seem to feel the ground beneath my feet for days.

But it was okay with me.

I had Tyler, I had family, I had a past I could be proud of and a future to look forward to. I had lessons I'd learned I couldn't wait to pass on. I had love in my heart and hope in my bones.

Everything was going to be okay.

THE END

Bonus Epilogue

APRIL

"You ready, peanut?" I scooped Jonah up from the changing table and set him on my hip. "We need to find Daddy and Frankie and get a move on. Where do you think they are, huh?"

"Dah!" my nine-month-old said happily. He'd just begun using an actual word here and there, although to hear Tyler tell it, both our kids were linguistic geniuses speaking in full sentences already.

"Where is Dah?" I asked, slinging the diaper bag over my shoulder and flipping the light off in the nursery. "Is he outside with your big sister? Are they playing catch again?"

I went down the steps carefully, balancing Jonah's weight on one side with the heft of the diaper bag on the other. It was only an overnight road trip to Grand Rapids, but traveling with two kids under age four meant we had to take a lot with us.

"Yep. There they are," I said, reaching the bottom of the

stairs. A glance out the window confirmed what I'd suspected before—Tyler had our three-year-old daughter Frankie out on the front lawn again, where he was teaching her how to catch and throw a foam ball.

My car, a family-friendly minivan, was parked in the driveway with the hatch open. I went out the front door and pulled it shut behind me. "Are we all set?"

"Just waiting for you," Tyler called, tossing the ball in a gentle arc. "Car is all packed. Atta girl, Frankie. Good catch!"

"I'm ready," I said, enjoying the way our little dark-haired girl lit up when her daddy smiled at her. It never failed to make my heart flutter with happiness when I watched Tyler with the kids. He was such an amazing father. "And we'd better hurry up or we'll be late for Chip's game."

"We're not gonna miss the game." Tyler looked at Frankie. "Okay, honey, one more throw. Can you do it? Right to Daddy."

Frankie threw the ball back to Tyler and he cheered. "Yay! Great job!"

"Can I bat, Daddy?"

"Not today, sweet pea. We have to go see Chip." He walked over and picked her up, giving her a kiss on the forehead before setting her on his hip. "We'll practice more with the tee when we get back."

"Okay."

"Is Chip going to strike anybody out?"

"Yes!" she said, clapping her hands.

"And what will we say?"

Frankie hollered at the top of her lungs, and I laughed.

Second only to watching Tyler with the kids on the list of Things That Melt My Heart was seeing Chip interact with them. He'd been a sophomore at Clemson when Frankie was born, but he visited us every time he came home during summers and holiday vacations, and we FaceTimed often. He was so sweet and patient with Frankie, maybe because he'd been such a great big brother to Cecily, who was now *fifteen and three quarters*, and excited about getting her driver's license. She was also one of Frankie's favorite babysitters.

Chip had graduated from Clemson last year, and he'd had such a fantastic college baseball career that he'd been drafted by Tampa Bay. He'd spent this year playing what Tyler called "rookie ball" with a team called the Bowling Green Hot Rods. Tonight they'd play an away game against a Michigan team, and we couldn't wait to see him pitch.

We buckled the kids into their carseats, double checked that we had everything packed that we'd need, got to the end of the block, realized we'd forgotten the stroller, went back for it, and finally got on the road only a few minutes later than planned.

"See?" Tyler reached over and patted my leg. "Nothing to worry about, babe. We got this."

The ride was only a few hours, and luckily, both our children slept through the whole thing. They always fell asleep so easily in the car. When they were newborns, Tyler used to take them for a drive in the middle of the night just so I could get a couple hours of sleep.

I glanced over my shoulder at them, smiling at Jonah's chubby cheeks and sparse tufts of ginger hair, Frankie's lopsided pigtails and the smudge of dirt on her face. She was Daddy's girl through and through, from her deep brown eyes to her long legs and her love for playing catch. The only thing my daughter had gotten from me was a dimple on one side of her smile. Our little boy, on the other hand, was all Sawyer. He looked just like baby pictures of my dad.

"Did you ever think this would be your life?" I asked Tyler. "Driving a minivan, a wife and kids, a double stroller, changing diapers, burping a baby in the middle of the night . . ."

"Uh, no." He took my hand and kissed the back of it. "But I wouldn't change a single thing."

* * *

After the game, we briefly met up with Chip and congratulated him on an amazing win. Both kids were asleep again, Jonah in the stroller and Frankie chest-to-chest with Tyler, her head on his shoulder, her legs hanging limp.

Chip laughed. "She's getting so big. I can't believe how much she's grown."

"The pediatrician says she's going to be tall," I said. "Not as tall as her dad, of course, but definitely taller than her mom."

"Well, who isn't?" Chip teased. He leaned over to peek at Jonah in the stroller. "Hey, little man. Whoa, you're getting big too."

"They grow fast," Tyler said. "Pretty soon we'll be watching *their* games."

Chip straightened to his full height. "That's so crazy."

"Great game today," I told him.

"Thanks," he said, giving me a grin that looked an awful lot like Tyler's back in the day.

"The motion is looking smooth," said Tyler. "How's the arm holding up?"

"Pretty good." Chip shrugged. "I might actually be going up to double A in a few weeks."

"That's awesome," Tyler said. "Make sure you're resting it enough."

"I am."

"So how's life outside baseball?" I asked.

"Life outside baseball, what's that?" Chip grinned again.

I sighed. "I don't even know why I ask. One of these times, I guess I'm hoping you'll say there's a girl."

"Actually, there *might* be a girl."

"Really?" I asked, perking up.

"Yeah. But she lives in Louisville and I'm probably going

to Alabama at some point so . . ." He shrugged. "It's kinda hard."

Jonah woke up and started to fuss. "I should get him back to the hotel so I can feed him," I said apologetically. "But you're good for breakfast tomorrow? I want to hear more about the girl."

He nodded. "Definitely. Can't wait to see these guys awake."

Smiling, I rose up on tiptoe and gave him a huge hug. It never failed to amaze me that he was part of my life now. I wasn't the one he called Mom, but we were special to each other, and we'd always have a unique bond. "Get some sleep. See you in the morning."

Tyler said goodnight and we headed for the car, me pushing the stroller and Frankie still draped over his chest.

"He looks good, doesn't he?" I said softly to Tyler as we walked toward the parking lot.

"Yeah. He's really worked on that knuckle curve. His slider too."

I sighed. "I didn't mean his pitching, but yes—he looks amazing on the mound. So strong and confident."

"Yeah." He was silent for a minute. "He called me a couple months ago because he was struggling with his confidence. Wanted some advice."

"Whatever you told him must have helped," I said as we approached our minivan. "He said they're going to bump him up."

"I just reminded him to trust himself, and when that gets tough, go back to the mechanics. It's about the process, not the result." He chuckled as he pulled his keys from his pocket and opened the doors. "All the same stuff Virgil used to say to me."

I smiled sympathetically at him—Virgil had passed away right after our wedding, and I knew Tyler still missed him. "He'd be happy you're passing it on."

We drove back to the hotel and trooped up to our room. While I managed to get Jonah fed, changed, and into the hotel-provided crib, Tyler dealt with a crabby little girl who didn't want the princess pajamas I'd packed—"I want the *pirates*"—and refused to brush her teeth.

"Come on, Cranky Frankie," he said, getting down on his knees with her toothbrush in his hand. "I'll do it for you. All you have to do is open your mouth."

She eventually let him do it and was practically asleep on her feet by the time he finished. He carried her over to one of two queen beds in the room, where I'd already stuck foam bumpers beneath the sheets to prevent her from rolling off.

Eventually, both kids were down, the room was quiet, and the two of us slipped under the covers of the empty bed. "Think I should leave the bathroom light on in case Frankie wakes up confused?" I whispered.

"Yeah. I'll get it." Tyler got out of bed, and a moment later the bathroom light snapped on. He shut the door partway so it wouldn't be so bright that it kept us awake, and returned to bed.

I cuddled up next to him, resting my head on his bare chest. "Boy, staying in a hotel these days sure is different from how it used to be, huh?"

He laughed a little. "Yeah. We used to make a lot more noise."

"Definitely." I picked up my head and kissed his scruffy jaw. "But like you said earlier, I wouldn't change a thing."

"Me neither." He pressed his lips to mine. "But you just gave me an idea."

"What?"

"Think your parents would take the kids one night next weekend?"

"Of course. They're always begging for them."

"Perfect. I'll get us a hotel room and we can pretend like

it's the old days—order room service, have lots of sex, make all the noise we want."

I giggled. "That sounds amazing. But you know what's going to happen the minute you and I hit the sheets in our nice quiet hotel room."

"We'll fall asleep."

"Exactly."

He sighed. "Are we that old?"

"We're forty. That's not *that* old."

"But we're too tired to even imagine having hypothetical sex in our hypothetical hotel room *next* weekend. That's lame."

I laughed. "Tell you what. Let's promise each other we will stay up long enough to at least have sex one time in our hotel room. I bet once we get going, we won't be able to stop. It'll be like the return of 'The Rifle.'"

"It's a deal."

"But bring the condoms. The rifle has a tendency to knock me up."

"You don't want any more kids?"

I picked my head up. "Do *you*?"

"I don't know. Maybe. I love being a dad. Our family is my favorite thing in the world. Why wouldn't I want to add to it?"

My throat grew tight. "You're going to make me cry."

He reached up and brushed my hair back from my face. "I guess I should tell you those things more often. I always think it's so obvious how I feel that I don't think to say the words out loud."

"It's okay." He showed me every single day what I meant to him—I wasn't hung up on words.

"But you know how much I love you, right?"

"I know."

"And you know that there's nothing I wouldn't do for you?"

I nodded. "Yes."

"And everything that I went through—all of it—I'd go through it a thousand times more if it brought me to you."

"It would, every time." I kissed his hand, the one that threw a hundred mile per hour fastball, the one he'd slipped into my hair late one July night, the one on which he now wore his wedding band. "This was always meant to be."

Bonus Prequel

TYLER

Standing in the crowded kitchen, I watched from across the room as April Sawyer whispered something in her friend's ear and giggled. She looked so cute tonight—she was wearing a short flowery dress that was kind of fitted over her hips and butt and had a little ruffle at the bottom. The top had skinny straps, and after a good amount of time trying to stare at her chest without being caught, I'd decided she wasn't wearing a bra.

Lately I'd spent a lot of time staring at April Sawyer and trying not to get caught.

We were just friends, but I'd hung out with her quite a bit this year. There had been many times I'd thought about kissing her, just to see what it was like, but I'd never made a move. Now that I was leaving town for good, I'd probably never get another chance.

"Shaw! Want another?"

I glanced at my friend and baseball teammate Pete

Matthews, who stood at the fridge holding up two cans of cheap beer. "Nah," I said. "I'm good."

We were at another teammate's house for his graduation party, and I'd already had a couple beers earlier in the night, but I'd stopped hours ago since I was driving. The last thing I wanted was to get pulled over and blow a breathalyzer test the night before I was heading out for Instructional League. Plus, it tasted like shit. My MLB signing bonus had been two million dollars, which was now sitting in my bank account. I did not need to drink crappy cans of cheap beer for a good time.

"Suit yourself." Pete put one can back in the fridge and shut the door. Cracking open the can, he came over to where I stood against the counter. Following my line of sight, he laughed. "Dude."

"What?"

"You want her so bad. Just go do it already."

"Do what?"

He gave me a sideways smirk before tipping up his beer. "Whatever it is that you're thinking about doing when you're staring at her that way."

I frowned. "Fuck off. We're just friends. I'm not going to mess around with her the night before I'm leaving for good. That's a dick move."

"Isn't a dick move the idea?" he joked.

I gave him a menacing look.

"Kidding. Look, I'm just saying, it's obvious you're into her, and it might be your last chance. She's going to Penn State, right?"

"Yeah. That's sounds right."

"And you'll be all the way across the country in Arizona."

"Exactly." I shut up when she and her friends walked past us on their way outside.

"Hey," she said, giving me a smile that showed off her dimpled and made my heartbeat quicken.

"Hey," I said with a nod, my eyes on her ass as she went out the door.

Pete laughed after it banged shut. "Dude."

A little while later, Pete and I went out to the backyard too, where a few dozen classmates were standing around a bonfire. It was late—after midnight—and all the adults had left hours ago.

"Hey, Tyler." Jenna Holmes, a girl in our graduating class that I'd made out with once with earlier this year, came up and slipped her arms around my waist. "What's up?"

"Not much." I didn't return the hug because I didn't want to give her the wrong idea. She was nice enough, but I only had one night left in town, and I was sort of hoping to drive April home.

"You leave tomorrow, right?" Jenna kept clinging to me, and of course, April looked over at us right then, averting her eyes quickly when she noticed Jenna's arms around me.

Shit.

"Yeah." Gently detaching myself from her embrace, I stepped aside. "And actually, I should get going. I've still got some packing to do."

"You're leaving already?" She pouted. "That's no fun."

"Hey, *I'm* still here," I heard Pete tell her as I made my way to where April was standing. "And I'm a lot more fun than Tyler. Just ask me."

I approached April, who was stifling a yawn. "Tired?" I asked, giving her my signature grin.

She laughed sheepishly. "Yes. To be honest, I'm ready to go home, but Ari drove me, and she doesn't want to leave yet."

"I can take you home," I offered.

"Are you sure you're ready to leave?"

"Yeah." I shrugged, glancing around. Then I lowered my voice. "I'm kind of over all this, you know?"

She nodded. "Yeah. I get it. I'll miss everyone—and home and my family—but I'm so ready to leave. You must be too."

"Fuck yeah."

"Tomorrow, right?"

"Yep," I confirmed. "By this time tomorrow night, I'll be in Arizona."

She smiled. "I'm so happy for you."

"Thanks. I'm happy for you too."

For a moment, we stood in silence, and I noticed how the light from the bonfire played with her auburn hair, giving it streaks of gold. In the dark, the reddish color looked deeper than it did during the day. But her skin looked luminous, and I could just make out the dusting of freckles across her nose. Her smile deepened, and she laughed nervously as she tucked her hair behind one ear. "Why are you staring at me like that?"

I laughed too. "Sorry. Didn't mean to. I was just thinking."

"About what?"

"About how weird it will be not to see you at my house all the time."

"But you won't be at your house," she pointed out. "You'll be somewhere new. So it won't be weird at all."

"True," I admitted, shoving my hands in my jeans pockets. "Maybe what I meant was that it will be weird not to see you at all once I leave."

"Yeah." Her smile was a little sad. "It will be weird not to see you too."

"Thanks for being there for Sadie this year."

"Of course," she said with a pretty shrug of her shoulders. "I had fun. Sadie is a doll—I adore her."

"Yeah." I shuffled one foot in the dirt. Thinking about leaving my little sister put an aching pit in my chest, and I didn't like thinking about it.

"She's going to miss you like crazy."

"What about you?" I teased.

"What about me?"

"Will *you* miss me?"

"Nah." But she had a terrible poker face and burst out laughing.

I couldn't resist grabbing her in a headlock and pretending to strangle her. "I won't miss you, either. You're so mean to me."

She tugged at my arm, which held her tight across the collarbone. Standing behind her, I could smell her hair—a mix of fruity shampoo and smoke from the bonfire. Her body was warm, and I pulled her a little closer to me. "Say you're sorry."

"No way."

"Come on, apologize for all the mean jokes you made about my biceps this year."

Giggling, she kept trying to pry my arm from her neck and couldn't. "Your biceps are so big, they're choking me. I can't even talk."

I loosened my hold—a little. "Now say it."

"I'm sorry," she said, breathless with laughter. "Your biceps are great, and I did not intend to insult them."

"And admit you'll miss me."

"I'll miss you."

"Are you just saying that so I'll let go of you?"

She hesitated, her hands still resting on my forearm, but no longer pulling. When she spoke, her voice was softer. "No. I really will miss you."

My lips were almost touching the top of her head, and my arm was right above her breasts. For a second, I thought about turning her to face me and kissing her for real, like I'd done in all my fantasies.

But instead, I released her, dropping my arms to my sides. Too many people were watching. And what would be the point?

"Come on, Sawyer," I said. "I'll take you home."

"It's out of your way," she pointed out.

"I don't mind."

"Okay. Thanks."

After letting out friends know we were taking off—Pete barely smothered a knowing grin—we walked out to my truck. I unlocked the passenger door for her, and she hopped in. Once I was behind the wheel, she said, "I've never been in your truck before."

"No?" I started the engine. "I thought I'd driven you home before."

She shook her head. "Nope. Whenever I saw you, you usually had . . . *company* at the end of the night."

"Not always," I argued, although it was true that I never lacked for female company when I wanted it.

"I said *usually*."

"Well, I'd have given you a ride home any time you asked."

She glanced over at me. "Would have been a little crowded up here in the front seat, don't you think?"

I shrugged. "I'd have made you ride in the bed."

Laughing, she whacked me on the leg. "Jerk!"

We drove a few minutes in silence, and the turn-off to Cloverleigh Farms was approaching. But I realized I didn't want to take her home yet. An idea took root in the back of my mind.

A moment later, she gestured out the passenger window. "That was the turn-off to my house," she said. "You missed it."

"I know."

She hesitated. "Where are we going?"

"On a detour."

"A detour?"

"Yeah. I want to show you something." I glanced at her. "Unless you have to be home right now?"

"No," she said, a note of caution in her voice—or maybe that was anticipation. "I'm okay."

A few miles down the road, I turned off the highway onto an old road that had been paved once upon a time but was now riddled with cracks and potholes. I remembered well avoiding them with my bike when I'd ride to practice, my glove hanging off the handlebars.

The field was even older than the road, and since it wasn't used much anymore—new fields with nicer facilities had been built closer to town—this one was pretty raggedy now. Deep ruts along the baselines. Weeds overtaking the outfield. Paint flaking off the team benches. But as my truck's headlights pierced the dark, I got that feeling in my stomach—the same once I used to get as a kid before a game. A mix of nerves, excitement, hope, possibility, all laced with the adrenaline of a boy desperate to prove himself and confident that he could.

I turned off the truck, but left the headlights on. April looked around with interest. "Did you used to play here?"

"My very first games. Actually, I played here even before that. My dad used to bring me here to play catch and practice batting and running the bases." I thought back to those early says, feeling the sun and sweat on my skin, hearing his voice in my head. *Head up, Tyler. Eye on the ball. Elbow bent. Wider stance—you want your head centered between your feet.* "Later I used to drive out here with a bucket of balls to practice pitching. I liked throwing when no one was around."

"So maybe someday, kids will come here and point at the mound and say, *That's where Tyler Shaw got his start.*" She leaned over and poked my arm. "Maybe they'll even rename this old field for you."

"Ha. Maybe." I glanced over at her. "Come on. Let's get out."

We hopped out of the truck and slammed the doors. It was a warm night, but the breeze was cool and smelled faintly like fertilizer from the farms in the area. I walked through the opening in the fence and motioned for April to come with me.

"Are you sure it's okay to be here?" she asked, following me onto the field, looking around like the cops might show up and arrest us. "We're not, like, trespassing, are we?"

I laughed, stepping onto the mound and into the beams of the truck's lights. I squared off against the plate, squinting against the brightness. "Trust me. No one cares that we're here."

"Good." She reached the mound and stood beside me. "Is this where you first learned to give the mean stare?"

"Yep." I turned to the side, bringing my feet together, but keeping my eyes narrowed on the imaginary batter. "This is where I first learned everything."

"So let's see it. Show me what you got."

Her words sent a little rocket of arousal straight to my crotch, but I kept my focus, wound up, and went through my motion. In my head, I saw the fastball cross the plate at ninety miles per hour, the batter watching it go by.

"Strike!" shouted April.

I looked at her and grinned. "Damn right."

"Someday I'll watch you in the World Series, and I'll remember this moment."

God, I fucking hoped so. That was all I wanted—to prove myself that way. "Maybe."

"Maybe?" She moved closer and gave me a little shove on the chest. "That doesn't sound like the Tyler I know."

"He's usually pretty cocky, huh?"

"Exactly." She tipped her head, her smile turning playful, almost flirty. "But he can back it up."

Another rocket of lust to my crotch. "You think so?"

"I'm pretty sure."

We stood there for a moment, in the spotlight of the truck's headlights on the dark field. I'd never been so tempted to kiss a girl in all my life. I looked at her lips, and they fell open. Her chest was rising and falling quickly. The breeze blew her hair around her face, and I was dying to brush it back—I loved her hair, and I'd never touched it.

Off in the distance, an ambulance or police car siren went off, making her jump and turn her head in that direction. "They're after us," she said with a laugh.

I tried to think of something to say and couldn't.

She slapped at her ankle. "The bugs are getting me."

"Oh—sorry. I should have turned the headlights off, I guess."

We walked back to the truck, and I followed her to the passenger side. But I paused with my hand on the handle. "I don't really want to go home yet."

"I don't either," she confessed. Then she tipped her head back. "So many stars out tonight. I just wish the mosquitoes weren't out too."

"You just gave me an idea. Give me a second." I opened the truck door, switched off the headlights, and shut it again. Then I took her arm, led her around to the truck bed, and opened the tailgate. "Here, let me jump in and then I'll help you." I hopped up and reached down with one hand.

She looked down at her clothes. "I'm wearing a dress, but . . . okay." With a shrug, she took my hand and let me help her climb into the empty bed. "Pretend you didn't see my underwear while I did that."

"It's dark. I didn't see anything." And I'd looked, believe me. "Sorry it's a little dusty back here."

"That's okay." She dropped gracefully onto her butt and

leaned back on her hands, letting her head fall back. "This is nice."

I stretched out beside her on my back, hands behind my head. A second later, she lay all the way back too. For a couple minutes, we lay there staring up at the stars, the crickets doing all the talking. I felt like there were things I wanted to say to her, but worried they'd either sound stupid or fake—like I was saying them just because I wanted to put my hand up her dress. Which I did, of course. But that felt like a separate thing from what I wanted to say to her.

"We should make a wish," she said softly. "On the brightest star we can find."

"Okay." I picked one out and wished the same thing I always did—to pitch in the World Series and get the win.

"Did you do it?"

"Yeah."

"Was it about baseball?"

"Yeah."

She laughed. "Of course."

I got a little defensive. "What else am I supposed to wish for? Baseball is all I really care about."

"Then that should be your wish."

Another minute ticked by before I spoke again, quieter this time. "It's not just because of my ego."

She turned her face to look at me. "What isn't?"

"Why I care about baseball so much. Why I have to be the best. It's just something I've always felt from the time I was little—I have to prove myself."

"To who?"

"I don't even know for sure. In the beginning, I think it was my dad. My coaches. Then other kids who saw me getting all the attention. Then the crowd who came to see me throw. Then scouts. I knew I was good, but there's always that little voice in your head that tries to talk you down, you know? That says, *you're not all that, you're just faking it.* And when it gets loud, I talk back to it by being more arrogant. By throwing harder and faster. By saying stupid cocky shit. But I don't always feel it."

"But that's normal. If you don't occasionally have self-doubt, you wouldn't even be human." She chuckled softly. "And as fast as you can throw, you're still only human."

"Sometimes when it gets bad, I think about my mom and tell myself I need to make her proud." I swallowed hard. "That she's watching from heaven and she's on my side."

"Of course she is." April's voice was thick with emotion. "And I know she's proud of you. Your dad is too. I'm always in the bleachers near him and Sadie at all your games, and no one cheers you on louder than he does."

"Making my dad proud means everything. He sobbed when I got drafted. He didn't want me to see it, but he did."

"I think the whole town cried."

The lump in my throat dissipated, and I glanced at her. "Did you?"

"Maybe a little," she said, a touch defensively. "But it's a big deal, and you're my friend. I'm happy for you."

I smiled. "Thanks."

"Are you nervous to leave tomorrow?"

"Nope. Not nervous—just excited." I paused. "The only thing I'm a little sad about is leaving Sadie. I feel like I'm going to miss her growing up."

"She won't let you," April said confidently. "I know how crazy she is about you, and she's probably going to call you every day."

I groaned. "You're probably right. I bet she'll call you too."

"I'd love it if she did. I'm going to miss her."

I rolled onto my side and propped my head in my right hand. "I know I said this before, but thanks again for being there for her."

"You're welcome."

"And for me."

She was staring at my mouth. "Of course."

My left hand was just inches from her hip, aching to touch her. "I couldn't have gotten through senior year without you."

Her eyes closed as she laughed, and although it was too dark to know for sure, I had the sense she was blushing. "You'd have been fine."

"Maybe. But it was better because of you."

Her eyes opened and met mine. Her smile faded.

I reached out and slid my hand up the back of her neck, into her hair. It felt like velvet under my fingers. "April."

"Yes," she whispered.

"Come here."

But I didn't even give her a chance to move before pulling her head toward me and pressing my lips to hers. They were soft and sweet and willing, opening beneath mine. I tasted her hungrily, my tongue seeking hers. My hand moved from her hair to her thigh, snaking up beneath her dress. I paused when my fingers reached the edge of her underwear, swearing to God I'd stop there if she said no or pushed me away. Instead she drew up one knee and wrapped her arms around my neck.

My cock surged to life, bulging against my jeans as I rubbed her pussy with only a thin layer of material between my fingers and her skin. When she made a little sound of pleasure, I grew bolder, moving the crotch of her panties aside. She was warm and wet, and I groaned as I slid one finger inside her.

You asshole, said a voice in my head. *She trusts you and you brought her out here in the dark to this abandoned place and now she's going to think you did it just so you could get your hand in her pants.*

I nearly stopped right then and there, but suddenly she moved her hand down my chest and put it between my legs, rubbing me through my jeans. My body instinctively moved against her touch, thrusting into her palm as I fucked her with my finger.

Just this, I told myself. *Just this much.*

But then it wasn't enough. And somehow I was on top of her and her panties her off and my jeans were undone and I was so fucking hard for her and I wanted to be inside her so badly and she was reaching for me and opening her thighs and I was easing my cock into her body saying *just a little more, just for a minute, just for tonight, just because it's her . . .*

And then before I knew what was happening, she was holding me so tight and crying out beneath me and I was fucking her hard and fast and deep and for real, because it felt so good to be that close to her and she was all I wanted in that moment and nothing could stop us from going all the way to the top together and then beyond, our hearts pounding, our bodies slick with sweat, her face buried in my neck as I poured myself into her.

I was so oblivious to everything but her, I couldn't even see.

When my vision cleared, I panicked and pulled out. "Oh, fuck."

"It's okay." April hurriedly shoved her dress down.

"Are you sure?"

"Yes."

I lifted myself off her and did up my pants while she tugged her underwear on. If she was sure it was okay, did that mean she was on the pill or something? I felt weird asking her, so I decided to just trust that she was telling the truth.

"God, that was—" I struggled for the right word.

"Unexpected?" she suggested.

"Well, yeah. That, but also . . . fun. At least for me."

"For me too," she said quickly.

"I'm sorry I lost control."

"It's okay." She was smoothing her dress over her hips,

her eyes following her hands. The silence grew a little awkward.

"Guess I should get you home, huh?"

"Yeah."

I jumped out of the truck and reached for her, grabbing her by the waist and lifting her down. When she was on her feet, I slid my arms around her and pressed my lips to her forehead. She placed her palms up my chest.

There were things I wanted her to know, but the words refused to take shape in my head. We stayed like that for a moment, and then I walked her to the passenger door and pulled it open.

As I pulled around the driveway in front of her house, I turned off the headlights. When I shut off the engine and started to get out, she put her hand on my arm.

"Tyler, you don't have to walk me to the door."

"I want to." I got out and met her in front of the truck, then took her hand as we climbed the front porch steps.

"Well, thanks for the ride," she said, giggling a little. "That was, um, quite a detour."

"It was," I agreed. "But I don't want you to think that was my plan all along or anything."

She shook her head. "I don't. I promise."

"Really?"

"Really. It just kind of happened."

"It's not that I hadn't thought about it," I said, then wondered if I'd just made things worse.

"I'd thought about it too," she admitted.

"Seriously?"

She nodded. "So we're even."

"Okay, good." I tugged her into my arms and gave her a hug, inhaling the smell of her one last time. "Friends?"

"Friends."

But we held on the that hug a little longer than friends should.

Never miss a thing!

For exclusive behind the scenes information, sales and freebies, cover reveals, recommendations, and sneak peeks to what's coming, subscribe to my mailing list using the QR code below!

Unforgettable

The Bellamy Creek Series
Drive Me Wild
Make Me Yours
Call Me Crazy
Tie Me Down

Cloverleigh Farms Next Generation Series
Ignite
Taste
Tease
Tempt

Co-Written Books
Hold You Close (Co-written with Corinne Michaels)
Imperfect Match (Co-written with Corinne Michaels)
Strong Enough (M/M romance co-written with David Romanov)

The Speak Easy Duet

The Tango Lesson (A Standalone Novella)

Want a reading order? Click here!

Acknowledgments

Much love and gratitude to the following people!

My friends Sammy and AJ Palace, who were so open and gracious about sharing their love story with me. Congratulations to them on being a family of four now!

I am especially indebted to Sammy for helping me better understand the hopes, dreams, struggles, and mindset of a professional baseball player.

This book was finished under coronavirus quarantine, and there were definitely days where I wasn't sure I could get it done. But the amazing humans listed above and below were there for me as I tried my best to deliver a story of love and hope amid the uncertainty. They cheered me on, made me smile, and lifted me up!

Melissa Gaston, Brandi Zelenka, Jenn Watson, Corinne Michaels, Kayti McGee, Laurelin Paige, Sierra Simone, Lauren Blakely, Rebecca Friedman at Friedman Literary, Nancy Smay at Evident Ink, proofreaders Julia Griffis, Michele Ficht, and Shannon Mummey, the Harlots and the Harlot ARC Team, bloggers and event organizers, my Queens and CH, my readers all over the world … and my beautiful family. I love you. I appreciate you. I am so grateful.

About the Author

Melanie Harlow likes her heels high, her martinis dry, and her history with the naughty bits left in. In addition to UNFORGETTABLE, she's the author of over twenty additional contemporary romances and a romantic historical duet.

She writes from her home outside of Detroit, where she lives with her husband and two daughters. When she's not writing, she's probably got a cocktail in hand. And sometimes when she is.

Find her at www.melanieharlow.com.